WHAT THE
RAVEN
BRINGS

Born and raised in Eastern Canada, John Owen Theobald moved to the UK to study the poetry of Keats, and in 2009 received a PhD from the University of St Andrews. He lives in London, England.

The Ravenmaster Trilogy
– BOOK II –

WHAT THE RAVEN BRINGS

JOHN OWEN THEOBALD

HEAD
of ZEUS

First published in the UK in 2016 by Head of Zeus Ltd

9 7 5 3 1 2 4 6 8

A catalogue record for this book is available from
the British Library.

Map and feather © Sarah Carter

ISBN (HB) 9781784974381
ISBN (E) 9781784974374

Typeset by Adrian McLaughlin

Printed and bound in Great Britain by
CPI Group (UK) Ltd, Croydon CR0 4YY

Head of Zeus Ltd
Clerkenwell House
45–47 Clerkenwell Green
London EC1R 0HT
WWW.HEADOFZEUS.COM

For Grammie
Jean McIntyre (*née* Murray),
RCAF 1941–1945

TOWER OF LONDON

1. WHITE TOWER
2. CHAPEL

3. BARRACKS
4. HOSPITAL

5. ROOST
6. TOWER GREEN
7. KING'S HOUSE
8. CONSTABLE TOWER
9. SALT TOWER

10. BLOODY TOWER
11. MAIN GUARD
12. CASEMATES
13. TOWER SCHOOL

14. TRAITORS' GATE
15. DEVELIN TOWER
16. BRASS MOUNT

17. WEST GATE
18. MOAT
19. RIVER THAMES

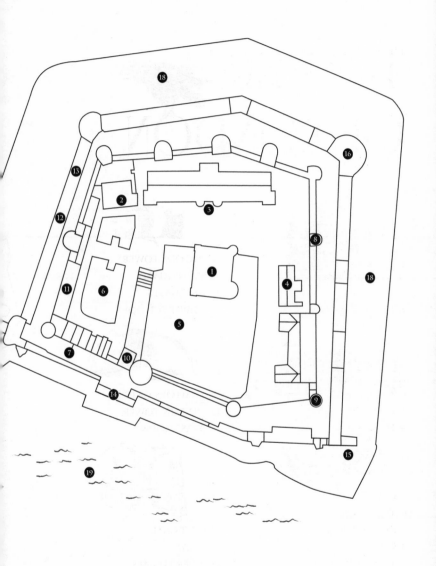

'You shall go as the others have gone,
Lay your head on a hard bed of stone,
And have the raven for companion.'

Dylan Thomas, *The Ploughman's Gone*

I

SHADOW OVER ENGLAND

MESSERSCHMITT "ME. 109"

'that thick and formidable circle of ancient stone, where so many drums have beaten and heads have fallen, the Tower of London itself.'

Virginia Woolf, *The Docks of London*

1

Saturday, 16 May 1942

My run of luck is over. During the Blitz, luck's the only thing that keeps you alive. Every bomb that falls next door, every fire that whips up just as you reach the shelter, every scrap of food you find before someone else – that's your luck, draining away. After a year, it's flat gone. And you're left trapped in the belly of a cement monster with the most annoying person in the world.

'Squire. You asleep over there?'

I turn to face the grinning voice. 'Working hard as you are, Lightwood.'

'I'll be the judge of that.' From above comes the quartermaster's voice. My head is down, focused on tying together the steel bars with wire. I don't need to peek over my shoulder to know that Lightwood's done the same.

'Timothy Squire and Arthur Lightwood. I should not have to remind you that one word from me and neither of you will ever wear a uniform.'

'Yes, sir.'

'Yes, sir.'

I grit my teeth. Three months of demolition training to become a sapper – a Royal Engineer in His Majesty's armed forces – and here I am reinforcing concrete down at the docks. Tie the steel bars together with a figure-eight knot, cut the wire free with pliers. Repeat until death.

Lightwood and I work together, apart. *As far apart as you can be in a ten-foot cell.* Even in the shadows cast by the walls, sweat drips into my eyes. We're in a giant hollow concrete box, with twenty compartments, sunk into the earth. All that's needed is a top, and we're as good as in a coffin. If we were truly dead and buried, at least we wouldn't notice these bloody midges.

It's hard to imagine a smaller space to work with another human. I could well do with some light, or air. The river is so close, but the dry dock blocks it. Seagulls cry out, mocking us.

My luck has run to empty.

I keep working, not daring to check if the quartermaster is still atop the ladder, watching like a riled hawk. *Crabby little apple, that one.*

The armed forces have taken over the docks, and brought their discipline with them. I suppose I should be happy to be here. As long as I'm close to these sappers, I can find another chance to become one myself. Truth is, I'd rather be anywhere else.

Finally, I glance up and risk turning full around. Cranes on tracks swing and swoop high above, intent on their own work. The walkway that runs down the centre is clear. He is gone. Long gone, I'll bet, smirking as he left.

Pressing a hand against the small of my back, I watch Lightwood working away, furious, tying the wire, yanking it firm. *Did I look that stupid?*

'Lightwood.'

He stops, panting, and turns to me, face bright as a cherry. 'He gone? Thank Christ.'

Letting the pliers fall to the concrete, he leans his back against the wall, closing his eyes. I watch him with a smile. Arthur Lightwood – sounds like he rides a white horse in some poem from school. Looks a bit like it, too. The horse, that is.

'You know what I should be doing right now?' I turn and spit in the opposite corner. 'Learning about mines. But some fool – some *blighter* – added a Type 70 fuse instead of a 67.'

His eyes still closed, he looks almost relaxed. 'I reckon another day in Aberdeen and you'd have been dead as a doornail. Can't keep your sticky fingers out of TNT for five minutes at a time. One of 'em was bound to go off eventually. Fag?'

Lightwood's eyes blink open, and he's rummaging in his pockets.

'Bleeding liar.' I wave the offered cigarette away, casting a look up at the walkway. 'Better get back to it. This bloody Phoenix isn't going to build itself.'

Who knows, maybe it will. No one here's got the first clue what a Phoenix is, and no one is allowed to ask.

The armed forces brought that with them, too – no questions, just make sure the concrete is reinforced.

Not even Lightwood knows, and he knows everything. Doesn't stop him from guessing, of course.

'Think about it, Squire. There's a ton of sappers down here. Obviously it's vital to the war. So what could it be?'

I almost guess a battleship, but the thought of Lightwood's horsey laugh makes me want to clobber him. And we really should get back to work.

'Massive old block of concrete,' he says after I fail to respond, then snorts when I don't understand him. *Man's a bleeding talking horse.* 'You sink it, you've got a foundation underwater.'

'A foundation for what?'

'Harbours. Roads. Whatever you want.'

I shake my head. 'You were wrong about the clockwork fuse.'

'That was your fault, Squire.'

Lightwood is full of it. No one knows what anyone is building. At least three other Phoenix units are under construction here, and similar work's going on at the other docks. And the clockwork fuse *was* partly my fault, that's the worst bit. How could I get the fuses mixed up?

'The Germans hold all the ports, right? If we're going to land over there, we'll need to bring our own—'

A voice booms from above. 'Another peep out of either of you, and you're both gone. Final warning.'

'Yes, sir.'

'Yes, sir.'

Don't lose your wool, mate. Didn't think it would be possible to miss the training, but two ticks and I'd go back and start it all over again. Who'd have thought I'd ever miss the endless buckles and buttons of the uniform. The marching drills were the worst, of course. The day my blistered feet finally burst, flooding my boots with blood, I thought I was done. But I learned a few tricks – get your boots one size too small, urinate on them, and never wear socks – worked a treat.

Lot of good marching tricks and rifle drills will do me stuck down here. At least when we spent hours in a bomb hole, we'd wonder what would happen if the bomb went off. Here we know nothing is going to happen. Ever.

Only two weeks away from completing sapper training; written tests, live demolitions, working with time-fused and magnetic response bombs – I'd finished it all. All I needed to do was blow the fake bridge. A single bloody bridge.

I was better than all those Kensington boys.

A whistle cracks the air. For what seems like the first time in hours, I look up. The sun has dropped behind the wall. Workers are hurrying across the wooden walkway. Another hellish long day. Midges cloud around me.

'Lightwood.'

He looks over, eyes wide. I already have my hand on the ladder.

'Let's close up shop, yeah?'

He nods, adds the final touches to some work, drops his pliers. We climb up to the light. I slide off my cap, take in as much sun as I can.

The docks had been hit hard during Hitler's fire-works. Many are now unusable. Ours, the South Dock, was badly damaged and turned into a dry dock – drained and sealed with a concrete barrier at the lock. And in the middle, four great Phoenix units. Nearly 200 feet long, I'd wager each must be, and close to 60 feet high. A giant harbour, and not a drop of water. Just cranes and concrete boxes.

The Greenland Docks are just to the east. From here I can see the shining water, with a ship in dock. When the day comes that we're done here – *if* that day comes – they'll open the gates and let the tide rush in, lifting this giant concrete bastard off the ground.

'It'll be over soon,' Lightwood says.

He grabs my shoulder, his grip exaggeratedly strong. Wants to be the big man, can't help himself. *Arthur Bleeding Lightwood*. I didn't get on with most of the kids at the Tower, but Arthur and I have palled up since training together in Aberdeen. He slept in the bunk above mine in the Aberdeen barracks. Now I'm stuck inside a concrete box with him.

Some day I'll have to tell Anna the truth.

In the quiet of the pub Lightwood once again guides me through his injuries working with our ill-fated fuse.

'You wouldn't believe the pain.'

'Hard luck, mate.'

I take small sips of the beer. You get a good pint in the Fox and Hounds, but Lightwood always goes for broke. Not that I can really complain to the guy. He is, after all, saving me from humiliation. Lightwood's mum lets me sleep in his room, though I'm shoved away in the corner like old socks. She keeps a fine eye on us, too.

I don't have enough for a bit of grub – I am skint – and Mrs Lightwood barely feeds us beyond a slap-up meal of bully-beef sandwiches and the odd sardine. *I could always go home. Mum and Dad would make sure I got a proper meal with potatoes and all.* But I've told them we're only at the docks for a few weeks and then we're being sent back up north to finish our training. If I stayed at home, Mum would weasel the truth out of me in no time. No, it's safer to stay at Lightwood's with a growling belly.

'There was blood on my *helmet*,' Lightwood is saying. 'The cut didn't look so bad, but the blood, I tell you, it was everywhere. The wrench just slipped—'

'Who is that?'

Lightwood blinks, startled. 'Who?'

'The bloke over there. Third table from the bar, brown hat. He keeps looking over here.'

Lightwood peers foolishly across the room. 'I don't know. That pipefitter, isn't he? From the unit next to ours?'

I nod, turn back to the beer. *Bloody hell, I'm going mad. Seeing Anna's dad in every face at the pub.* Coming to England was a mistake that man won't make again. They'd shoot him on sight. I'd shoot him myself.

'Fag?'

Lightwood tilts the pack towards me. I slide one tube free, hold it between my thumb and finger. Well, maybe I wouldn't shoot the man. But I'd at least chase the bastard away.

You already did. He's long gone back to see Hitler. I still can't wrap my head around it. Anna's dad – a German!

'You gonna smoke it?'

'Yeah.' I light it, puffing out a huge grey cloud, and swallow the itch that seizes my throat. 'Thanks.'

'What is it, Squire? You've gone all white.'

'Lightwood, I couldn't tell you, mate. Not even if I wanted to.'

He lets it go with a snort, intent on his pint.

'You shouldn't have used a wrench,' I say. 'A magnet would've got the fuse out. Lot less blood and whinging.'

He looks up, surprised I'd been listening to his ramblings about slippery wrenches. 'A magnet, eh? They were in short supply on the training ground. Unless you had one on you the whole time?'

''Course not. But a sapper's got to use his head. Not that we're sappers, though, are we?' I glance down at my plain work clothes. 'We're just labourers, Lightwood, that's the truth of it. No sense bantering about bombs.'

I crush out the cigarette, swallowing the harsh dry taste. I take a long sip of beer. Another. *How does Lightwood suck these things back all day?* I feel like I'm going to lose what little food is in my stomach.

I will go, tomorrow, to the Tower. My first day off – might as well get it over with. I will talk to Anna; she'll believe me. She isn't likely to guess the truth: that I'm sleeping in Lightwood's flat in Shadwell, pretending to live in the barracks.

A voice comes back to me, a horrible sing-song voice from school.

Timothy Squire is a rotten liar.

'Come on, Lightwood. I'm knackered and I ought to get some proper sleep. Tomorrow's set to be a long day.'

Sunday, 17 May 1942

'What do you mean, "Not the real Ravenmaster"?'

'It's a ceremonial role, Anna.'

'I know more about ravens than Mr Sickhouse—'

'Mr *Stack*house.'

'—ever could and it's not fair at all.'

Oakes sighs, drops his spoon. The clink echoes throughout the Stone Kitchen. Life in the Tower of London is filled with echoes and long silences. It is also filled with Beefeaters – Yeoman Warders – and their *traditions*.

'It's a ceremonial role, Anna. You need to be a Warder. Serve in the army. Be a man.'

'Why all these rules? Uncle was the first Ravenmaster.'

I stop the moment I say it, but it is too late. Oakes's face falls. It has been a month since Uncle's funeral, and neither of us has said much about it since. I feel quite terrible. Yes, he was *my* uncle, but Oakes was his greatest friend. Since Uncle passed away, Oakes is mostly quiet. Sometimes, after school, when he speaks I can smell whisky. At least he does not smell of whisky yet.

I can still see Uncle Henry's thin, grey-cold features – how old he looked before he died. He became like this place – old and grey as stone. It is strange not to have him here, it feels *wrong*. Despite the roaring fire behind us, the room is suddenly very cold.

'You can't just make up traditions as you go along,' I mutter.

'Sometimes you can.' A rueful smile and Oakes lifts his spoon to his breakfast. 'Finish your porridge, Anna. It's the first real milk we've had in ages.'

I eye the bowl suspiciously. Is this even real milk, or is Oakes just saying that so I will enjoy it? I have long forgotten the taste of real milk. Now the hens have all stopped laying, we have dried eggs – everyone calls them 'dregs', which is just what they taste like. I am so tired of these Blitz dishes. Mum used to worry we were living a 'pinched existence' on Warwick Avenue. What would she say about this? The thought is enough to make me laugh.

But I am not in the mood for laughing.

'And who decided on Mr Sickhouse—'

'Stackhouse.'

'Shouldn't there be a test – or a vote – or something?'

There isn't and there won't be. After only six months on the job, I have been demoted. And only one of the ravens tried to escape. And if Malcolm got pecked on the skull, well maybe it's Malcolm's own fault for trying to pet the raven like it's a cat.

14

'We're going to open to the public soon, Anna. As soon as the war is over. And they expect certain things about the Tower of London – Warders in uniform, for example.' He casts a look down at his very unWarder-like shirt and tie.

I am sick of the Warders and their stuffy traditions. *Always there have been thirty-five Yeoman Warders at the Tower – for six hundred years.*

Everything is planned perfectly. I will act as Ravenmaster, with Timothy Squire as my assistant, and one day when we're older we will live in Maida Vale, bringing three ravens with us to look after there. They will have plenty of trees and space to fly around, and on Saturdays Timothy Squire will bring them meat from the Warwick Avenue butcher.

Working with – working *under* – this new Warder is *not* part of the plan.

'I just don't understand *why* we need him.'

Oakes clears his throat. 'It was my suggestion, actually.'

'Yours? But, Yeoman Oakes, I know the ravens better than anyone.'

'Yes.' He frowns, or maybe smiles, it is hard to tell the difference these days. 'But now that school is over, and you've no wish to attend another school, I thought perhaps you might be interested in… *other* things. Volunteering at the canteen, for example?'

'The canteen? Like a NAAFI girl?' All I can think of is that horrible Elsie that Timothy Squire used to fawn over.

Most of the students have gone – shipped off, called up – and the teachers have left, too. (Miss Breedon has joined the navy!) Even Kate went north with her family. As the only students left were me and Malcolm, I wasn't surprised when Oakes told me Tower School was closing for good.

In fact, the Tower is now more of an army barracks than the village it's been these past two years. The Scots Guard parade and drill across the grounds, and in the (drained) moat new encampments of soldiers seem to crop up every week. The school is set to become a first-aid post, and the other buildings are being turned into fire stations. Now the cobblestone courtyard is empty, the kids gone. Only the ravens are still here.

'Don't look so worried, Anna. The ravens will be fine under the care of Yeoman Stackhouse. You can see to his training yourself.'

I barely hold in a shout. I've already trained Timothy Squire, and he's still hopeless. The day before he left, he thought the youngest raven, Stan, was moulting when he was only preening. When Timothy Squire returns from Aberdeen, I shall have to retrain him – and now I have to train some bumbling old man on top of it. The whole situation is mad.

'Anna. Your uncle spoke very highly of you. He said that you always did what needed to be done.'

I try to smile. *Well, that doesn't sound like the best compliment.* Surely Uncle said nicer things than that about me…

'He thought you could do anything you set your mind to. I happen to agree with him. What I mean is, your uncle wouldn't have wanted you to stay here, looking after the ravens, on his behalf.'

'But I want to stay here. Timothy Squire will be back

soon and he can help out. There'll be plenty to do once spring comes and the birds begin to moult… and the legend of the ravens says—'

Oakes waves his hand. 'Yes, yes, there must always be six ravens at the Tower or else Britain will fall. Yeoman Stackhouse will look after them.'

I mumble something, which seems to satisfy Oakes.

'So, will you go to the canteen tomorrow? See if they'll take you on?'

'Yes, Yeoman Oakes, sir.'

Oakes apologizes for abandoning me with the washing up and soon his footsteps echo away into the distance. Echoes and silence. Maybe it won't be so bad, volunteering at the canteen. But if Oakes says I can do whatever I set my mind to, why do I have to be a NAAFI girl like horrible Elsie?

I shiver in the stone room, with its stored cold of a thousand winters. Thoroughly underwhelmed with the dregs, I collect the plates and cutlery. At least Stackhouse won't be joining us for meals, too. He has a family of his own.

Well, good for him.

I have eaten. Now it is the ravens' turn. And they're always hungry.

'Good morning, Portia. Good morning, Rogan.'

I pull open the first cage. It is still cold in the morning air. Two ravens emerge. Their feathers reflect sunlight

– catching the light and sending it back. As if the sun cannot touch them. There is little enough sunlight today.

When Uncle first told me about the legend of the ravens, I didn't believe him. But to see it now, printed out in big letters in newspapers – it almost seems possible. Of course it's not true. I let the last two birds escape – I *helped* Grip and Mabel escape. And the kingdom didn't fall.

Not yet.

We have a full roost of new birds; they should be up to the job. *You lot are staying right here.* That is the least I can do for Uncle. I whistle Raven Stan over but he keeps on bouncing off, biscuit in his beak ready to stash away.

I look past Stan, over to the sounds of the Scots Guard garrison. They are still here in the Waterloo Block – drilling on the Parade Grounds and dancing in the White Tower. *As long as they're here, no one can sneak inside.*

I've started seeing his face everywhere. The ruffled hair, pale as moonlight, the ears sticking out. *My ears don't stick out. And my hair is red, same as Mum's.*

I shake my head to clear it. *Now who's being mad?*

My eyes are pulled away by an approaching figure. It must be Stackhouse, in full blue uniform, with long cloak billowing behind him. I turn back at the birds. They hop, croak, oblivious to the confusing life of people.

'They're the real Beefeaters, eh?'

I don't look up at the voice. 'Yeoman Stackhouse, hello.'

'You are Anna Cooper, yes? I hear you've been taking pretty good care of these birds.'

Of course I have. 'Thank you, sir.'

'Want to give me a hand feeding 'em?'

My whole body screams in protest. *Give* you *a hand?*
'Yes, sir. Let me introduce you to the ravens.'

Uncle wanted everyone in the Tower to care about the
ravens, so he let the Tower residents name them. So I have
Malcolm to thank every time I call 'Cronk' over for feeding.
The others have more suitable names – Corax, Lyra, Stan,
Oliver, Rogan, and Portia.

Portia and Rogan are mated. And though I miss Mabel
and Grip – the mated couple from the earlier group of
ravens – there is *something* about Portia. She is the smart-
est bird I have ever met. She is the dominant female, puffing
out her throat feathers as she stalks past and glances up at
me. *Recognizes* me, I am sure of it.

Uncle always spoke of how sophisticated ravens are;
only once did he talk, gently, about a feeling of connection.
Maybe he thought I'd laugh at him, at the idea of having
something in common, something important, with these
croaking black birds. But Portia is definitely looking at
me. She knows me. Well, I chose her name myself. *She's
probably just grateful not to be called Mrs Cronk.*

Rogan, of course, is Timothy Squire's choice of name
– something to do with his favourite comic book. I only
casually mentioned that I named my bird after a character
in Shakespeare. *I'm not certain he will ever grow up.*

*It will take more than three months in Aberdeen to
make Timothy Squire grow up.*

Hard to believe they took him at all. I told him he was
stupid, that no one would take a sixteen-year-old boy, but

he told the recruiting officer he was seventeen and a half and they took him at his word.

'Good morning, Raven Oliver,' I say, opening the last of the cages. 'You must always say hello when you release them in the morning.'

Yeoman Stackhouse smiles, looks around as we walk. 'Whole place'll be different come peacetime.'

'Yes, sir.'

I feed the ravens in the welcome silence that follows. Surrounded by the high stone walls, the towers and turrets and the Warders in blue cloaks and uniforms, you could feel like a proper princess from an old story. I don't. It is *always* cold inside, and the only room with a reliable fire is the Stone Kitchen.

Stan is wandering off. I don't dare try my whistle, in case he ignores me in front of Stackhouse. He is the youngest of the ravens, almost bursting with energy. *Stackhouse is going to have his hands full with him.*

'Hitler sure did knock hell out of the place, didn't he?' Stackhouse makes a *tsk tsk* sound. 'Lost the whole batch, didn't you? Well, let us turn our minds to the future, shall we?'

Batch? No, they didn't all die. I let them go. But I say nothing, thinking that might be even worse.

People believe the ravens saved us from the Blitz. The *Evening Standard*, where Mum used to write lots of articles about the coming war – she was a 'very important journalist', Oakes says – even called the ravens 'heroes' for fulfilling the ancient legend.

They even seem to believe it. Oliver is strutting across the Green like he's a film star. The ravens have done their part. Timothy Squire is off doing his.

What about me?

'Well, happy to have the help for the next little bit,' Stackhouse says, smiling for an unpleasant amount of time. 'But then you'll be off – working in a factory likely as not. Conscription will extend to the women – to everyone but us old folks. Guessing from what I've heard of you, missy, you'll leap before you're pushed.'

'She always does.'

The sudden voice jolts me upright. I can't believe it. It's too early. There is no way... but I turn and see him and know that somehow it is true.

Timothy Squire is back.

'You're early.'

I am standing, amazed, in my old blue jumper and plain trousers. Timothy Squire is standing beside me; the same dark, bushy hair; the same almost too big forehead. He smells of some kind of shaving soap, which he clearly doesn't need. *He hasn't been gone* that *long.*

He is eight days early. And wearing a tweed jacket. *I expected him to be showing off his uniform. I expected him to come back Tuesday next.* I wish I'd put on cold cream this morning.

21

'Who's that then?'

I turn in confusion. Stackhouse has just wandered off without even saying hello.

'Oh, that's Yeoman Stackhouse. The new Ravenmaster, apparently.' I turn back, all thoughts of Stackhouse and ravens gone. 'Training ended early?'

I know that look in his blue eyes. *Something's up.*

'Yeah.'

'So you're a real bomb expert now, Timothy Squire?'

The barest of nods. *No sticking his chest out, no long lectures.*

'How long are you staying?'

'For now. Here,' he says, fumbling in his jacket and handing me a one-pound jar of marmalade. 'Getting paid a proper soldier's wage now. Oh, and this.'

From another pocket, he locates a slab of toffee and offers it.

A soldier's wage. I stare at the delicious food, stunned. There is something – a measured pace – to his speech that is surely the work of officers in Aberdeen.

I hug him tightly, adding a squeeze to remind him how long he's been gone.

I'll take this toffee to Flo's for dinner tonight. The marmalade, though, is all mine. *No more dregs in the morning.* We walk on, Timothy Squire a little stiffly. He must be exhausted from the training. It is strange to see him so quiet – so serious. He was always silent around other people – like during class – but never when we were alone. Then he was in dogged high spirits. All this, from

22

a few months of drills? Whatever it is, he'll not keep it for long.

'Where are you billeted?'

'I'll be at the docks. Important work down there.'

'The docks?' I laugh, loudly, for a moment overcome with delight. He'll be a ten-minute bike ride away. 'Go on, tell me all about it – what are you doing?'

He shakes his head, and a glimmer of life returns. 'I couldn't tell you, Magpie, even if I knew. But it feels good, you know, to be doing something to help. Other than trigonometry.'

So it's a secret, is it? Well, you're no good at keeping those, Timothy Squire.

'You have to tell me if you're leaving again. Even if it's a great secret.'

He nods, going a little red. 'I will.'

'Good. Well, school's all done for me, too, so I'll be volunteering,' I say proudly. 'Starting tomorrow. You can come up and get something from the canteen.'

Now he turns bright red. 'Well, I likely can't. I mean, I can't just go wandering round, can I?'

'You mean you're not allowed to have lunch in the armed forces?'

He snorts. 'Not really, no. But I'll try and find you, yeah? You'll have proper sausage rolls, I wager, like the ones at Borough Market?'

I take his hand, a little more rough and callused than before. 'I'm glad you're back, Timothy Squire.'

'Me, too, Magpie.'

Now he's grinning like he's found a piece of shrapnel to take home and polish. Just when I think everything is going swimmingly, a terrifying sound wails. A sound we all know too well.

The air raid siren.

Once, the thought of spending the night in a shelter was hard to take. The smell of the paraffin lamp, the feel of the clammy darkness. But not today. Instead of the whole Tower crammed into the room, it is just me and Timothy Squire.

I decide not to wait until Flo's for the toffee. The sweetness is almost painful on the tongue.

'So what kind of bombs did you work with up there?'

He shrugs. *Shrugs.*

'Timothy Squire, are you OK?'

'All right, Magpie, just knackered.'

It's just like back in school, when we first met and he'd ignore me in class. *What's going on?*

He's got a new watch, too, which makes my stomach turn to see. Timothy Squire no longer 'goes to see the ruins' but the memory of the things he took will never go away. That watch looks old – it looks expensive – but there is no way he stole it. *He doesn't do that any more.*

'So you didn't miss school, then?' I ask, inching a little closer.

The planes are nearly overhead, but no sound of bombs yet. *Maybe just a scouting mission?* We haven't had a daylight raid in months.

'School? 'Course not. I doubt Miss Breedon was going to train me to defuse a delayed-timer bomb.'

Timothy Squire takes a piece of the toffee. Even in the near darkness I can tell he still bites his fingernails.

'I'd like to see you, sometime – as a proper sapper. In your uniform.'

He looks down at his tweed coat. 'Bit hot to wear it when I don't have to.'

'You don't want me around?'

'Magpie. That's mad.'

'You *do* want to see me, then?'

He smiles, his blue eyes brightening with their old mischief. He has not kissed me since he came back. He kisses me now.

The door heaves open, and Malcolm Brodie staggers into the room, catching his balance after three steps. He stares at us, his eyes impossibly wide, before he slinks inside the shelter. The door thunders closed behind him.

'Hi Malcolm,' I say.

'Sorry to interrupt,' he mutters before slumping into the far corner. Malcolm, Yeoman Brodie's son, never says a word unless you force it out of him.

'All right, Malcolm?' Timothy Squire says. 'Doesn't sound like a lot of action up there.'

Malcolm shrugs thin shoulders, keeps his eyes fixed on the door. 'You're a sapper now, Dad says.'

'That's right,' I answer, the pride clear in my voice.

'Nothing to worry about, Malcolm. Even if a bomb falls, Timothy Squire can help put it out.'

A strange choking sound in the darkness.

'One in five is a dud, ours as well as theirs,' Timothy Squire says, sounding a bit strangled. He must have taken too much toffee. 'Ones that are going to go off, though, we've learned how to stop 'em.'

Malcolm doesn't move. 'Everyone knows the saying. *Join the army and see the world. Join bomb disposal and see the next one.* I'd be too frightened.'

'Well,' Timothy Squire says, 'it is a bit scary. At times. Mostly it's brilliant, though.'

There is more, of course, prised out of him like rotten teeth. He *must* be ill. We learn that at the height of the Blitz we were getting three thousand bombs a week dropped on us. He also tells us of rumours of a new German weapon so powerful that *nothing is left* of the people killed.

'We'll have to put sandbags in the coffins,' he says matter-of-factly.

Hitler's new secret weapon: launched from bases in France.

The silence is solid enough to touch. *I shouldn't have encouraged him.*

'Malcolm,' I say, 'would you like a piece of toffee?'

He waves the offer of food away but I can feel his eyes across the room, watching us. The minutes ooze past.

All the Warders seem to have gathered on the battlements. Apparently white-haired Yeoman Sparks, the oldest Warder at the Tower, is in charge.

'Might as well be off to see your friends, dear,' Sparks says as we approach. 'No bombs from this lot.'

I stare at him through the grey mist, barely comprehending. It's not his thick Glasgow accent, but the words themselves.

'No bombs? But the planes – they flew right over us—'

'None were dropped,' Oakes says, stepping forward. 'You can go off to Mr and Mrs Swift's, Anna.'

Well, it wasn't long enough to be a raid. Timothy Squire and I spent less than an hour in the shelter, trying in vain to make conversation with Malcolm.

Despite Oakes's words, I gaze around for the smoke, the flames, the signs of damage. I could tell from the roar, even from the shelter in the bowels of the White Tower, that the bomber flew directly over us. There is nothing.

Well, not nothing, exactly.

Dozens of white shapes flutter in the wind. Paper. One skids close to us; I reach down, pick it up. It is a leaflet, painted with red flames engulfing Tower Bridge, while two people – a man and a woman – dash through the ruins. No words are printed. Just large white letters:

V1

So this is it then. The weapon Timothy Squire lectured us about, Hitler's new secret weapon. *Why do we always have to be so afraid?* Ever since that taxi brought me here on the day Mum died, to start a strange new life with Uncle Henry, I have been hiding behind these walls.

I can't hide here any more. Everyone else is doing their part to make life normal again. I have to do mine.

Oakes's laughter takes me by surprise. I didn't hear him approach. 'German propaganda has become feeble.' But he takes the leaflet from my hands.

Timothy Squire is staring at me in that way he does when he wants to get my attention – when he has something he's desperate to explain to me. *Something he's managed to leave out.*

But I don't need him to explain this. I know what the V means.

Vengeance.

The Thames slides past. I put V1s from my thoughts as I bike up to see Flo's parents. She wrote last summer to say she'd be back in October – but they stayed another six months in Montreal. I don't know why she was delayed but it doesn't matter; she is here now. She has been back in London for six days and I still haven't seen her.

At least she wrote a letter. Timothy Squire couldn't find the time to do the same.

I still cannot believe that he is back. I left him standing in front of the roost, silent as an old stone. A good night's sleep and he'll be rambling on and on like always.

Flo's letter said they have actual beef! I can't believe it – but Flo is here now, so anything is possible. Even a proper Sunday roast.

I am free to come and go at the Tower. No longer the hovering presence he used to be, nosing around all the time, Oakes treats me like a grown-up. Almost. So long as I stay between Blackfriars Bridge and Tower Bridge, and don't go further south than Borough, I can ride the bike wherever I like.

To go and see Flo, though, I was granted special permission. Maida Vale is well outside our agreed-upon area, but I know the way perfectly. And all the shelters are clearly marked.

I ride alongside the river for another few minutes, then turn on to the Strand, climbing north-west. The afternoon is chilly, the cobbles wet from the earlier rain. Summer is still a long time coming. I have been back here many times since the Blitz ended. The first time was with Oakes. It was after that walk that he bought me the bike. We visited my old street, the tall, stately houses, but didn't spend too much time at my house. It was a surprise to see that the gate posts were so low, the windows so close together.

We looked at it from across the street, but for some reason I didn't want to go any closer. Despite dreaming of coming back, it didn't feel quite right. It didn't feel like home any more. All our things are inside, but it is a hollow shell. For a moment I glimpsed it. Another life, barely recognizable now, separated by a great gulf. But it is still there.

A photograph is inside – of me, Mum, and Father.

He looked different then, not the thin, wild man who went mad at the Tower gates. *But still a German, even then.* I don't need to go inside to get it. The photograph is always at the edge of my thoughts, stronger than memory.

At least the house has not been bombed. At least I know it is still there.

I bike past Buckingham Palace, not even flinching at the heavy roar of the Hyde Park guns being tested, and turn left towards Paddington. I fly down Warwick Avenue, the canals and coloured boats coming into view. I am getting close now. *Some day Timothy Squire and I will live here with our ravens.* Portia and Rogan, and maybe Stan, once he calms down a little.

Much has changed in the past two years. Most of the flats, even the great tall ones, have gone to powder. The city is just… different. Blackout curtains can still be seen in the corners of windows, ready to be drawn at nightfall. I keep my eyes skinned for any shards gleaming amid the cobblestones. At least there is no more rubble in the streets.

It is easy to imagine how the city used to look. It comes to me like a picture. The orange glow of torched houses. Jagged craters left from parachute mines. Everywhere, fire-hoses. Your ears still ringing, the breath sucked from your lungs, eyes stung red with dust.

If Hitler had his way, the whole city would be nothing more than a cloud of smoke. People talk of the 'world after the war', clearing up all the mess and starting again. Do they mean it – can they truly see an end to it, a new world after this one?

I swing up the lane – and stop. Behind me, approaching slowly, is a silver car. I watch it come, drive right beside me, and disappear down the turning road.

Who is that? I recognize the car somehow. Petrol is impossible to get, Oakes says. I shake my head, find the pedals, and bike on.

The silver car is in front of me, now stopped. The driver's door swings open and a man steps halfway out.

'Anna?'

I blink in recognition. 'Mr Swift?'

'Just had to pop out and get some more wine. Come on, hop in – I'll take you the rest of the way.'

'Oh, that's OK, sir. I have my bike.'

Flo's dad looks down, acknowledges the bike. One foot is still inside the car. I can hear the running engine from here. 'Aha. Well, we'll see you in a minute then. Be careful on the roads, Anna.'

'Goodbye, Mr Swift.' I wave, embarrassed. 'See you in a moment.'

I am hugging Flo like it is a dream. She is taller – she always was – but somehow *younger*. Or not as old as the rest of us.

'You couldn't have written a few more letters?' She laughs, pulling back to stare at me.

'I know. I'm sorry, Flo. I tried… it is wonderful to see you.'

Again she is hugging me and again my face feels hot. It is so like a dream that I cannot fully understand where I am.

No, I know I am in Flo's sitting room. The room where we read *King Arthur* and *Stories for Girls* before going outside to follow the afternoon sun around the garden.

'There,' I say, and point to the blue mugs on the counter. The mugs we always used for tea. 'So many nights hiding in a dark shelter and I thought about those.' Staring at them now, I almost feel tears come to my eyes.

'Anna!'

Mr Swift greets me as though we hadn't said hello mere moments ago.

The sitting room is just as I remember it. White curtains on the wide windows, heavy rugs, high chairs with cushions. I was here, just before they left, when the furniture was covered in dust sheets and the vases and lamps packed away in newspaper. Flo's two brothers and sister – older, almost plump now, especially Peter – give me subdued hellos.

A black blur rushes past and I cry out. It is wonderful to see a happy dog. Last year, when the rule banned dogs from air raid shelters, many of the animals were put down. People couldn't care for their pets while spending days and nights in the shelter. Geoffrey, however, looks as happy as any dog can be.

'Did he go to Canada with you?' I ask, incredulous.

'Geoffrey *loves* the snow. You're going to miss all that snow, aren't you, Geoffrey? And the food! Anna, I wish you could have been there. Doughnuts with sugar. Apple juice, caramels, peanuts – chewing gum!'

Her voice is the same – soft and laughing, just as I'd imagined it these past two years. Soon we are in the dining room, a room we only ever passed through on the way to the garden. Even her family never had dinner in this room. Heaps of beef on china plates. Beef. *No way they ate better than this in Canada.* The beef is *fried*. As butter and oil are impossible to come by, all food is boiled. Already my mouth is watering. Peas *and* beans.

The only thing that is different is the absence of white-uniformed maids, who used to bustle around the kitchen. *Not a maid in London now*, Oakes once said. *They've followed all the rich families to their country homes.*

I didn't know Mrs Swift cooked, but this looks incredible. *Extraordinary.* Flo's brothers and sister occupy the other side of the table. But I only have eyes for Flo. And the beef.

It feels like Christmas dinner, and Mr Swift has a shiny smile. It is warm, happy – apart from everything horrible that has happened. Safe and removed. Flo takes little, tiny bites of her food and I almost laugh – *she has not changed*.

There is no weight, none of the heavy feeling always present when sitting down to dinner with the Warders. It feels like, well, family. *I suddenly imagine Timothy Squire and I having such a life. It will be perfect.*

'Living in the Tower,' Mr Swift says, munching his bread. 'There's a story for the kids.'

'Yes, sir. And I am volunteering at the canteen.'

I am only waiting for him to say 'the juice is worth

the squeeze' with that giant smile, or 'something to think about while you help with the dishes'. I've had so many dinners here – and been sent home with so many left-overs. What would Timothy Squire say if I brought him roast beef?

Mr Swift turns to Flo, smiling. 'So much history. We took you, didn't we, sweetie? When you were – what, six or seven? You saw the Crown jewels. I don't suppose you remember much of it now. I wager Anna could show you around. Maybe jump the queue.'

'We're not open to the public,' I say. 'Not during the war.'

No Crown jewels either. My mind skips back to Uncle's words, and I almost laugh and make a fool of myself. *The ravens are the Crown jewels.*

'Oh, well, that makes sense.' Flo's mum turns to her soup, slurping. 'Things'll be right as rain soon enough.'

A distant rumble. A passing truck? Or the V1s? Instinctively, I glance around. I saw through the windows to the back garden when I first came in; no Anderson shelter. *Is there a cellar? Flo and I spent most of our time in her room or in the garden.* Mr Swift's stack of wine bottles in the kitchen confirms there isn't a cellar.

'How long to get to the Warwick Avenue shelter?'

Mum and I had put up an Anderson in our garden – well, Mrs Weber's husband helped, before he was sent away to the Isle of Man. *He was an Austrian – not as bad as a German, but close.*

We can only trust our own.

34

The prospect of a night in the shelter is far less enticing with Flo's family and half the neighbourhood, but walls will keep you safe from the blast. Out in the open, you can be thrown ten feet in the air by the impact. *Unless it is the V1s. No one knows* what *they'll do.*

Mr Swift exchanges a long look with Mrs Swift.

'All that is behind us now, Anna dear.'

I look between them, too surprised to hide it. Abruptly it occurs to me why the white-curtained living room looks so strange. 'You don't have blackout curtains.'

Mrs Swift smiles. 'No need to worry.'

No need to worry? Blackout curtains are thick enough to catch the broken glass. Usually.

'Our bombers went to Cologne last night,' I say. 'Hitler always retaliates. And the Germans are developing new weapons, new bombs. That's why the Tower is still closed. We all have to go to the shelter when the siren sounds.'

Mr Swift coughs into his napkin.

'We took Florence to see the ice hockey,' he says, suddenly smiling wide. 'She was quite taken with it. Who was it you liked, Florence? Number eleven, for the Canadiens – fast as a pistol.'

We all turn to Flo, who appears to be near bursting.

'Father says you must come and live with us now,' she says. 'Especially now that your – Oh, it will be grand, Anna.'

I am still. I can feel Mr Swift's eyes on me.

Flo has not *changed. None of them have.*

'Well, what do you say, Anna? It's not a castle, but we'll

keep you warm and fed. "Bread in the bin, cake in the tin." And you two girls, reunited.'

I say nothing at first. It *isn't* a castle. And it isn't home.

'Thank you, Mr Swift, Mrs Swift. Thank you both so much. But the Tower – I live there now. I mean, I have a life there. I am the Ravenmaster. I am needed, and especially with these new birds; some of them don't get on at all. And I start work at the canteen—'

'Come back to school,' Flo says, more confused than angry. 'Mrs Munro is still teaching maths and I bet even Mr—'

'No, Flo.' I stop her. 'I can't.'

Everything is very quiet.

'Anna,' says Mr Swift. The shiny smile has vanished. 'Please. There is no rush – to finish your dinner or to move house. We only thought, given what happened at the Tower…'

'Do you mean the war? The war is not over. The Germans are planning a whole new attack – are you all blind?'

He looks cross now. 'Anna, we know it has been a difficult time for you – and we shall pass no judgement here. Now, if you want to come back and live in the old neighbourhood, if you want to share a room with Florence instead of a suit of medieval armour, we'd be happy to have you.'

Flo's eyes are wide like a puppy's. I have to look away. 'Thank you for dinner Mrs Swift. And thank you for your kind offer, Mr Swift. But I have to go home now.'

Monday, 18 May 1942

'Glad to hear of your interest.' The old lady smiles down at me. 'You'll not be our youngest, so don't go worrying about that. Come on, let me show you how to do it.'

I am to be part of a canteen, run with an iron fist by Mrs Barrett. Girls in dungarees and tin hats – some of them looking younger than me – are handing out food and drink.

'A wonderful thing, isn't it?' says the old lady, glancing over at the sea of volunteers.

It is different, now that the daily bombing has stopped. Now, people are rebuilding. And what they need is decent food and drink.

I give a tight smile as a dirty man calls up to me. Already my feet itch.

I *am* like a bloody NAAFI girl. To think I used to want to be one myself. Elsie changed all that. Elsie and Timothy Squire's little romance had the whole Tower wanting to sick up.

A queue of hopeful women snakes around the street. They have caught a rumour that the empty stall will later be selling fish. I think of the stories Oakes told me about the Russians, running away as the Nazi army approached, and smashing their own homes so the Germans couldn't use them. Burning their own crops so the Nazis wouldn't get them. Could we ever do something like that? Destroy our homes, our markets? It is so very cold in Russia.

But the Germans are that evil. All of them. We have to do what we can to stop them.

37

The canteen is mostly frequented by the defence gunners – 'the battery boys' – starving for sandwiches (sardine paste or tomato and marge), which cost eightpence with a canteen cake and a cup of tea. Otherwise it is filled with a lot of conchies – conscientious objectors to war. They help clear up bomb damage. Some of the battery boys carry on a bit of banter with them, but mostly the conchies keep to themselves.

'Dunkirk took Roger,' Mrs Barrett says, seeing me watching them and adding a glare of her own. 'No help from this lot. Should all be locked in Brixton gaol.'

Despite her hard looks and words, Mrs Barrett treats the conchies fairly, selling food and drink to them with a tight smile.

After a few hours I am exhausted. My whole body is sore from lack of sleep. *Just like everyone else.* Except Flo, who will be enjoying the summer holidays.

'Your hot chocolate, sir.' I push the steaming cup across the counter, and the soldier takes it with a grateful nod. A frontline soldier.

Frontline soldiers appear among the crowds, on leave or receiving treatment, and groups cluster around them. From these interactions, rumours spin and grow. Whispers of something – something huge, something never before attempted. The Germans are about to invade. No, it is us – we are about to sail an army across the Channel and invade Germany. Whatever the details, one thing is always true: this war is about to change.

I think again of the V1 leaflets: the red flames dancing around Tower Bridge, the man and woman screaming among the ruins. *Is it true?* And even though Hitler seems to have stopped bombing London, with each passing full moon, my heart clenches.

With a mumbled thank you the soldier takes the hot chocolate, wanders to a patch of sunlight. Something *is* about to happen. And I can't be handing out hot chocolate when it does. I should be like these soldiers, in a proper uniform, fighting alongside the men.

I can do more than work at the canteen. But I will need some help. Then I remember – there *is* someone who can help me. And I know just where to find her.

Victory House in Piccadilly could be a palace, with great marble columns catching and pooling the light. A crowd of women stream past in their pretty blue uniforms. *That* is the type of uniform I could wear with pride. I gaze out over the sea of faces, some smiling, others blank – with exhaustion, or boredom?

'Nell!'

I recognize her the instant I see her. She is with a group of women, blurry in the heat, but I would recognize her anywhere.

'Nell,' I say. 'Hello. It's me—'

'Anna Cooper,' she says, grinning. 'All grown up.'

She remembers *me*? Her Cockney accent sounds almost musical to my ears.

I stare at her, her uniform starched, pressed, and perfect. And me, dirty and exhausted in my dungarees. A day at the canteen and it already feels like the longest summer of my life. Mrs Barrett doesn't seem to feel the sweltering temperature.

'Volunteering are you?' Nell looks me up and down. 'I did my time at the canteen. How long have you been down there?'

'Not long.' I glance hastily away. 'Yeoman Sparks told me you were helping out with recruiting. For the Women's Auxiliary Air Force.'

'Just for a while longer. I'll be off to the airfield any day now.'

How can I ask her? Well, I am here now.

'The truth is, Nell, I want to be in the WAAF, too. I would love it, in fact.'

'Of course you would, sweetie. All the top-drawer girls are here. You don't want any of that navy stuff – staring out at the sea all day. The air force is the place for talented girls like you. Hitler's Blitz is done, so now it's our turn to drop some bombs.'

I nod, feigning knowledge. 'I would love to help, however I can.'

'You'll need to know someone to get in – but then, you know me. And you're a strong one, I remember that much. How old are you?'

'Sixteen. Well, I will be next year.'

Another smile. 'Well, there are ways around that, if you're truly keen.'

'Really?'

'Of course.' She laughs. 'You were a Vacuee, right? Do you even *have* a birth certificate?'

I shake my head. 'I don't know – I mean, no, I doubt it. All is know is that Oakes is now my guardian, and I'll need his permission—'

'Gregory Oakes is your guardian?' She has stopped smiling, her perfect pencilled eyebrows knitted together in worry. 'Well, my dear Anna Cooper, you're just going to have to wait another year or so. No way he'll go down to the register office with a bucket full of lies. That man wouldn't break a rule to save his own life.'

I nod, sure that she's right. After Uncle's funeral, Oakes became my guardian, for which I was very happy. Otherwise I'd have been sent God-knows-where. Of course I once thought very differently about Yeoman Oakes. The whole of last year I was certain he was a spy, not realizing that he was the one keeping Father from finding me here. I still flush with shame to remember how sure I was that he was a traitor. *But he truly wouldn't break a rule to save his own life.*

I fight back an abrupt surge of helplessness. But it isn't his life he'll be saving.

'Leave it to me, Nell.'

I remember what Uncle said about me. *I can do anything I set my mind to.*

She frowns, clearly not confident in the possibility of Oakes ever changing. Women in uniform continue to file out around us. Nell plucks a cigarette from her breast pocket, lights it.

'Tell you what, Cooper. There's a film playing down in Leicester Square next week. About a female pilot. Make sure you've got a real passion for all this before you go begging Gregory Oakes to give up being a statue?'

'Oh, Nell. Are you sure?'

'Of course, love. My date's been called away on a mission, so I've got a spare ticket. You up for it then?'

I nod, already imagining myself in the WAAF uniform, living on base with Nell, planes roaring into the sky around us. And one day, somehow, I will be needed to fly one. With Nell as my co-pilot, we will chase out the roving Nazi bombers.

Saying goodbye to Nell, I make my way back to the Underground, my mind racing. If I am going to leave the Tower, I must train the new Ravenmaster as best I can. And there's no way it's going to be Yeoman Stackhouse.

Uncle named *me* the new Ravenmaster, so it's up to me to pass the title on.

And I have my work cut out for me.

2

'Rogan is the dominant male – see?'

Anna gestures to the bird standing in the sunlight. I have already helped her lay out the meat for the birds. Even wearing thick gloves and carrying around that tin bucket, her red hair all messed up in the wind, she is the prettiest girl I know. Well, there is Nell, but she is more *beautiful* than pretty. And she's like twenty-five, besides.

I need to get Anna a present.

All I got her was marmalade and some toffee. Expensive enough, sure – I had to borrow ten shillings from Lightwood – but it wasn't quite right. Bought it in a hurry, as we were suddenly sent home. It's a wonder she didn't get cross with me.

I sneak another look at her. I know if I say it now, it will never happen. The time isn't right; it will be gone, lost, for ever.

'Timothy Squire, are you even paying attention?'

''Course.'

She is pointing at Rogan – I can tell that it is him even

43

without the blue plastic ring around his foot. The others, though, I can only tell apart by their coloured bands: Portia (white), Corax (yellow – and terrifying), Lyra (red), Oliver (green), Stan (purple), Cronk (orange).

'See? Look at his ear feathers.'

I shake my head clear. *Ear feathers?*

'And see how he flares the feathers on his legs – like baggy trousers.'

Am I looking at the same bird? Ears? Trousers?

'Right. Got it.'

'And watch how Cronk begs when confronted by him?'

That much I can see. *Come on, Cronk, stand up for yourself, mate.* But Cronk shrinks, giving little cries, and Rogan, beak held high, shoulders spread, chases him off.

Anna also told me about trimming the birds' wings – how there's no need to cut the boys' wings. 'Only trim the females' wings, because the males just follow them around.' I thought she was teasing at first. But Anna knows everything about these birds.

What else do girls like? Well, Anna's not a regular girl anyway – she'll want a new raven or something impossible.

We walk slowly over to where Rogan and Stan are playing. Each step I take sends them a hop away. *They don't recognize me any more.* Anna said ravens can recognize a face for years. I haven't changed *that* much. I hold out a biscuit in a gloved hand ('always wear gloves when feeding the ravens'). My *own* biscuits. An expensive bribe, but it seems to do the trick. Stan hops back towards me.

'So will you be down at the docks for a while, then?'

'Dunno,' I say, pulling my hand away before Stan can take a bite of that, too. Can't I just give Anna some flowers? All girls like flowers, even Anna. No chance of sneaking off at lunch to visit her canteen. We're barely allowed out of Quarter's sight. *You're not allowed out of it at all.* 'We'll all be down there for a while.'

I hand over a square of chocolate to Anna. She puts down the bucket, tugs off her gloves.

'Where did you get this?' she asks, suspicious. *Even more suspicious than the bloody bird was.* What is that look? It's as if she wants me to apologize for every mistake I ever made. We don't have *that* kind of time.

'Bloke I work with. Trade my cigarette ration for his chocolate cards, one for one.'

'Your friend Lightwood? He's a sapper, too, right? How many of you sappers are down there? Sounds like a big project.'

'There's only one like him. Clever little bugger. I'm good, but he's absolute mustard on disposing bombs. Knows it all,' I laugh. She wants to know more, of course – what we're building, and why. *Like I could tell her even if I knew.*

A harsh *kraa* from one of the ravens – green, that's Oliver. It's a bit much, spending all this time with the birds, and all you get is angry croaking in return.

'So you don't mind,' she says, with her habit of reading the thoughts right out of my head, 'spending a little time with the ravens? When you have time, I mean. I don't trust Stackhouse, and if you'll be at the docks for a while…'

Spend *more* time with the birds? A person can only

handle so much raven chat before they go barking mad. And in the morning, after a night at the pub with Lightwood, the noise'll do my head in. I'll have to teach the birds to croak a little softer...

'Ah,' I say, giving her my best smile, 'I just thought of something.'

'What?' She raises an eyebrow, *still* suspicious. 'A convenient reason why you can't help with the ravens?'

'Just the opposite, Magpie. I'd be happy to look after them for you.'

From his perch on the Green, Oliver growls and rumbles. But I've heard him make all sorts of calls, *yips* and yells, clicking noises and whistling sounds. Ravens *are* meant to be proper smart.

'It's a surprise. Might take a little time, but don't worry. You're going to love it.'

Saturday, 20 *June* 1942

'You're sure you're allowed to go out like this?' Flo is trying to sound calm but I can hear the nervousness just underneath.

'Oh yes, I come down here all the time.'

'With your friend?' She nods darkly towards Nell.

In fact I've never been to Leicester Square, with Nell or on my own. And I did have to get special permission from Oakes.

But there is nothing dangerous in us going to the cinema.

(Flo wanted to bring her dad along – but the thought of a talk with Mr Swift in front of Nell was too much. I have not been over to their house since the horrid dinner.) My head is pounding, but it will clear once the picture starts.

Either way, it feels good to have Flo here. When she was gone in Montreal, I would dream of us laughing during a film together. She was delighted when I offered for her to join Nell and me. Nell didn't seem as thrilled. She figured Flo would never get a ticket, but somehow Flo's dad got his hands on one for her. That only seemed to anger Nell more. But she'll come around. Everyone always ends up liking Flo.

'They could sure use a soda fountain here,' she says.

Nell rolls her eyes, lights another cigarette without slowing her pace. We are practically racing to the cinema, Nell's clicking heels leading the way. Flo for the most part seems to ignore her, speaking softly to me and edging away from the clouds of cigarette smoke like they can hurt her.

This is not the first time Flo has told me all about the wonders of Canada and soda fountains. I'll have to ask her boring questions about ice hockey – her stories of milkshakes and beefburgers only make me more hungry.

I'm beginning to think I should not have brought her at all. But I just couldn't forget, when I left her house, the look on her face. *She looked so hurt*. I should not have been so hard on them. I was carrying on like Oakes, one step away from asking them to do gas-mask drills. I used to dream about moving in with Flo and her family. When Mum was mean or cross with me, I would dream about Flo and I being sisters, and how Mr and Mrs Swift would let us do whatever we wanted.

Flo moves a little closer to me, braving Nell's cigarette smoke. 'Sorry you left so early – you missed pudding! But I understand.'

Her tone makes me want to scream. Sympathy! I know what she really means. *Of course there was no bombing – you're mad, Anna Cooper!* There *was* a bombing – a retaliation bombing – but Canterbury was the target, not London. Another historic city. Hitler will destroy our past and then our future. Or has he already?

Flo knows nothing but thinks she knows everything.

Why am I so mad at her? It's not *her* fault. And I did see the pudding on her kitchen counter. Butter and plum jam. Plum jam! Still, I had to leave.

Of course Flo didn't bring a torch with her. When she was last here, streetlights and shop entrances were lit up. Now no sliver of light shows the way. I can feel her, groping through space. If only she could have seen me when I sneaked through the city at night to find Mabel – the Blitz was still on then, and wardens chased me through the streets. Even she couldn't have run any faster.

'Here.' I pass her the torch but she shakes her head. And quickly bumps into a woman, muttering pardons. *As stubborn as ever then.*

Flo was always good at everything and in no time she gets the hang of it, letting her feet slide off the kerb so as not to fall.

'Only for ever, that's putting it mild,' she hums, repeating the line from some song. She seems to have developed a number of annoying habits in Canada, including always snatching at her hair.

There are crowds as we reach the square. Women in skirts calling boldly to the passing men. Flo stares in fascination but I hurry her along, trying to equal Nell's pace.

'I know why you want to live in the Tower of London,' Flo chatters on, a smile in her voice. 'It is where Guinevere fled, and Mordred laid siege to the Tower – until Lancelot came and saved her, as she knew he would.'

I glance swiftly up, but Nell is thankfully too far ahead to hear in the commotion of people.

'King Arthur is not real, Flo.'

'So?'

'Well, real things happened there. Real stories.'

'I thought you liked King Arthur,' she says, loudly, her tone hurt.

Clearing my throat, hoping Nell can't hear us, I turn to Flo. 'Do you know who Rudolf Hess is? The second-in-command of the Nazis. He was stood right in front of me, talking to me. And the night that Leslie… God, you don't know anything, do you? No one cares about King Arthur or ice-hockey games, OK?'

She flinches as if stung.

'He's not coming back.' Her voice reaches me as I stalk away. Nell has stopped, too, watching us. As I reach her, I turn back to Flo, staring hard. 'What?'

'You think if you stay at the Tower, he'll come back. He won't. He can't.'

'You think I want him to? A *German*, to come stop by and visit me? Maybe we'll have breakfast with the Warders, some schnitzel.'

'He's your father—'

'I don't know this person. I don't know a single thing about him.'

People are looking at us, watching, listening. I offer Flo a half smile, go forward and link her arm.

'Can we just enjoy the film?' I ask.

She mutters something that might be agreement. It is an uneasy silence as we walk on, but I can think of nothing to say. I *did* talk to Rudolf Hess. The newspapers say he is mad, that he deserted Hitler. He even handed me a piece of paper – a poem. I almost kept it to show Flo. To prove to her that I was brave.

'School was *much* easier in Montreal.' Flo laughs, squeezing my arm. Nothing keeps her down for long. 'I was worried it was all going to be ghastly and all in French, but Mr Beaudet spoke English almost as well as an Englishman. It's much harder with Mrs Jordan.'

We turn the corner and there are flashbulbs everywhere. Two women are in the heart of it, one serious as a school teacher, the other regal as any queen. Both blonde, but the grand lady's hair gleams like platinum.

'Cooper.' Nell's voice is barely a breath. Her eyes are wide and bright – I have never seen her like this. 'That's her.'

'Who?'

'*Anna Neagle.* The film star.'

50

I've never heard of Anna Neagle, but instantly I know which of the two is the film star; and she is certainly stunning. *My name is Anna*, is the first inane thing to pop into my thoughts. We stand in the cool night, staring at Nell staring at Anna Neagle.

Flo squeezes my arm again. 'That summer we went blackberrying. Oh, do you remember blackberry tarts?'

'Blackberry tarts,' I repeat, turning away from Nell's rapt face. The thought of blackberry tarts is almost enough to make my mouth water.

Flo gives me a sidelong look. 'Anna, don't you think you should come back to school? I mean, you don't have to right now, if you don't want to – but next year…'

'It's not because I don't want to, Flo.' I sigh, certain she won't understand. *Leap before you're pushed.* 'I just… can't.'

'Well,' she tries again, 'at least pass your school certificate so you can go on to sixth form.'

'I'm not going back to school, Flo,' I say, my voice as steady as I can make it. 'I need to do something… useful.'

'You mean for the war?'

'It's our duty to help out, Flo.'

'Anna, we're fourteen. Our *duty* is to finish school.'

'And then what?'

Astonishingly, she looks angry. 'I don't know why you have to be this way.'

'What way?'

'You're so mad – so serious all the time. I know the war is wicked—'

'How do you know that?'

'I'm sorry I left, Anna. I'm sorry my parents wanted to protect me. I'm sorry that most of the city left *like we were told to*. I'm sorry you had to stay.'

The film is about a female pilot named Amy Johnson, played by Anna Neagle, who is stunning throughout. Smoking a cigarette in the cockpit, waiting for her aircraft to be refuelled, she is heroic and beautiful. She reminds me of Nell, in a way, but somehow even more glamorous. But as we leave the cinema I am not thinking about Nell or Anna Neagle.

Was any of that real? Did Amy Johnson actually fly from London to Cape Town, South Africa? Imagine being the first woman to fly solo to Australia – *Australia*. Twenty days and eleven thousand miles away. All thoughts of blackberry tarts have been swept away.

'Cooper.' Nell lights another cigarette, blows the smoke straight up into the sky. 'What do you think? Romantic enough for you?'

I can only nod.

'But... she died.' Flo stands at my side, visibly shaken.

Nell smiles vaguely. 'A dangerous life, being a pilot.'

Amy Johnson died in a flying accident – trapped in the clouds, no way out and no petrol left, she parachuted out but drowned in the Thames. She was helping the war effort, ferrying aircraft back and forth.

As we squeeze through the Leicester Square crowds I can still hear Amy Johnson's voice, when she's warned the weather is too dangerous to fly. *I'll crack through and fly over the top.*

Alone.

Wednesday, 15 July 1942

Uncle was buried in the Bow cemetery on a wet freezing day, but I put a cross here at the Tower, too. Next to those marked *MacDonald*, *Cora*, *Edgar*, and *Merlin*, is a small wooden cross that reads *Henry Reed, Ravenmaster*. The Raven Graveyard, he called it, when we decided to honour the ravens that had died in the Blitz; to make sure they wouldn't be forgotten. Nothing fancy like all the stone monuments and ancient gravestones around here, but Uncle thought it was perfect. Less than a week later, he was gone.

The exact spot was our secret – no one else comes here – and I won't tell anyone, not even Timothy Squire. It is a quiet place to think of Uncle and the ravens and that terrible year. I often come here after we've filed out of Chapel, my ears still full of the droning organ.

Today there is nothing in my ears, only the wind across the stone. I sit down beside the markers, quiet as a statue.

The new roost will be safe. The Blitz is over. They will live here, and thrive, and protect the legend of the Tower.

I think of the two markers without names – Uncle and I agreed they should remain blank – Mabel and Grip. Maybe out there somewhere, flying free. It's been a hundred years or more since a wild raven has been seen in London, Uncle said. Well, maybe one day they'll come back.

And maybe I will, too.

'I did what I could, Uncle,' I whisper into the quiet. The wind across the stone is the only answer.

Tuesday, 13 October 1942

'I hardly think this is the sort of protection expected of me as your guardian, Anna.' Yeoman Oakes shakes his head.

I try to keep my voice calm. 'Nell says they may take me at sixteen – it's only one year's difference.'

'Well then, in another year I will be happy to help you.'

'In another year the war will be over!'

He laughs, low and humourless. 'God willing.'

'Yeoman Oakes, I want to help out. And not in the canteen. Uncle said – you said – I could do anything I set my mind to, remember? Well, this is what I want to do. I want to join the WAAF with Nell. Maybe I can't be a pilot myself, but I can help other pilots. Some ravens aren't meant to stay in the Tower – remember, you said that?'

Oakes sighs. 'Anna, your birth certificate is a serious matter. I can't just lie, simply because you want to join up with Nell Singer.'

'But my whole life is a lie! My father is a German, and everyone lies about that. Mum told me that Father drowned when I was five, and yet he's still alive. Mum even changed our name. And then she killed herself, and everyone lied about that! So why can't I have a new life? Even if the age is wrong, it will be more real. My mother was Margaret Cooper, a journalist. My father was John Cooper, a sailor. And in October, I turn sixteen years old. Why not? Why can't *that* be true?'

I stop to take a breath, the speech not coming out quite like I'd planned. I know I shouldn't mention Mum – or Father – to get what I want, but Oakes is always so stubborn.

'Just because she's not here, doesn't mean she abandoned you, Anna.'

I have heard all this before. She was ill, Uncle said, and in her ill mind, she thought she was sacrificing herself to save me. *She made a mistake. She loved me.*

The ache of it never goes away.

'That's not how it feels, Yeoman Oakes, sir.'

'I'll wager you can still feel her love here. She sent you here. She knew you'd be looked after, protected at the Tower. Looked after better than she could with her illness.'

'How could anyone look after me better than her?'

'She was ill, Anna.'

'Uncle Henry was ill, too,' I say. 'But he didn't leave you.'

Oakes falls silent, hanging his head in defeat. *I am sorry, Yeoman Oakes.*

'But... how...?'

I am smiling at Nell. 'Right? Nothing easier than back-dating a birth certificate.'

She shakes her head, clearly impressed. Her cigarette burns away between her fingers. 'I can't believe it, Cooper.'

'Neither can I, to be honest. But I'm sixteen now.'

She remembers her cigarette, brings it to her lips. 'Yeah. Seventeen would've been too much of a stretch, let's be honest. But you're a doll of a young sixteen.'

I am beaming, brick-red and without a care. 'Thank you, Nell. For helping me do this.'

Reaching in her bag, she pulls out cigarettes and tips the pack towards me. 'Thank me by doing a hell of a job for the WAAF, Miss Cooper.'

I reach, drawing out a slender tube, holding it gently between my thumb and forefinger. Nell strikes a match, holds it steady between us.

And just like that, on my fifteenth birthday, I turned sixteen.

The Tower is less welcoming in the grey evening light. The new birds still feel so different – even the sounds they make. Far more *quorks* and honks, mainly from Rogan and Portia, and rolling, gurgling calls between Oliver and Stan. I never heard Grip or Mabel make those noises.

The ravens squabble around me, Stan and Oliver locked in playful battle. I shake my head to clear it. I must round up this lot and get to bed. What will Timothy Squire say when I tell him I am signing up to be a WAAF? Oh, the look on his face when he sees me in the uniform.

It can't be as hard as working in the docks – he barely leaves off complaining about it. First I must pass my interview, and a physical test, and I should definitely start learning something about planes.

I close the last of the roost doors with a heavy clang. 'Goodnight, you lot.'

Looking out at the ravens in their cages, snapping beaks and flailing wings, a certainty grows in me. Madness, perhaps. I *can* do anything I set my mind to. *I can learn to fly.*

The sky darkens to purple as I walk to the Bloody Tower. All I can think about is Amy Johnson and a single plane soaring above the clouds.

Thursday, 15 October 1942

Quarter lounges at his desk, pouring a tall glass. I don't take the seat opposite. I can see, from here, his stash of single malt whisky. He just leaves it out in the open, so confident no one would dare.

I wouldn't.

'It's your lucky day, Squire. Seems they're desperate enough to give you another shot. Demolition training. Something we can both celebrate.'

A great smile threatens to engulf my face but I fight it back. 'Thank you, sir.'

'Take this.' He shoves a letter across the table. 'You'll be off to Aberdeen at first light tomorrow to rejoin Major Roland.'

I stare down at the page, reading and rereading the looping words.

'Aberdeen?'

'What? You have a problem with sheep, Squire?' Quarter laughs, enjoying his drink.

'No, sir. It's just…'

'What is wrong with you, boy?'

'What about Lightwood?'

'They don't want him. You've been offered a second chance, Squire. No time for mooning over your mates.'

'If I'm invited back, he must be, too. It was *my* fault the fuse didn't work…'

Quarter squints at me, lowers his glass. 'What are you talking about?'

'It's the truth, sir.'

His hand abandons the glass, tightening into a fist. *How I hate this man.* 'Major Roland is happy to give you another chance to join their ranks as a sapper so long as you don't make a fuss. Why are you making a fuss, Squire?'

I drop my head. I can't believe I am going to do this – throw away my chance to become a sapper. I *must* be mad.

'I'm sorry, sir. I thank them for the offer, but I can't accept it unless they take Lightwood, too.'

'Accept it? This is the armed forces, Squire. You'll do as you're told or you'll be off to gaol.'

I can look nowhere but at my boots, though the words come out solid enough.

'Actually, sir, I won't. I'm not properly eligible for the armed forces. I'm only sixteen, sir. So I'll just have to carry on my work here at the docks.'

Thursday, 22 *October* 1942

Timothy Squire wants to know why I've been acting so queer. He will find out soon enough. But first he is trying to give me something: lavender soap for my birthday. He has again managed to make it for the dawn feeding, something I am barely able to do with Mrs Barrett's crushing schedule.

'Thank you, Timothy Squire.'

'Hey, it's nothing. Bought it myself, of course.' He tries to smile, but his face says he wishes he hadn't spoken at all.

Looting is not a joke, Timothy Squire. I won't forget what you did just because you actually paid for something now.

Did you tell him about your theft last year? Did you mention how you broke into his room and stole from him – how you let the Tower think an incendiary had landed, just to create a distraction so you could escape?

No, I haven't said a word. If Oakes is happy to keep it quiet, I am, too. And I have something more important to say. *He's going to scoff at me.*

59

'Matter of fact,' he goes on hurriedly, 'I have something else for you. Well, not really, I mean it's not quite ready yet.'

'What is it?' I know I sound distracted – I *am* distracted! I just need to tell him, to tell him that I've made my decision. I have to tell him now.

Right now. *Before I lose my nerve.*

'I am teaching Oliver to speak,' he says.

'You are not.'

'Don't believe me? I'll show you – tomorrow at the dawn feeding.'

'Timothy—'

'If you listen hard, right, you can sort of make it out.'

'Timothy—'

He reaches out and takes my hand. 'It's sort of another present, I mean, it's not ready yet, but maybe by tomorrow morning—'

'I can't. I'm sorry, but I can't help tomorrow morning. Or for a while. I'm joining the WAAF.'

He pulls his hand away as though scalded.

We stare at each other. I must look just as confused.

'But you're working in the canteen, aren't you? I mean, you're not old enough to join the air force.'

'Are you mad at me?'

'No,' he says, though his voice sounds anything but calm. 'I just thought you'd work at the canteen. I thought you'd live at the Tower, and I'd be close by down at the docks. The WAAFs have bases all over the bloody place – you'll likely be in Cornwall or Orkney or some place.'

'You were happy to go to Aberdeen.'

'That's different,' he says. Timothy Squire is thinking. When he thinks, his forehead wrinkles with lines.

'Besides, they could send you anywhere, Timothy Squire – I'm sure you'll be in the desert before Christmas time.'

He gives me a strange look. 'I'll be here,' he says, 'in the docks.'

We are silent.

'It's not so bad,' he says, 'sticking around here. And the birds – they'd not last long with just me taking care of them. I think Corax hates me.'

'You have to be careful until they are familiar with you. You're too aggressive.'

He's far too aggressive. Half the time I'm worried Corax is going to take his hand off.

'The canteen is a good fit for you, Magpie.'

'I don't want to work at the canteen. I don't want to be a NAAFI girl.' I keep my voice as firm as I can. *God, why do I sound so sulky?* 'I am joining the Women's Auxiliary Air Force, if they'll have me.'

'Is it the V1s? Don't worry. A self-propelled missile is impossible. They'd never be able to aim it. The Nazis may've come up with all sorts of mad weapons – but that is impossible.'

'It's not the V1s.'

'What then?'

'I'm doing this for me, Timothy Squire. And for us.'

'For us?'

'Yes. As long as the war's still on, we can't do any of the things I've... planned.' His eyebrows shoot up in alarm.

'Never mind.' I sigh. 'I have to help. It's my duty.'

'But – you're not old enough.'

'Fake documents, same as you.'

'Magpie…'

'It's routine, remember? You told me everyone's doing the same thing.'

'What about the ravens?' he asks, looking at me from the corner of his eyes. 'What about them?'

'I was hoping you'd help me. Until I get back. I am coming back, you know. I just have to do my part. I have to. In the meantime, I was hoping you could be the Ravenmaster.'

'You can't do your part with the canteen? What's wrong with being a NAAFI girl, anyway?' He gives a grunt that could mean anything. 'I think it's stupid.'

I raise my eyebrows at him. 'Stupid?'

'Yes. Joining the WAAF is stupid, Anna.'

'Well, I'm leaving, Timothy Squire. Goodbye.'

'Churchill and his men are in for a surprise, when this is all over,' Oakes says. 'Rationing food, sharing space. People are unified now. How can we go back to the rich taking it all?'

Oakes sounds like Mum again. I care nothing for politics, but Oakes has agreed to sign my consent form and I don't want to ruin it.

'Thank you, Yeoman Oakes. Nell is going to help me, too. I mean, she is going to help me apply, even though she can't be at the application centre because she has been sent to the airfield. She really wants me to join. I will miss being here, though. Truly.'

And I will miss Yeoman Oakes, as mad as that once would have sounded. I feel like he needs me here. He scarcely leaves the Stone Kitchen any more. When I asked how long it was since he'd last visited Hew Draper's carving in Salt Tower, he said, 'Oh, I haven't been there in ages.' That carving is one of his favourite things, and it's hardly five minutes from the kitchen. I will ask him to take me there when I'm next home.

'I'm sure other people raised objections to you leaving us,' he says now. 'As a canteen worker, you'd be able to live in the Tower. Close to the ravens – and the docks.'

I go as red as my hair. Oakes always knows more than he lets on, and I am grateful for him not saying it out loud. *Timothy Squire said it was stupid.* And what will Flo say? She thinks I should still be in school.

'I know.' I *do* know. Of course Timothy Squire wants me to stay, to be close. But I have to follow my own path. 'But I still want to join the WAAF, Yeoman Oakes.'

'See.' He gives a slow smile. 'They will be lucky to have you. And your uncle would be very proud.'

'I think Stackhouse will improve. And I have Timothy Squire helping out,' I say. 'It's just that Uncle named me the Ravenmaster – and I can't bear to let him down.'

Oakes clears his throat roughly. 'Oh, Anna, you mustn't think of it like that. Your uncle would be so proud of you, and so would your mother. It's your life, Anna, and you have to find a way to get on with it, do you understand?'

'I know, Yeoman Oakes. It's just I always think about Mum, about what I could have done differently. If only I—'

'Anna.' Oakes's voice is suddenly firm – the old, stern Oakes I remember from last year. 'There is nothing you could have done. Nothing. It was not your fault. She loved you.'

She loved you. That's what everyone tells me. *She loved you.* But she still left. I think of all the times I would shout to get what I wanted, like going to see some stupid film or spending the night at Flo's house.

'You couldn't have known, dear.' Oakes's voice has already softened. 'And there is nothing you could have done. Nothing anyone could have done. Your mum was ill, and so was your uncle, and we've lost them both. We'll just have to do our best now, you and I, won't we?'

We shall have to do our best.

I will miss Oakes – and all the Warders. This *is* home now. Somehow I feel connected to all the people and the history of the Tower, those who have been imprisoned in the dark towers and the thousands who have lived their lives in the school, pub, and the stone halls of this ancient castle. Mad as it sounds, it no longer feels like a gaol to me.

Each time I return to the Tower, pushing my bike across the stone bridge, I feel the enclosure of the Tower, the cool air. Coming back to the Tower is like walking into a mountain, with cliffs, ridges, and lookouts, and full of caves and valleys. A strange, ancient, impossible place. But *home*.

I stay awake into the night. Somewhere a fox barks.

In reply, a raven cries from the roost. Everyone is hungry. As the night deepens even these sounds fade.

Monday, 2 November 1942

The sergeant gives me a doubtful look.

'Name and age.'

I draw a breath, wishing it was steadier. 'Anna Cooper. I am sixteen, sir.'

He glances down at the form. 'Anna Winifred Cooper?'

'I'm afraid so.'

'Sixteen, huh?'

'Yes, sir.'

'And what, dear girl, is a "Ravenmaster"?'

'It's my job – my old job. I looked after the ravens. At the Tower of London, where I live.'

The sergeant is looking at me with a glazed look. 'Where were you at school?'

'Tower School, inside the Tower, sir. Closed now, due to the bomb damage.'

'And you didn't think to continue your school elsewhere? A school at Buckingham Palace, perhaps?'

'That would be an awful commute, sir.'

He eyes me, unsure who is mocking who. 'Right you are. Do you read *The Times*? Yes. The *Evening Standard*? Anything else? What about games?'

'I play netball, sir. And running.'

'Good. How many battleships are there in the Far East?'

'Battleships…? I couldn't say, sir.' Nell did *not* prepare me for this. Why does this man care about battleships – and how could I possibly know that? Does *anyone* know that? *Oh, Nell.*

'Hmmm. And what is the cosine of a right-angled triangle?'

I feel my breathing relax. 'The cosine is the length of the adjacent side over the length of the hypotenuse.' Trigonometry is something she did warn me about.

'Fine. Take this slip to the attendant and you will hear from us in due course.'

'Thank you, sir.'

I take the blue slip from his hand and hurry away.

Wednesday, 6 January 1943

I have also missed Timothy Squire's birthday – he turned sixteen last week. But he has barely been at the Tower since our talk. He is hiding from me. Like a child. He is *busy down at the docks*, he said, the one time I caught him crossing the Green. I almost believed him until he added, *Good luck with your air force application.*

He is insufferable. I enter the Stone Kitchen and coloured light falls through the high windows. There is an envelope on the table. A heavy, brown envelope. The room is quiet, the others having gone off to the Hut already – all except Oakes, calmly drinking his tea.

Oakes stands, tries a smile. 'I received a communication from the Air Ministry.'

WHAT THE RAVEN BRINGS

'Is this…?' I can't form the question.

'It's for you, Anna,' he says and walks away, taking his cup with him.

I wait until his footsteps have vanished before I tear open the envelope. I scan it quickly, none of the words sinking in. *It is an acceptance letter. They want me.*

The letter shakes in my hand. *Bases all over the bloody place. Cornwall; Orkney.* I finally focus, comprehend the words on the page.

Report to Victory House in Piccadilly at 8 a.m. for a medical exam.

Saturday, 9 January 1943

I walk down to Mark Lane Station, in my new Austin Reed skirt – I had just enough coupons for it – and I am feeling very grown up. I remember what Nell said to me last summer, after she helped me pick out an outfit. *Looking snappy.* What will she say when she sees me now?

I actually searched for Timothy Squire (even he would snap out of his sulking to wish me luck) but I could not find him. Maybe he really is busy down at the docks. *Hopefully not too busy to check up on the ravens.*

Victory House is overwhelmed with queuing recruits. As crowded as a Tube carriage at rush hour. Some of the girls smile, returning brisk hellos. A few look even younger than me. A WAAF sergeant appears before the eager faces and her voice sails down the hall.

67

'Pass today's medical examination and you will report for three weeks' basic training in Dorchester. Train departs at 5 p.m. Fail the examination, and you will be going straight back home.'

After hours of queuing I met every type of doctor – arms and legs stretched, elbows and knees knocked with a little hammer, ears, eyes, and feet examined, hearts listened to and breath measured. In the end, I was deemed suitable and sent to get a sandwich and tea.

Sunday, 10 January 1943

Pick-up point is a small railway station in Dorset. The night is clear and frozen. As always, a gas mask is in my pack. An open-backed lorry is out front.

'Throw your packs inside, girls,' calls a voice. A rough man appears. 'Go on. Toss them in and then find a place to hold on.'

I almost laugh at the absurdity. But the girl in front of me throws her bag into the back and finds a handhold. The other girls are doing the same and I scramble to get a place. My bag rolls away but I don't care. I grab a place on the side, the metal cold on my hands. *Is he serious? We're going to just hang off the side of the lorry? How far away is the base?* I hope Nell will be there when we arrive.

I am sorry, Timothy Squire.

Without so much as a word of warning the engine rumbles to life. We are moving. My hands clench around the hold. The girl beside me is laughing. The wind pushes as we pick up speed, bouncing along the wet road. I can see little aside from the dark shapes of houses in the distance. The stars are out above the long fields.

The other girl is laughing now. The wind gusts, a jolt of life, as we speed through the countryside. Dark shapes above, too. Aircraft, coming in to land? I cling hard to the side of the cold lorry, blasted by the night air.

I am laughing, too.

II

THE GHOSTS
WE CALLED

"LANCASTER"

'The ghosts I have called, I cannot get rid of them now...'

Goethe, *The Sorcerer's Apprentice*

3

Sunday, 10 January 1943

In the frozen darkness, I slip out from my sheets on the sofa and force myself to dress. Pausing – *did Lightwood just roll over?* – I stamp my feet into my boots. Serves him right if he does wake up.

Oh, how he smirked at the whole idea. It was worse than I thought – I knew the moment I said it that he would laugh, but I didn't fancy him dining out on it quite so much.

'Timothy Squire, the bird tamer,' he's started calling me. 'Right, who tames more birds than you? The birds love you.' He gave an awful wink. I can only imagine what he'd say if he knew I'm supposed to have the title *Ravenmaster*.

The door squeals murderously as it swings open. *Good.* I slip out, blinking in the surrounding dark. Ships glow wetly in the moonlight.

The moon is still up, and I'm wandering the city.

I shiver through the dark streets, heading north to Tower Bridge. I can't believe Anna's gone. And like that. Pure madness that we'd have that argument again – she's running off to join the WAAF, and we're arguing about looting. I know why she's so mad and unreasonable about it. Her mum died, and all her old stuff's just sitting in the house. She doesn't want to believe that someone might come along and take it.

'I'm sorry, yeah,' I said, calm as you like. 'I haven't nicked a thing – from anyone – in years. The Blitz is over, and God willing it will never come back. So there's no need for you to go running off.'

We walked back from the roost not touching or talking. And now she's gone. Dead set on being a WAAF.

The docklands are slow to recover from Hitler's fire-works. I remember the swarms of rats, basically taking over these streets. Those warehouses are gone, burnt to rubble. Where'd those rats go? There must've been thousands of them. *Stray cats couldn't have got 'em all.*

Dawn is wet, heavy. You could cut the air with a knife. The dark stone of the Tower seems always shadowed, cold. Fingers crossed not to run into old dreary pants bloody Oakes. Mr Thorne, the Watchman, observes my approach from his post at the West Gate.

'Morning, Mr Thorne, sir.'

'Morning, Timothy Squire.'

'All right if I come in?'

'Your dad expecting you?'

'No. No, I only have a few minutes before I'm due at the docks. Just need to feed the ravens, sir.'

'Yeoman Stackhouse requested some help?' He raises his eyebrows.

'Not exactly, sir.'

Suddenly he smiles, and I go red. 'Anna sent you along, did she? Well, better get a move on.'

I walk as calmly as I can through the gate. *Bloody Mr Thorne.* Anna *sent* me? I am doing her a favour, becoming the bloody Ravenmaster. She'd better appreciate it. Once Lightwood's done telling the story, half of the city will be laughing at me.

You shouldn't have tried to stop her leaving.

I *should* have gone to Aberdeen, and finished my training. Instead I'm here, feeling like a drowned rat. *I had my chance and I made a hash of it.* The whole thing's gone to buggery.

I'm so early to reach the Stone Kitchen that even the milk's not here yet. *If there's any milk left to come.* Chilled to the bone, I prepare the ravens' food in the cold empty kitchen. The stained glass was set in the windows to catch the sunrise, but I'm an hour too soon at least. Seems like Yeoman Stackhouse has not left any supplies out. Why is he messing about? What is he feeding them, grass?

Not a single piece of meat in the stores. I find the biscuits – about the only thing left in the counters – but without the meat there's no blood. *Soaked in blood* is how they eat. Will they even eat them dry? I've got little choice but to try it now.

What would Anna say if she saw this? No supplies for the birds; not so much as a mouse. She must have been too busy to notice the state of things. *Rushing off to buy her fancy uniform.* When Yeoman Stackhouse turns up I'll have to chat to him. He'll be more than a touch surprised to see me here.

I hurry across the wet cobblestones and past Traitors' Gate, climbing the slick steps to the battlements, and loop back towards the Green and the roost. I scan the grounds below, seeing only a few Wives crossing to the White Tower. Dad will already be working away inside the White Tower. Not that I'm afraid to run into him. I just don't have the time.

As I walk on to the Green, I can hear them. Dry, insistent croaking, like a saw across wood. Or bone. They know I'm here. I catch a glimpse of a curved beak in the darkness. I pull open the cages, one by one, thankful for the gloves against the cold wire.

'Sorry, gents – ladies. Grub's fallen off a bit, I'm afraid.'

The birds do eat, which is a relief. But I feel their gaze – a questioning, an anger. *It's not my fault! I never let the stores run down when I was here, did I? You lot have the memory of goldfish.*

Back in Aberdeen, living in the barracks, there was always steak and kidney. We earned them, no doubt about it. The whole company of engineers drilled together, marched together – twenty miles every day, with the bloody piper keeping time. Run for ten minutes, march for five. At the end we'd stop at the rifle range, exhausted but ready to put in some rounds. And then some steak and kidney.

I rush around depositing the dry biscuits into frowning beaks. 'Anna will be back soon, all right? I'll do my best in the meantime.'

That one's Stan, the youngest. *I hope you're not moult-ing again.* He swoops his wings, almost flying already. I try Anna's whistle, but he flaps away unconcerned, off to hide away his food again. *Caching*, Anna called it. Hardly enough here to save more for later.

The wings on some are almost too long, which means Stackhouse is not clipping them. They'll all fly away given the chance; now that's a headline for the papers – *Bird Tamer Loses Tower Ravens, Britain Falls.* Oh, Lightwood would talk of nothing else.

'What are you doing?'

'Ah, Yeoman Stackhouse. Good morning.'

He appears to disagree. In his uniform, hat in hand at his side, he gives the distinct impression he was on his way elsewhere. Breakfast, I'd wager.

'I just thought I'd give you a hand with the morning feeding. I kind of missed doing it, that's all. I used to do it – to help Anna do it – before you came here, sir.'

'Don't you have other duties now, Private? Why are you not in uniform?'

'Straight after this I'm down at the docks. I'll kit up then, sir.'

He narrows his eyes. 'I'm sure the country needs you more at the docks, don't you think, Private?'

'It's Sapper, sir, and more to the point, Anna named me Ravenmaster while she's away. And I'm a little concerned about the food for the birds. They need four ounces of meat – the size of your palm – and the biscuits need to be soaked in blood. The butcher at Smithfields knows the order.'

'No tourists coming this year, Ravenmaster. Not until the war's done.'

'We still have to feed the birds. Keep them alive and all that. You know the prime minister himself came to check on them last year. I can't imagine what he'd say if he comes again and the birds are starving.'

'I'm sure he'll manage.'

'Sir, the ravens are well important. Legend has it that if they ever leave the Tower, the kingdom will fall. That is why Churchill is so interested in them. That is why we have to clip their wings, sir. If not, they will simply fly away. If the newspapers got word that the ravens of the Tower have flown away – well, I can only imagine what Churchill would say then.'

We stare at each other.

'If you don't mind, sir, I will just finish up here.'

I can't quite make myself say the last bit, but I think he as good as hears it. *And when I come back tomorrow morning, do me a favour and have the meat ready in the storeroom.*

Maybe the quartermaster is right, and I'm running from the action, scared I'm about to get clobbered. *No, I know the real reason why I am here.*

And it's far more foolish than that.

Sunday, 10 January 1943

It is almost midnight when we arrive. A guard at the gate waves us inside. A red-brick building looms ahead, huge and unfriendly. Runways shoot out from all angles, lit up by two lines of paraffin lamps – 'goosenecks', someone called them – like giant candles disappearing into the darkness beyond.

I can't help but think it. What would Timothy Squire make of this?

We are led by torchlight into the giant building. Warmwell is not the central training facility for new recruits, and they still get five hundred girls a week. And they are *girls*. Men have to be seventeen and a half to join the RAF, but some of the girls here look as young as me. *All the top-drawer girls*, Nell said. The building is cold, even with all the bodies, and we are marched into a huge lecture hall. I don't see Nell anywhere.

'Hair off the collar in your uniform,' a girl in an officer's uniform says. 'That means put your hair up, girls. No jewellery, no make-up. And if you're signing up because you like the uniform, well – wait until you get the knickers. They don't call them "passion crushers" for nothing. Now, on you go.'

I have turned beet-red, but keep walking. The horrible woman, yelling about knickers in front of the crowd. *She is an officer, and we all have to listen to everything she says.* She leads us to our billets, endless rows of wooden huts, leading to the giant hangars beyond. We follow like ghosts, silent, barely there. Iron cots run along both sides of the hut, each cot separated by a locker for kitbags. Only a few feet between us and our neighbours.

'Hi. I'm called Anna Cooper.'

'Anna Cooper? I'm Samantha Nicholson. I was at school with Sergeant MacKay at North London Collegiate. How do you know her?'

'She's my sergeant,' I say, somewhat lamely. *I did not attend some posh school.* 'I haven't met her yet.'

There is a pause, when Samantha doesn't seem to know quite where to look.

Another girl rises from her bunk, tall and skinny with dark blonde hair. 'Samantha Nicholson? I'm Isabella Pomeroy. My uncle told me to keep a lookout for you. He was at Fighter Command with your father.'

Squeezed out of the conversation, I move back to my cot when Sergeant MacKay herself comes in, her eyes straight ahead. 'Stand when your Commanding Officer enters a room,' she barks.

We hurry to find our feet, even her old school mates. I am about to get my first taste of drills.

Sergeant MacKay tells us to make up our 'beds' and then wait to be taken to the Mess. The billets are simple iron cots, a few feet apart. They don't look comfortable. The hut itself is grim. Long, with low ceilings and cement floors. There must be twenty-five of us in here. I cast sideways glances, but the girls around are intent at their tasks.

Sergeant beckons us to follow her to the Mess. It is much warmer here, though the food is mashed potato and minced beef, which is more water than beef. We are given our first kit items – our 'irons', a knife, fork, and spoon. In silence and nervous laughter we eat. There is something, I notice, in the faces of the girls here that I can't quite place. A glimmer.

Kitchen hands come out to serve tea, which is spooned from a giant bucket – *tea from a bucket* – and I watch in horror as the woman ladles tea into my enamel mug.

'Welcome to the WAAF,' mutters a dark-haired girl at my side, but she, too, is smiling.

I lift the mug and try not to grimace. Whatever these girls are excited about, it isn't the tea. But I am here.

Tuesday, 12 January 1943

Three weeks of training have begun. We are woken up at 6.30 a.m. and sent to bed at 10.30 p.m. In between, we are marched around in groups – to sports practice, RAF history lectures, gas drills, physical training, first aid, and, finally, meals. Of course everything is still rationed – meat, eggs, tea, cheese, butter, milk, fats. I chewed a last bite of Terry's bitter chocolate this morning.

Parade is horrid, especially after getting hardly a wink of sleep. The iron cots are *not* comfortable. The mattress is made of three separate sections – 'biscuits', the girls call them – which bunch up and slide apart when you twist or turn. I feel as stiff and sore as if I'd spent the night in a shelter. And I've not seen a glimpse of Nell.

We are numbered and ranked, and already I have heard more than enough lectures about the 'King's Regulations'. Once I finally figured out how to put the uniform on, it somehow felt uncomfortable, as if it's *too* shiny. It's only that it's new, I suppose. *And clean enough to suit Flo's mum.*

It is an effort to do anything – brushing my teeth or combing my hair feel like real challenges. Several of the girls cried softly in the night. *I will not cry.* Even if Warmwell is the most horrid place in the world.

Most horrid of all is the parade ground, which is wide and featureless, leaving us exposed to the full brunt of the wind as we practise drilling.

'We do what we do. Because any day now, the sky is going to be filled with parachutes.' I *must* try to remember the sergeant's words. Everyone calls her Queen Bee, and I understand why.

I'm grousing as much as Timothy Squire.

Today we are marched away from the screeching wind of the parade ground to a wooden hut for injections. *More* jabs – *inoculations*, they call them – what for, I can't imagine. But a hard-faced nurse gives us them all at once. I'm sure at least one has left me feeling swiftly ill, but I say nothing.

Act like a child and they'll start asking questions.

As I head back to our hut, the air is as cold as it ever was in the Tower.

The night *is* cold, I know it is, but my body throbs with a strange heat. I am sweating. Those bloody inoculations. I can't let the girls see me like this. What would Isabella

82

Pomeroy make of the girl who *got* a fever from her shots? *Oh, why does everything have to be so bloody difficult?*

I do a small walk around the huts. I can't be sick in my uniform. *What would Timothy Squire say?* And I'm on probation.

There, a tree, just wide enough to hide me if I'm lucky.

I am, and the trunk covers me completely. Clutching the trunk, I fall to one knee and vomit heavily.

Monday, 1 February 1943

The three weeks of training come to a dull close. I am now an Aircraftwoman 2nd Class, which is about as glamorous as it sounds. Now we are to learn a specific trade. And Nell has finally arrived, having requested to help with my training.

Perfect as always in her uniform, she is not quite as friendly as I'd hoped she'd be. I follow her clicking footsteps down the hall, trying to keep up.

'Can you type?' Nell asks over her shoulder. 'WAAF needs fast shorthand typists. The pilots must be interviewed as soon as they come back, while their memories are still fresh.'

'I've never learned.'

I awoke feeling almost myself again. Whatever that shot was, it did not pass quickly. None of the girls saw a thing. My stomach is well enough now, but I still feel utterly lost. *No one told me I would have to be able to type.*

'Cooper, wake up,' she says, and my back stiffens. 'Can you draw?'

'Draw?'

'Draw, paint, whatever. Are you actually still asleep?'

I shake my head and force myself to match her pace. *We seem to be heading towards the toilets.* 'I am awake.'

'Well, if you can draw, there's the model-making course. That's what all the art-school girls are doing, building model cities to help Bomber Command.'

My experience feeding ravens at the Tower of London has yet to come in handy. 'I'm sorry – I... I can't do any of those things.'

A long moment passes with the sound of her heels the only sound in the world. But instead of some mean comment or just laughing in my face, Nell's face relaxes. She offers a smile, and looks once again like the girl who took me to the cinema.

'Don't worry, you'll find something, Cooper. Just stick with it as best you can. There's a reason why so many new girls come here. Lots of them go home on Christmas leave and never come back. We pack up their stuff and ship it along. We'll find you something once you're done in here. Everyone hates this first job, but we all have to do it. Stick with it, OK?'

It's not long before I realize how difficult it might be. *We were headed towards the toilets.* Nell swings the door open with the ghost of a smile.

'Dustman's daughter or Baron's little girl...' She shrugs

84

before turning to leave. 'The toilets aren't going to clean themselves. Everything you need is under the sink.'

The door thuds closed. Finding the bucket of supplies, I hoist it over to the stalls. *Maybe my experience at the Tower has come in handy after all.* I cannot bring myself to smile at the thought.

I sigh, lowering myself down to scrub the toilet. I can't believe what a misery this whole WAAF training is turning out to be. Was Nell wrong? Maybe I don't belong here. I am only here because so many of the girls refused to come back. *And why was she smiling when she brought me here?*

It is too much of an effort not to be sad. But there is no privacy in the barracks, so I can't crumple under the bed – the *cot* – and let it wash over me. *I can't.* And I will not cry in some toilet stall while Nell marches off to a real job.

Let her smile. I promised her I'd do a hell of a job for the WAAF, and I will.

Gritting my teeth, I scour the stupid toilet.

My probation period cleaning the toilets is over. I'm trying my hand as a parachute packer. Nell, to her obvious frustration, is still tasked with discovering my talent. With a stern face she leads me to a long table crowded with other girls. She must regret agreeing to help me.

'Untangle the rigging lines,' she says. 'And fold the parachutes like so, do you see? If they're not properly packed, they won't properly open. Pilots' lives are in your hands, Cooper.'

I watch the other girls, trying to follow along. I fold a piece of the white fabric over, realize it is backwards, fold it again. They work fast.

'Right,' Nell says. 'It's like this.' She brings her fold down in a smooth motion.

I nod, silently. This is the longest I've seen her go without a cigarette.

'Not too bad, isn't it?' she says with a smile. 'Escape from that freezing bloody Tower, meet girls your own age.'

Blushing red, I press the corners down. *There*. I pass it to the right, where a plump girl ties the pack shut. *Was that right?* It must have been, or the plump girl wouldn't have tied it up. She'd notice if I got it wrong. *Wouldn't she?* It is now tossed in the corner. A newly mended parachute is pushed to me by the curly-haired girl to my right.

'These posh girls.' Nell shrugs, taking a pin from her mouth. 'Can't even sew their own things. Can you believe it?'

'Yes.' I can still see the pack in the corner. Should I check it again?

Nell has worked hard her whole life, she tells me, and has countless hardships to look forward to. But I see it in her face too, that glimmer of happiness, and I suddenly know it for what it is: her world has opened up. She never dreamed she could be in a place like this. *Neither did I.*

I see, too, the red gemstone on her finger.

'Oh, Nell, congratulations—'

'Cooper.' She frowns at me, then quickly lowers her head. 'It's not that sort of ring. Just a gift.'

'But he must love you then—'

'Love me?' a pencilled eyebrow is raised, and her voice drops almost to a whisper. 'You're supposed to be sixteen, remember? It's only a gift from a boy, so I'll remember him when he gets back from wherever they've sent him to.'

For a second her smile falters, and I know to say no more. Was this boy her date to the film? She said he was being called away on a mission. *Should he have returned by now?*

'Rule is no jewellery, but I'll keep wearing it.' She sighs. 'A girl in my hut keeps stacks of Elizabeth Arden make-up in her pack, and no one dares throw it away.'

Nell finishes mending another parachute, then hands it to me.

'Nell,' I say, still watching the tied parachute pack in the corner. 'How can I be sure – I mean, what if I didn't fold the corners just right...'

'Cooper.' Her voice is abruptly stern. 'Don't start with all that. A girl in here a few weeks ago got it in her head she packed one of the chutes wrong. Started opening them all up, mad to find it. They had to wrestle her out of here, in the end. CO said she needed a week's leave.'

'So she got it?'

Nell shakes her head, takes up her sewing. 'Found her in her hut. Hanging from the rafters. Now fold the corners tight, that's the way.'

Tuesday, 2 February 1943

I see Nell again at the watch office. The parachute packers have deemed me unfit – *I guess I really did mess up that parachute* – and the barrage balloons workers just laughed at me.

'You'd need to be twice your size, Aircraftwoman. Next.'

So now I am to begin training as a R/T operator, using the radio and telephones. Nell tries to explain how to transmit and log communications, signal Morse code, and memorize ciphers. I mostly just make tea. I learn that the boy who gave her that ring has been gone for nine days on a bombing raid.

Earphones tight, cramped in a small room, we help the bomber touchdown. Nell leans into the microphone at my desk, waiting to hear the voice, and she talks down planes returning from raids.

Off duty, I head back to my hut, Nell muttering alongside me about the poor cigarette ration. Could I ever become a controller, helping guide the aircrafts to the targets? *How could you? What if you directed the bomber that…?*

All at once Nell stops. 'Well, now, would you look at that?'

A huge bomber has just landed, and there is plenty of activity on the runway. Ground crew are on the strip, in balaclavas against the cold, refuelling the engines and putting oil in, while the newly arrived air crew – in their battle kits – cross the grounds to the Mess.

The bomber is huge – more like a house with wings. There's a great cockpit on the top floor, another on the ground floor for the bomb aimer.

Timothy Squire will be properly jealous.

The pilots look fairly ordinary, though with a confidence about them that is not unappealing. And they all seem to have shiny, slicked-back hair.

I notice Nell is wearing a huge grin. 'Just in time for the party tonight. Of course.'

'Is that him?' I hazard a guess. One man does stick out above the others – in the back, with dark hair and wide shoulders.

'Captain Cecil Rafferty,' she says.

'He is very handsome, Nell.'

'They'll be there tonight,' she says. 'Drinks at the Links Hotel. Evening dress, cocktails and port and all that posh bother. You *have* to come.'

She sounds very excited. I look away. *Sounds like another ball at the White Tower.*

'Sorry,' she says. 'I forget how young you are. One day you'll be interested.' She says the last words with a smug certainty. I am not so young. I really will be sixteen in the autumn. I'm only half an inch shorter than Nell, at any rate.

'Dancing all night. Steak and kidney pie. Plum pudding.' Nell is still lost in her vision of a grand ball with Cecil Rafferty.

But for once, I am right along with her. *Plum pudding.* I missed it at Flo's; I can't miss it again. 'I'd love to come dancing, Nell. But I don't have an evening dress.'

Her smile is huge, but she keeps one eye on the runway. 'Don't worry, Cooper. I'll take care of you.'

Friday, 5 February 1943

I couldn't imagine why Nell had brought evening dresses to the WAAF training centre. Now it doesn't seem so strange, surrounded by balloons and paper streamers. Nell of course looks stunning in her sleek blue dress with a thin belt at the waist – as she would in the green dress with wide shoulders that I'm wearing. On me, it just hangs like a great curtain past my knees. *She always did make me feel thoroughly second-hand.*

I am wearing a little of her red lipstick – she was aghast that I didn't own any myself ('good lippy is more essential than food'). Luckily she had a pair of flat shoes (only slightly too big) for me; there is no way I could glide around like she does in those great heels. I'd be tottering around like a fool.

What would Timothy Squire think if he could see me now? I know what he'd think if he could see Nell. Timothy Squire regularly goes to pieces around Nell. He pretends not to, of course, but it's plain for everyone to see.

But I forget all about Timothy Squire when I notice who is standing directly across from us. *Nell no doubt led us straight here while I was trying to smooth the bunches from the dress.* Wings pinned over his left breast pocket, Flight Officer Rafferty smiles at us. The curve of his lips, directed at us, makes my mouth go dry. He is holding a glass of strong-smelling whisky.

'Well, hello, Nell Singer.' He sees me, nods his head.

'You girls keep us airborne. Every one of us owes you a great debt.'

Once again his hair is shiny and slicked back – I remember that Nell called the RAF men the Brylcreem Boys. It certainly is a clean, smart look. Trying to imagine Timothy Squire with his hair so shiny and neat is impossible.

'Allow me to thank you personally, Nell. I could not see a thing coming in.' He's lying – the afternoon was almost cloudless – but she is blushing red. 'I was exhausted today, I fear. Longest mission I've done, and with the new aircraft... I put myself unreservedly in your hands.'

Nell is silent as the grave. I glance at her in shock. She has the same bright-eyed look she wore when we saw Anna Neagle. I cough. I want to leave. Suddenly, I want to be anywhere but here, with smiling Cecil and stunned Nell. She's clearly in love with this pilot and my being here is not helping. He senses my discomfort, and his eyes flick from beautiful, wide-eyed Nell, to me in my too big dress. I stand a little taller.

'I must apologize, we forget that not everyone finds aircraft talk fascinating.'

The flight wings on his uniform really do gleam in the candlelight. My words come out in a rush. 'I do find aircraft fascinating. I just wish I knew more. I wish I had studied more... about planes.'

'Ah,' he smiles, 'I feared that some other pilot had already cornered you with chat as boring as mine.'

'She's new,' Nell says, giving her dress an adjusting tug it doesn't need. 'In training. She doesn't know anything.'

His eyes widen in mock surprise, and he turns back to me. 'Well, would you care to ask any questions of a pilot who has just flown the much written about Lancaster?'

'Cecil, darling.' Isabella Pomeroy slides over and takes his arm. She locks eyes with Nell, and suddenly the old Nell rears to life. Isabella only spares one disdainful look for my wilting dress. 'Shall we?'

He nods, the gesture almost a small bow. 'Another time, perhaps. Pleasure to see you again, Nell. And to meet your friend. Best of luck with your future studies.'

I laugh to cover my nervousness. 'You, too. I mean – goodbye.'

'Steady on, Cooper,' Nell mutters at my side. She is fidgeting with the ring on her hand. *What kind of man gives a woman a ring and then ignores her to dance with some snobby git?*

Together Isabella and Cecil move to the dance floor. On her way she pauses, turns back, swings her hair, and smiles. Suddenly, and for the first time, I feel terrible for Nell.

Sunday, 7 February 1943

I could be living peacefully on a farm somewhere. With chickens. Farms always have chickens. And they never look ready to sink their talons into your arm. *The first thing ravens eat is your eyes*, Anna once said, plain as you like.

Croak.

'Go on.' I stop myself from helping Corax along with a toe. 'Get in your cage. Bedtime, isn't it?'

I push it shut. I watch her for a minute, behind the bars. What am I doing feeding these birds when I could be feeding myself? Mum'll have dinner ready by now, and I haven't had a bite since noon. Why starve myself half to death just to drop bloody biscuits in front of some fat crows? No, I have to do it. It's my job to look after them. I'd better not make a cod's head of it. Anna's expecting that.

'Come on, you.' I squint at the approaching bird – Lyra. 'We're all hungry here, let's crack on with it.' I throw the slop in ahead of her, and close the gate once she's inside. *That's the lot.*

But I don't head straight to dinner. Not yet. I double back to the first cage along the roost. 'Oliver,' I say. 'You still awake? It's me, the new Ravenmaster.'

The raven gives me a look. *He's not having that title from me.* Well, better off him razzing me than Lightwood.

It's not razzing me, I remind myself. It's a bleeding bird. But a smart one.

I hope.

'Right, Olly. Let's practise again. Just once more, then I'm off to dinner. You remember what we practised?'

Arrk.

'No, that's not quite it. Try again.'

I kneel down, down to the bird's level. I speak, slow and soft. He repeats with an nonsense croak. *That won't do.* Again, and again, that rusty, metallic caw. Finally, I abandon the task.

'You're getting worse, Oliver.' I stand back up, and the stiffness of ten months at the docks fills me.

Something is about to happen. Soon. Whatever I hear, I have to forget. But the truth is clear to anyone with their wits about them. Something is about to happen, something... massive.

The war seems to be turning in our favour. News has come that the Germans have surrendered at Stalingrad. Looks like I am destined to miss it.

How to explain this feeling then? I have a... black feeling. As if things aren't going to turn out all right. A lot of people will die in this war – I may be one of them. It's a *strong* feeling, and I can't seem to shake it.

In truth, the black feeling seems to cloud my thoughts. Seems to happen more and more these days. Just scattered thoughts, black – like wings. I know what it is they remind me of, and I know what they mean. If I wasn't so knackered, I'd feel like a right fool.

I give my head a good shake. Looking at these bloody birds all day isn't going to help: like little grim reapers, always eyeing you. I'm just sore and starving. Some food and a fire, and I'll feel like myself again. Imagine, going down to Smithfields. But I don't have enough points for a steak.

I glance at the Bloody Tower as I pass; Anna's room. I laugh at the thought of her chasing some RAF uniform. *All the girls are wild for the pilots' wings.* Well, we can't all be the sons of lords, some of us have to get by on skills and hard work. I have written her a letter, apologizing for acting like a fool. I will post it today. Tomorrow at the latest.

Once she's through being cross with me, I can tell her the truth about what happened at training. All of it. If I can keep these blasted birds alive, she'll forgive me for certain.

Shoving open the Jewel House door, I begin to climb the many steps. This building used to be Wellington's old barracks, they say; but now it's all fixed up into flats. Thankfully, home is nothing like the real barracks used by the armed forces. *Imagine Dad living in a proper barracks... Where would he keep all his books?*

Before I even reach the door, Mum swings it open. She hugs me; Dad says hello from behind a newspaper. *I'd have wagered my ration card it would be one of the dusty old volumes.* Dinner is already on plates, soggy-looking Brussels sprouts and boiled potatoes. We sit down to eating without any further fuss. *It won't take long; and Lightwood will be waiting at the pub.*

'It's nice to see you, dear.' Mum smiles. 'Too bad your friend Arthur couldn't join us. It's wonderful of his parents to take you in, so you boys can be together.'

'It's only for a few months, Mum. Then we'll go back up north to finish training.'

'Months? Oh, well, you're always welcome to come home. Your friend is welcome here, too. So, were you feeding Henry's birds, dear?'

'They're Anna's birds now,' I say, immediately regretting it. 'The Tower's birds. They are the Tower ravens.'

And they're eating better than this.

'It's too bad Anna's left us,' Dad says, folding the paper away. 'She was a real help around the White Tower. I have a new display in mind for when we reopen. I could use an extra pair of hands cleaning that old samurai amour. A gift to King James I, nearly five hundred years ago.'

'She's a wonderful girl,' Mum adds.

We manage to eat for a few minutes in silence. *No doubt one of them is planning a clever way to ask more questions about Anna. Or talk about how I need to finish school.*

'Watch looks good, son,' Dad says, stabbing at his mushy potato. 'Kept your grandfather safe in the Great War. It'll keep you safe now.'

Dad never talks about the war we are currently fighting. Usually, he sticks to lectures about things that happened a thousand years ago.

'I'm at the docks, Dad. Only the seagulls to look out for down there.'

The watch is heavy on my wrist – I never seem to get used to wearing it. *But I'll take any piece of good luck I can get.*

'If you had managed to finish up at your school first—'

'William,' Mum cautions.

'I'm only saying what the boy already knows, dear.'

I'm not about to take this bait. Not with Lightwood waiting for me at the Fox and Hounds. He's had a chance to bring up Anna, school, and correct my language. *We must be done here.*

I spoon the last of the potatoes into my mouth, chewing as I talk.

'Thanks for the grub, Mum, Dad. I'm off.'

Might as well change first. Be good to have a night out in clothes not stiff with dust. Maybe the tweed coat? With the cap? *We'll see who's stuck at the docks for ever. I'm headed to Europe, you just wait and see.*

Oh, and the bloody letter. Should I even bother posting it to Dorchester? Or wait and give it to her myself? That seems the sensible thing to do. But I remember two Christmases gone, when I slid a book under her door. She was so mad at me before that, and then everything came out good afterwards. *Might work again.*

I will race up to her room, slide the letter under the door, and get cracking to the pub. *Sod the new clothes.* I hurry up the Bloody Tower stairs. No need to worry about Yeoman Oakes. He's changed more than a sight since Henry Reed died. Not all there, if I'm honest. He'll be no good at spotting me like he used to. *Years ago when I stole a cake from the Martin Tower kitchen, he saw me sneaking away all the way from Salt Tower.*

I reach Anna's door. The memory of when I borrowed the knife from her room – she even punched me! – reminds me not to make a joke of it in front of her. *I thought we might need that knife. I've said I'm sorry a thousand bleeding times.*

I push the letter under the door, a bit more roughly than I intended. *Well, I did apologize! How many times can I say I'm sorry before she believes me? Enough to do my head in.*

The door nudges open.

I look up, startled. I didn't push the letter *that* hard, and why isn't the door locked anyway? Oakes locks everything around here, even in his current gloomy mood. Before I can stop myself, I have creaked it open and wandered inside.

It is Anna's room, just as she left it. The books, the small bed. Even the smell. *That's the soap I got her, I'll wager.* I walk towards the books by the window and blink when I see the notebook I gave her. Not that I'd expect her to take it to WAAF training. *Of course not.*

I stare at the notebook for a moment, thinking. I have no intention of reading it – I just want to be *certain* it is the book I gave her. Picking it up, I gingerly turn the first page.

'You're not who I expected.'

I stumble and almost fall at the voice behind me. I whip around, willing in that instant to trade all the world for my training rifle.

A man rises from the chair in the corner. Calmly, almost casually, he crosses the room and presses the door closed. I cannot move an inch. He is dressed in a suit and tie, somewhat worn. He removes his hat, a dark trilby. Does he have a weapon? I can't see. *Of course he has a bloody weapon.*

'Well,' the German says. 'I believe we've met before.'

'How did you get in? Why are you here?'

'I am here for Anna.'

'Anna?' I manage to say. 'She hates you.'

He laughs, a low sound without any humour in it. Despite his composure, one thing is terribly clear – this is a desperate man.

'Anna is my daughter. I am not leaving without her.'

I try to meet his gaze, but my eyes slide away. 'I think the Warders might have something to say about that.'

The Warders and the Scots Guard. How did no one spot a Nazi wandering the castle grounds – there is a whole bleeding garrison of them drilling in front of White Tower?

'Oh, yes. They can chase me out of their little castle. But I am not leaving this city. I am not leaving without Anna Esser.'

'Anna *Cooper* lives here now. Why don't you just leave her alone? Christ, you did it once already. That was easy enough, wasn't it?'

My whole body is filled with anger. He is almost as shocked as I am, but quicker to recover. He looks down at his feet, then back at me.

'How would it feel to never see your family again? If someone took them from you?' He steps closer, holds out a tightly folded piece of paper. 'Since you are her friend, give her this for me. This is where she can find me.'

'No.'

It's all I can say.

He nods to himself, strides out of the door, leaving it open. It creaks in the cold air. A full minute passes in stillness. I unfold the paper.

78 Catesby Street.

4

Wednesday, 10 February 1943

Queen Bee hates me. I know, as I reach the door, that nothing good waits for me on the other side. When you're called to see the Commanding Officer, you're either getting a medal or a kick in the arse.

And I'm not getting any medals.

I knock, wait for the call, take a shallow breath, and enter. Giving a swift salute, I stand to attention. Queen Bee stares at me. Stares and stares, for minutes at least. I fold my hands behind my back. I will not let her see them trembling.

Oh God, is she going to send me home?

'You don't know why you're here, do you, Miss Cooper?'

I almost stagger at the 'Miss' – I am Aircraftwoman 2nd Class. Unless it is already too late. *Oh, God, don't let it be too late.* Transfer me to Equipment Branch, or make me an orderly or a cook, transfer me far away, just don't send me back to the Tower as a failure.

'No, Sergeant.'

'Why are you here at all, Miss Cooper?'

'Here?' I say, stupidly.

'Here, yes, here. The WAAF. Why are you here?'

Perhaps this is a great horrible dream and at any moment I will awake screaming in my billet. After Oakes agreed to sign my birth certificate – after he gave me permission to come here – what will he think? And Timothy Squire, a proper sapper helping win the war – he will know I am weak.

Don't send me back to Flo as a failure.

'I am here because I want to help the war effort.' *I am here because I can do anything I set my mind to.*

Queen Bee sighs. 'Miss Cooper, your skills are not only below par, they are frankly non-existent. I can't imagine what you possibly thought would come of your time here. You have proven yourself something beyond a disaster.'

'I know, Sergeant. I know you are right and I am sorry, but I didn't mess up the RT—'

'For goodness' sake, be quiet, Miss Cooper. You are exactly the type of girl who makes the rest of us look bad. Because of people like you, we must all work harder, harder than you can even fathom. You have done nothing but waste our time and resources, in a time of war, when our future as a country, as a people, hangs in the balance. Yes, you do well to cry, Miss Cooper. This is absolutely your final warning. If you wish to remain here in your training, you will endeavour to make yourself worthy of the WAAF.

'That is all. Now go.'

Cecil is coming out of the all-male Mess, his hair slicked back and shining. *Not now. Oh, God.* Head down, I try to wipe away the tears but the buttons on the cuff of the uniform stab my eye.

'Heavens, are you all right?'

'Oh, yes.' I keep my head down, wishing him away, but knowing I will at some point have to look up. And he will still be standing there.

'Are you certain? I can call for a medic—'

'No, I am fine. Truly.'

I look up, realizing there is no way he'll remember who I am. *I doubt he even remembers who Nell is.* I arrange a smile on my face, my eyes red and streaming, and meet his eyes. *His deep brown eyes.*

'Allergies,' I offer weakly.

'Yes,' he says with a nod to the closed office door. 'Sergeant MacKay has that effect on people. I suffer from it a bit myself.'

I manage a laugh though it sounds more like a sob.

'You are at the watch office, isn't that right? An excellent place to resume your studies. Aircraftwoman…?'

I swallow, hard. *He does remember me.* And he won't forget me now. The girl who wept in the hall.

'Cooper. You may as well just call me Anna. And I don't need to learn about planes any more.'

'Leaving us so soon?'

What do you care? Unless you're planning on giving me a ring, too?

'Sergeant MacKay just kept saying the same thing over and over again, *Why are you here, why are you here?*'

'Not a completely absurd question, given the nature of this place. It's something we all have to ask ourselves every now and then.' He smiles. 'So. Why *are* you here, Miss Cooper?'

I make a noise suspiciously like a growl, but Cecil keeps looking at me, his brown eyes wide and sincere.

'I don't know, I think I'm in the wrong place. I thought I would fly planes. But all I do is scrub toilets and fold parachutes.'

'Well, perhaps you are in the wrong place. The WAAF does not pilot aircraft. You want the ATA.'

'What?'

'Air Transport Auxiliary. They recruit all sorts of pilots, men and women. Mind you, you won't be locked in dogfights with German Messerschmitts. The work is mainly taxiing planes from one airfield to the next, wherever they're needed most. It's a civilian role, but a vital one.'

The thought floods into my mind. Anna Neagle. No, she was the actress – Amy Johnson was the pilot. She ferried planes back and forth to help the war effort.

'Miss Cooper, may I go so far as to make a bold suggestion? The new Lancaster has to be seen to be fully appreciated. Would it be excruciatingly dull if I asked you to join me?'

'What? What do you mean?' I am shocked into blathering.

'If you don't mind me saying, you can read every book and flight manual in the world, but nothing can replace the real thing. And I am so very sorry that Sergeant MacKay has come down so hard on you.

'Let me take you up. Tomorrow morning, just a quick loop around the countryside, before I'm off abroad. The old man'll give me the green, don't worry,' he says, misunderstanding my silence. 'I need to check on the equipment anyway, ahead of the mission. Not that I'd tell any of the WAAFs, and certainly not Sergeant MacKay. She'll come down on both of us, then.'

He gives another one of those smiles.

'Well, what do you say, Miss Cooper?'

Meeting Anna's dad has shaken me up. What do I do? What can I do? I can't go and tell Oakes. Not until I've told Anna first. *But can I tell Anna?* She doesn't want to know.

Is she safe? And what about Mum and Dad? Bloody hell, I should tell Oakes right away. Get the Warders on high alert, make sure no one gets in the Tower.

Oakes'll be no help in his current state. Who then, Sparks? The bloke's a hundred years old, but I'd wager he's tougher than he looks. And Yeoman Brodie could pick the Nazi up by his neck and fling him back over the walls.

No, I mustn't tell the Warders. They will turn him in, likely after Brodie tosses him over the wall. And he will be executed.

And it will be my fault. No, I have to talk to Anna first. But I can't. I can't tell her. That black feeling is back. In truth, it never really goes away – sometimes it is less strong, but it is always there. I look out through the wooden slats above the gate to the crashing waves beyond.

Luck is a ration, too, and I used up all mine in the Blitz.

Thursday, 11 February 1943

Of course it is a joke; no one will be there. I am a fool, and a silly girl pretending to be sixteen. But Cecil is standing there, in his flight suit, smiling as I approach. His breath puffs in the air like Nell with her cigarettes. *What will Nell say to this?*

'I must apologize, as there were no suits in your size. But here's an umbrella just in case.' He hands me a parachute pack.

Umbrella? Is that supposed to be funny?

He hands me a life vest. 'And you'll need a Mae West.'

'Mae West?'

'Ah.' He holds it up to his chest. 'The chaps think it reminds them of her… you know.'

'Oh.'

'Sorry,' he says, turning a little red. 'That was hardly proper of me.'

'No. It's funny.' *Well, Timothy Squire would think it's funny, at any rate.*

A salvaged smile, and he says, 'Let's go up then, shall we?'

He feels bad for me – I cried in front of him. He thinks I'm a child. This is why I'm here.

'Don't worry about anything,' he says. 'Like I promised. You and I are both coming back.'

'Right,' I say stupidly. *Right?*

'Here she is,' he says, approaching the giant Lancaster bomber. It is soot-black; the colour of a raven. Up close, it really is the size of a house.

'Can you really fly this alone?'

'Takes a seven-man crew, but you only need one pilot. This here is Harris. He's going to help us take off, aren't you, Harris?'

I turn to see a flight engineer watching us with a stone-faced expression. *Will he report me?* He doesn't seem too concerned.

'After you.' Cecil pulls the door open. I step up and inside the Lancaster.

I sit in the low seat beside him, on the right side. So many buttons and switches, some with red on them, but everything else, the sides, the ceiling – is green. The world has shrunk to the size of this cockpit, with only the smell of metal, petrol, and the leather of the helmet and gloves. I breathe it all in deeply. I push Nell and her reactions out of my mind.

Cecil gestures to Harris, who pulls the chocks from the wheels. Huge propellers fire up.

'Four engines,' he says, switching them on one at a time.

Noise and vibration rumble through me until my teeth start shaking.

'What are those?' I say, weakly, as I stare at the terrifying leather contraptions.

'Oxygen masks. No need for that, we'll keep it well under 10,000 feet. Might still be cold, though, so do bundle up.'

I am still fussing with my wool coat over my uniform as we rumble forward. I look at the side of his face – serious, handsome – and go back to fumbling with my coat. *Cecil Bleeding Rafferty.*

The power swells behind me, the great machine roaring to life. We are moving across the tarmac, the world humming. I am pressed sharply back against the seat as we gather speed, the humming growing louder, the huge plane heading straight for the road beyond.

With a great roar the ground lunges away. The plane slides into the air, shooting into the morning sky. And stays there.

We climb, higher and higher. There is nothing underneath us, only air. No, the world is underneath us. And I can see *all* of it. It is so small.

'Go on,' he yells out as we level off. 'Have a look around. Best view is from the top gunner's turret.'

What? Get up? Part of me – a large part of me – wants to stay right where I am. But another voice, Timothy Squire's voice, pops into my head. *The view, Anna. It'll be kicks.* Timothy Squire has a knack for appearing at the worst possible times.

I unbuckle the belt, and make my stumbling way across the plane. It is not so bumpy – more like an Underground train than anything. I look at the window across the wing, seeing two huge propellers roaring and England below. It barely feels like we're moving at all. It feels – *unreal*. The ground does not seem like the ground I know. Surely that is not where we just stood. Surely that is impossible.

All around us, the sky. Bright blue, blindingly bright.

I make my way – terrified of touching anything, even to keep my balance – to the top gunner's turret.

Timothy Squire will be so jealous.

The view is amazing, yet I still hurry back to my seat.

'So what do you think?'

'Brilliant,' I say, breathless from it all.

Friday, 12 February 1943

'You told Queen Bee?'

I can only stare at Nell in wonder. She has her arms crossed and looks decidedly less beautiful than normal.

'Flying an RAF aircraft is not a joke, Cooper. Pilots risk their lives up there.'

'Nell – I—'

'It's not some little game, right?'

She turns and marches off. Well, I imagined many angry reactions, but not this. I do actually feel horrible for not telling her myself – especially after that whole business with Isabella Pomeroy – but did she have to sell me down the river?

She could have yelled at me in private – she didn't need to bring Queen Bee into it. *Nell never did know when to keep her mouth shut.*

Just because she fancies Cecil. I didn't fail to notice that she isn't wearing her ring any more. I should have known she'd be jealous. It doesn't matter; it's too late now. I'm in for it.

I will just wait for the call into Sergeant's office. And I won't have to wait for long.

Monday, 15 February 1943

'Get up, Miss Cooper,' she says. 'Pack your things. You're out.'

'Out?' I say, still not quite awake.

It is not a raid. No bombs have come for me.

I blink into the blackness. Sergeant MacKay is leaning over me. *Of course she comes in the middle of the night. Of course she can barely hold back a grin.*

'Your distinguished career as a WAAF is over.'

I sit up, stunned and silent. My skin burns with the humiliation. Murmurs and squeaking bunks tell me other cadets are stirring. *Oh, please let Isabella Pomeroy stay asleep.*

'The air force life does not appear to agree with you, Miss Cooper,' Queen Bee continues, her voice definitely loud enough to wake the entire hut.

'It seems not, Sergeant.'

'You're being transferred to a civilian post.' A distant intake of breath; a barely concealed snigger of laughter. 'Now pack your things.'

I am awake. 'Transferred…?'

And in the same tone of voice that she says everything, she says, 'That's right, Miss Cooper. You're headed to the ATA. Some fool thinks you can be a pilot.'

Wednesday, 24 February 1943

At first glance, dinner in the Stone Kitchen appears to be in my honour. Even Yeoman Stackhouse has joined the table. But soon it is confirmed that dinner is merely an opportunity for me to take on some advice.

'But have you seen all the photographs of the women pilots, modelling in their uniforms?' Stackhouse asks. 'Flying aircraft when there are so many men qualified to do the work…'

He lets the thought hang in the air.

'Actually, Yeoman Stackhouse, the Air Transport Auxiliary is in great need of pilots,' I say. 'They selected me because I was in the WAAF, I passed the medical, I'm under thirty, and I'm happy to be sent anywhere, at any time.'

In truth, I'm not sure how this possibly happened – I was certain I was getting sacked. But there's no reason for the Warders to know that. *There's no reason for anyone to know.*

A loud crack as the logs settle in the fireplace. I turn towards the heat, absorb as much as I can.

'*Well* under thirty, I'd say,' Stackhouse replies. 'I'm not sure I can trust an organization with such recruitment standards.'

'Oh, now it's considered quite glamorous. First they had to have motor cars, now they need aircraft.' Yeoman Sparks laughs into his wine glass.

I say nothing. There is nothing to say. Half of them think it is a glamorous tea party, and the other that it is a 'perversion of decency'. I take a small sip of wine, wishing against hope that it will be both.

Oakes clears his throat loudly. 'Well, Anna. We are all proud of you. It is a real honour to join the ATA.'

'Thanks, Mr Oakes.'

He is holding a tall glass of whisky. 'You are off to Gloucester then? To White Waltham?'

'Yes, sir, ATA Headquarters. I'm on the Paddington train—'

At that moment the giant Yeoman Brodie, Malcolm's dad, enters the Stone Kitchen. We smile at each other – I like Yeoman Brodie, but we have never been truly friendly since I discovered that he killed one of the ravens, MacDonald. He was in a great panic about his son, and he worried that the ravens were bad luck – Uncle explained it all to me so I wouldn't hate him too much – but it is hard to laugh at his loud jokes as if nothing had happened.

'Ferry pilot, eh?' He looks at me disapprovingly. 'Those Hurricanes weigh near to ten thousand pounds, you know?'

'I'm not planning to carry it, Yeoman Brodie. I'm going to make it carry me.'

He laughs – a great booming sound destined to echo throughout the castle.

I say my goodnights and march away as the talking and laughter crash on, afraid of overhearing anything. I learned that lesson. *You don't always want to know what people really think.*

I never imagined I would long for my old mattress. Hard, yes, but at least it doesn't sag in the middle. I am sorry to have missed Timothy Squire. Before dinner I wandered down to the docks, but no one seemed to know of Sapper Squire; I got only blank looks and shrugged shoulders. *Perhaps he is at work on his secret mission.* I will write to him, arrange to see him on my first leave from the ATA. *What will he say when he learns that I'm training to be a pilot?* I will write to Flo, too.

As I climb the stairs to the Bloody Tower, I cast a fearful glance behind me. I can feel eyes on me.

I am being watched.

Staring hard into the darkness, I tell myself to relax. Stranger things than watching eyes can happen in the Tower. Could there really be someone standing in the shadows? The Scots Guard are still here, and the Warders are no more than twenty steps away in the kitchen. *I am safe.*

He's not coming back.

'Hello?' I call out, without realizing I have spoken. There is no answer from the shadows.

My old room is much colder from my absence. Like it

113

felt when I first came here. Cold and empty, impossible to imagine a life here. Dust an inch thick. As I get ready for bed, shivering, I notice a folded leaflet next to the diary Timothy Squire once gave me for Christmas but which I have long since filled up.

My heart clenches as I unfold the strange paper. Flames reaching for Tower Bridge, a couple screaming in terror. Who did this I have no idea, but I'm certain what it is.

The V1 poster.

A *warning*.

III

ATTAGIRLS

"TIGER MOTH"

'Women who are anxious to serve their country should take on work more befitting their sex instead of encroaching on a man's occupation. Men have made aviation reach its present perfection.'

Aeroplane magazine, January 1940

5

Maidenhead is a large village, with elegant bridges spanning the Thames. I have brought my bicycle to speed back and forth from my billet to the airfield, and from the classrooms to the hangars, but now I push it through the uniformed crowds – many the dark blue of the ATA – my pack heavy on my back.

And after several moments, I am sure I've found my new home. I had assumed my billet would be in the barracks again, but this time I am in a small private house. I am not far, though, the constant roar of aircraft tells me that. The house is modest, and if the furniture is old and stuffy, it is still a far more comfortable situation than the WAAF barracks.

Mrs Wells, a carefully dressed lady with a searching look, greets me with a warm hello and sends me up to my room to get changed for tea. She is a widow and both her boys have been called up, so I will be alone. *I am very much looking forward to that.* Not that I have time to enjoy it; I have only a day to settle in, before I report to Headquarters at 9 a.m.

I do not think of the V1 poster. It must have been Stackhouse who put it there – who else? – but that means he was in my room! The thought is too much to consider.

I am a little taken aback by how clean the house is. When I reach the bedroom I am doubly surprised. Not because the room is covered in yellow wallpaper, but because it is not empty.

'Ah.' A girl stands, shakes my hand. 'The roommate arrives. How do you do?'

'You're not British,' I blurt out.

'You got me,' she says with a smile. She is wearing a dark blue uniform, the ATA wings on her left breast, the golden stripe of an officer on her shoulder. 'Joy Brooks, New York City.'

I don't know what to say. I'd heard that some Americans have come to help – 'cousins', they are called – but you hardly ever see one. And there is one other thing that is unusual about my new roommate.

She is black.

She notices my hesitation. 'They won't let me fly back home, but no one's asking questions here. I guess it's that bad, huh?'

I give a slight nod. I haven't seen a black person since Timothy Squire took me to the coloured quarter in the docks. But I've never seen a woman pilot, either.

'I'm called Anna. Anna Cooper.'

'Pleasure to meet you, Anna Cooper. Now let's fly some planes.'

118

Turns out I am not Joy's first roommate. Others have come and quickly left again, but Mrs Wells never thought to throw Joy out.

'I owe her for that.' Joy smiles. 'Almost enough to chew down the peas and boiled potatoes for dinner.' She sticks out her tongue.

'Tonight?'

'Every night.'

Nothing I'm not already used to. But my roommate is an American. *A black American.* I am still a little shocked, but when we come down for our peas and boiled potatoes I can see Mrs Wells takes it as calmly as the rain.

Joy tells me more while we eat. 'Anyone who can fly, can fly here, Cooper. I saw Jim taking off in a Hurricane – he's only got one arm. Ted's missing an eye and he's got to be nearing sixty.' She scoops up the peas keenly, despite her earlier complaints. 'You've never been up in a kite before?'

It takes me a second to understand. I finish chewing a large chunk of steaming potato. 'No.'

'Funny to think about, isn't it? Flying?'

Is it? My mouth is on fire, and I reach for the glass. Mrs Wells smiles at me from across the table. Taking a hurried sip of water, I try to smile back.

'My father runs an air circus. C. A. Brooks's air circus,' Joy is saying, 'and he taught me to fly his plane. I've trained a few others myself.'

'I can't believe it.'

'I'm from New York. None of those laws up there.'

What laws she's talking about I have no idea, but my tongue has finally stopped burning, so I hazard a question. 'You trained pilots as part of the circus?'

Joy laughs, a deep, husky laugh that I immediately like. 'I was a stunt pilot, Cooper. Mainly sixty-five horsepower trainers, but I got my hands on some of the four-hundred horsepower beauties. Bent a few in my time. Looking forward to some real engines.'

I nod, feigning understanding. *Bent?*

But she's a pilot. She can help teach me. Do I really want to fly? Being around Cecil distracted me somehow. But the actual experience of flying I remember with a faint and still present dizziness. I'm not so sure I want to do it myself, to be the pilot, the one responsible for the aircraft. Do I?

Some hours later, as I lie in the darkness across the narrow room from a strange American, I listen to the faint roar of engines, and wonder whether I ought to have stayed at the canteen.

Sunday, 28 February 1943

Snow dusts everything, making the ancient grey Tower look white and new.

'Timothy,' a voice says. 'What are you doing here?'

'Hello, Mum. I'm... looking for something. Is Dad at the White Tower?'

'Oh, who knows with him, dear. I assume he's where he always is.'

'Right.'

Mum offers me breakfast, which I wave away despite my hunger.

'Just be careful, Mum. Keep an eye out for anything, or anyone, unusual.'

'Of course, dear.' She is smiling, thinks I'm suddenly acting like the big man in uniform, telling the civilians to be vigilant. *Whatever works.*

'What is it you're looking for, dear?'

I've not given this any thought. 'Don't worry, I'll just get it.'

I go into my room. The oak panelling, the bed with the headboard, the comfy chair, the wide window; so much of my life, up here staring across the river. I thought the war would take me there, out into the world – Algeria, or Italy, or some island where we wait to plan our next move. I thought I'd be in a tank, or a great ship, sailing across the ocean to strike Hitler his killing blow.

I glance out of the window now, seeing the rectangle of the Green and the stone Parade Ground. No one out there but a Warder – Brodie, by the size of him, heading towards West Gate and the Tiger Pub no doubt – and a Wife, clicking away towards King's House. The black smudge of a raven, perched on the bench. Somehow, even from this distance, I can tell it is Stan.

Opening the thin closet, I check that the old hiding spots are still in place; bombs under the piled jumpers, shrapnel at the back of the drawer. I guess Mum only found that one incendiary. It was the best one, perfect condition, clean silver, as long as your forearm – a complete dud, only a small scratch from the landing. It would have been dropped as part of a breadbasket, one of seven hundred. Had this one caught fire, it would have burned at two and a half thousand degrees Centigrade.

Mum must have thrown it in the rubbish.

Well, so long as she doesn't mention it to Dad, I'll chalk it up to what's left of my luck.

I push the shrapnel well back in the drawer – no sense being sloppy. The only other stuff here is a pile of old comics and I flip through a few of them. I stare at the *Champion* – on the cover Rockfist is delivering a punch to the chest of a nasty polar bear, while his co-pilot hides pitifully inside the igloo – and slip it into my coat.

At that moment Mum appears in the doorway. 'Now that you mention it, dear, there was a man that came to the Tower this morning—'

'What man?'

She blinks. 'I don't know. A relative, I suppose, of one of the Scots Guards. Spent some time down at the roost looking at the birds. I would've said hello but I was tied up with work.'

'Don't,' I say. 'If you see someone unusual, stay away. Stay far away, yeah Mum? Tell Dad to do the same.'

'What's this all about, Timothy? Are you in trouble with the wardens?'

'I'm not in trouble with the air raid wardens. I'm not a child, Mum.'

I say goodbye to a confused but not suspicious Mum, and march down the stairs. There is no one at the roost now. It probably *was* a relative of a Scots Guard. Even Anna's dad is not mad enough to hang around the roost in broad daylight.

In Oakes's current state, he wouldn't notice if a Nazi sat down to breakfast with him. *I still can't believe he signed a consent form to let Anna join the WAAF. Some guardian he is.*

I prowl the area. The wind raises a wall of dust, which no amount of blinking will clear. *I should have just gone to Aberdeen. Mad fool.*

No, then Anna wouldn't know her father was lurking around. *She still doesn't know.* Well, no one would know and she'd have no one to protect her. Not that I'm turning out to be much of a guardian myself.

The sun dips beneath the clouds. A slight cool breeze – not cold, though, despite the snow settled around the Green. No one is around so I slide the comic free. I flip the pages – Rockfist dishes out his left hook, escapes in his Spitfire.

Someone is coming and I can see from here that it is not a vicious German madman.

'Hello,' says a girl. She is walking a black dog on a lead. How'd she get in here? *What is the point of all these bleeding Warders if tourists and German spies just wander in? Is Mr Thorne asleep at the gate?* Tourists aren't allowed in the Tower while the war's on. I don't say any of that, though. I put the comic face down beside me. 'Hello.'

We look at each other. I stand, abandoning the comic. *Stan will tear it to pieces in a second.*

'I'm looking for Anna – Anna Cooper – do you know her?'

I almost laugh. 'You might say that. Are you the friend I've heard all about – Flo?'

She turns a little red. 'And you're Timothy Squire.'

We stand there, not quite looking at each other.

'Is she with the birds, or…?'

'Ah, right. Sorry. She's away at the airfield.'

Her face falls. 'Oh. I thought she was volunteering at the canteen…'

'Don't feel too bad. *I* thought she was at the WAAF. One of the Warders had to tell me she'd joined the ATA. She's training to be a pilot, it seems. She must be well busy.'

'You haven't heard from her either.'

'Not a word.'

'Oh.'

'Who's this?' I point to the dog.

'Geoffrey.' She tugs at the lead. Then, 'Oh,' she says, pointing, 'is that one of the ravens?'

'That's Portia, yeah.'

'Portia? Nice name. It's from *The Merchant of Venice*, right?' Flo smiles. A nice, warm smile.

'Of course.' I move a little closer. She is tall, taller than Anna, and her hair is long and brown.

'I read all about them in the papers – the Ravens of the Tower. How all but one died in the Blitz and the prime minister ordered a new flock brought in to keep England safe.'

I nod slowly. Did Anna not tell her? That she let the last

124

of the ravens go free? That it was her uncle, Yeoman Reed, who ordered the new birds? Seems like Anna's happy to keep her great friend in the dark.

'Churchill himself ordered them,' she says, a little breathless. 'And it's up to you to look after them. It must be a lot of responsibility.'

'A little, yeah. They're well important. You, ah, want to go and see the roost? Most of 'em should be hanging around there, waiting for their dinner. Might have to keep Geoffrey on his lead.' Gesturing for her to go ahead, I scoop up the comic as I pass.

She looks up at me, her eyes big and pretty. 'That would be grand.'

But even as we cross the Green, walking in step, my eyes scan the battlements for any lurking figures.

'Look, mate, can you come or not?'

Lightwood stares back. He worries I am going mad. Too much time at the docks can do that. *Too much time in the pub with Lightwood can do that, too.*

'Is this about a bird?'

'No, I just need to check something. Can you come with me?' It burns me to ask him, but I am afraid to go alone. The truth of that burns even more.

He finally nods. 'Where are we going then?'

'Catesby Street.'

There's no one here. He's not fool enough to leave his real address. He knew I'd come down here myself and see him tossed in gaol.

Nah, even I know that's bollocks.

So where is he? He's checked out, that's easy enough to see. A crack through the curtains shows there's nothing but a dusty table and a few mice inside. Back home to Germany? In time for tea with Hitler?

Or has he found out where Anna is stationed? If he's mad enough to show up at the Tower when the Warders are looking out for him, he's mad enough to storm up to an airfield and demand to see his daughter.

Sure enough he'll mention he's had a nice chat with me. Yet again I'll be seen as keeping secrets from her. This time, I'll wager, she'll never speak to me again.

Speak to me? This man is mad – he's a bleeding Nazi – who knows what his plan is? Maybe he means to kill her, to kill us all.

She has to be warned.

'You planning to loot the place, or what?'

I shake at the voice. I forgot all about Lightwood. 'No… I just thought…'

'Stood you up, did she?' He is all smiles. 'No harm in it, Squire. Happens to the best of us. But I've never heard of a girl up and moving house just to avoid a bloke.'

I ignore him, gazing around. There is nothing. Only a

man in the window across the road, and a lady walking a little white dog by the stop sign.

He is not here.

'Don't sweat it, mate.' Lightwood clamps me on the back. 'Pint's on me. It'll take your mind right off it.'

Monday, 1 March 1943

Aircraft line the rough grass airfield, wingtip to wingtip. I have never seen so many planes together in one place. I didn't know there *were* this many. *Only the Germans seem to have endless planes.* There are more, many more, huddled in that lump of hangars like great tin sheds with rounded tops.

Timothy Squire with two broken legs wouldn't miss seeing this.

I cannot fly one of those machines – I simply can't. White Waltham airfield is surrounded by giant barrage balloons; grey whales, floating in the sky above. Watching them gives me a haunted feeling.

And the planes must take off amid those great looming shapes.

I took the bus this morning with Joy – it is far too wet to bother with the bicycle, though I miss the fresh air. Not that I noticed any of the Berkshire countryside. I felt quite important in my ATA uniform. The navy jacket is a slim cut, and it pulled close as I looped each black button in the mirror. I tied the tie and fixed the forage side cap so it stays put. I always thought the cap was a little silly, but now I like it. It changes my face somehow, makes it less round. Less like a girl's.

The whole uniform seems to transform me into a woman. Into a pilot. Most important of all are the narrow stripes, one on each shoulder, of the thinnest gold, which announce me as a cadet.

I glance over at Joy's ATA wings. *Someday it will be me.*

White Waltham is made up of huge, flat-roofed buildings, built of solid brick, and crowded with important people, gold bars of rank on their shoulders. Before the war this was the School of Flying. Now it's ATA Headquarters.

As we enter the main building I stare back at the congested traffic on the grass runways. Joy says she does two or three flights before lunch, sometimes coming back to base on a train.

'They come in like this,' Joy brings an arm down in a slow swoop. 'Easy as.'

But I hear something else, something I heard in the WAAF barracks. *One in ten pilots are killed. And* they *already know how to fly.*

Joy takes me to the female locker room, where I hang my coat and hat in the wooden locker, before leading me on. She has a cheerful appearance, almost carefree. She is taller than me, but not by more than a few inches. No taller than Flo.

'Here's the Met Office.' Joy points to the wall, where a blackboard lists the day's forecast – including everything from wind strength to cloud base to visibility. The forecaster sits in the corner, her desk covered in charts.

'A glance at that will tell you if you're likely to get a job, or if you should run for a place at the billiards table. Come on, I'll show you the Mess.'

I fight the urge to walk in tight single file, instead moving slowly, almost at a stroll. *I will not march.*

'How long have you been here?'

'Three months.' She smiles. 'Here it is. Where you'll get your tea. Honestly, I don't know how you all drink so much of it.'

There is a smile in her words. *She hasn't been here long enough. She'll come round.*

'Lunch is in here, unless you're flying, then you take a bag with you.' We reach the crew room and Joy spreads her hands wide. 'And here's where you'll spend most of your time.'

It is 9.30 a.m., and the room is filled. Many people are crowding around a table, a second away from pushing and shoving.

'Chits,' Joy says, as the pilots rummage through papers. 'The delivery orders. Type of ship, from where to where.'

A woman turns, face flushed and happy, clutching a sheet of paper. 'Connecting Hurricanes!'

Another pilot turns, her face curdled.

'What? What did you get, Helen? Taxi?'

'Worse. Bleeding Swordfish.'

The shocked looks are confirmation of this dire news.

'Most of what we do here is transport aircraft. Nothing too dangerous,' Joy says. 'But a Swordfish is an open cockpit, and in this cold…'

We move into the room with its large windows, big cushioned sofas, and leather armchairs. Newspapers lie untouched on the table – they are small, usually only four pages, on account of the paper rationing. Pilots push past us, parachutes slung over shoulders. No one says hello to Joy – or to me – or even takes any notice of us.

'Taxi planes are off at 10 a.m., so those pilots are off to check the weather along the route they're headed, and to pack up whatever kit they need. Some will fly back in new planes, a few will arrive in cars, and some will be back on tomorrow's train. Others you might not see for weeks, as they're stationed at various airfields. You understand?'

I nod. The 'transport' is not people, but planes. Planes needed elsewhere.

'Sometimes you'll take a stooge,' she says, using the term for passenger. 'Sometimes we fly as stooges with other pilots. Mainly, though, we fly an aircraft to where it needs to be.'

Sounds simple enough. *Except for the part where I fly a plane.*

One step at a time. *Elementary Flying Training School. Finish the training, earn your wings.* The ATA is not a military organization, but they still have uniforms and officers' ranks. No drills, at least. And no marching. *And no scrubbing toilets.*

But, of course, there is one truth that sticks in my throat. *One in ten pilots die.*

'So those pilots are off to work. The others…'

I follow her gaze to the back of the room. Now that the departing pilots have gone, the atmosphere has shifted. Women lounge on chairs and tables, smoking cigarettes and playing blackjack. Music from *The Strawberry Blonde* plays on the gramophone. The roar of departing planes hangs over it all.

Backgammon and darts, and a heated game of billiards. Clouds of smoke fill the room, pushing you out as much as holding you in. *A very different place from the WAAF break room.*

No rules about make-up here. The women are glamorous in lipstick, with long fingernails, and sunglasses on the side tables. None of them even look *tired*. But they must be exhausted. *Should I be wearing make-up?*

'They spend most days playing cards. Either waiting for a weather window to open up, or just enjoying a washout day,' Joy says. 'It never stops raining for two days together over here.'

I can tell already how these women will treat me – I will be ignored.

Amy Johnson was the first woman to fly solo to Australia. And she was the daughter of a fish merchant.

No need to worry. I remind myself of what Joy said about pilots being moved around so often that you hardly get to know them. Then again, Joy seems to know an awful lot about these pilots.

'That's Margaret Fairweather, the first woman to fly a Spit. Everyone calls her the Cold Front. I think the blonde one is called the Mayfair Minx in the papers. And Diana Gaines, another American pilot. From Kentucky, though.'

A thought suddenly occurs to me. 'Where are all the male pilots?'

Joy shrugs. I'm not sure if her smile is sarcastic or pleased. 'We get the odd RAF pilot. Most of them steer clear.'

Really? I think, amazed. *They steer clear of the Mayfair Minx?*

'The RAF doesn't love that we're here. Women can't handle planes and all that. Don't go expecting any salutes, Cooper.'

Joy must see something in my look. 'Don't worry too much. The boys just need some time to adjust. In no time they'll be cheering as you take off in a Spitfire.'

'I've never even seen a Spitfire.'

'It's the hottest ship around, Cooper.' Joy smiles. 'And flying strange ships without any instruction and in the face of grumbling men – *that's* what the ATA does.'

Wednesday, 3 March 1943

The Phoenix units have been completed. Not that it's put Quarter in a less foul mood.

'Now, the things you might have learned here – the things you *think* you've learned here – are never to pass your lips, do you understand?'

I'm not certain I could have lasted another day inside

this frozen great concrete box, held as a prisoner by this roving bugger. Right knackered, thoughts shimmer and disappear. Bed would be wonderful.

'Any hope of success in this war relies on you keeping your mouth shut. There are a thousand rumours, I hear them all – but you are not to add to them, or debate them, or even try to figure it out. Just do your job, keep your head down, and when it's time for people to know – for the world to know – rest assured, they will know. And your mommy and your sweetheart will understand why you couldn't tell them before. Does everyone understand me?'

A raving tosser, who wants us to keep his secrets. Which are what, exactly? That some day this thing will float off to Europe and, at the right moment, each compartment will fill with water, and drag the whole beast to the bottom of the sea to provide a foundation? *Who am I going to tell that to? It'd be just as useful to tell Rogan.*

I stand beside Lightwood in the cold air, waiting for the link between the docks to be reopened. We watch as the water from Greenland Dock pours in, filling South Dock.

'Man's a rotten bastard,' Lightwood says.

I spit in agreement.

The Phoenix units are floated through the cut – with only nine inches of clearance – and into the Thames.

'We're going to push a great bloody harbour ahead of us?' I mutter. 'Hitler won't see that coming.'

'The harbours would come behind, of course,' Lightwood shakes his head at my ignorance. 'Beach landings will do little good if there're no supplies behind them. The initial landing will secure the coast and allow us to set up the harbours.'

'Sounds dead easy.'

'No doubt the Germans have been busy gardening the coastal waters. They've had years to prepare for us coming. If we reach the beaches, they'll be mined like anthills. The whole of every beach, and the water leading up to it, will be fitted with explosives.'

Lightwood finishes his cigarette in silence. We watch as the Phoenix unit is towed downriver.

What happens now?

What can I do?

One thing is certain. We have to hurry up and get over there, whatever it takes. The news on the wireless last night has shocked everyone stiff. The Nazis have murdered so many Jews – thousands; tens of thousands.

There was some hopeful news at least. The Russians are pushing Hitler back across Russia. Now we must act.

I am not afraid to fight, but we are not like the Nazis. Everywhere, from the drunks at the pub to the Warders in the Tower, people tell stories about the Hitler Youth. They are armies, trained from childhood to fight to the death for their great leader. We are just – people. Lads from all over; many of who have never so much as seen a gun before joining up. Lightwood couldn't fight his way out of a bag.

Churchill seems a fine enough bloke, but I'd just as soon not die for him. But I have to do something. I have to help.

'Excuse me, sir.' I knock on the open door; mechanically, my right hand swoops to my temple, palm out, and snaps back to my side.

'Squire. No need to salute, boy. That's only for the armed forces.'

'Sir.' I fight to keep my voice steady. 'Now that the Phoenix unit is complete, sir, I was wondering... if there are any openings for the training battalion in Yorkshire? Even if they can't take Lightwood, too. I will go alone.'

His eyes go wide and stay wide. Then he laughs. 'You reckon they'd take you now? After you've turned them down? No one's taking you till you're eighteen, son. Better hope the war lasts. Plenty for you to do around here until then.'

I raise my hands just in time as he heaves a great empty bag into my arms.

'Here's a job for someone with your qualifications. Take this pack and have a run up to the chemist's.'

'The chemist's, sir?'

'On the High Street. Ask them for two hundred French letters.'

'Sir?'

'Condoms, Squire. You know what those are, yes?'

'Of course, sir.'

He is smiling – smirking – at me. 'Of course. Well, on you go. Take your pal Lightwood, if you need to have him around so badly.'

I look from the bag to the quartermaster. Surely this is just a big joke. *What do I do now?* Shift is over – I am too hungry for such a ridiculous task.

'But sir… why, sir?'

'You ever fire a gun when the barrel's hot?' The smirk is still there. Before I can respond, though, it is gone. 'The gun, lad, for Christ's sake, I'm talking about the gun. You have to keep it dry, keep the barrel dry, or there's no sense carrying the bloody thing around. You understand? Other boys *have* elected to fight, and you can at least do your bit to help them.'

I can't say no to him, but I can't say yes, either. I just turn and walk off in a daze. I feel his eyes like a shove. *Right, I'm going.*

French letters? I've only ever kissed two girls – Anna, and Elsie behind the curtain wall – in my whole life. Now I have to march into a chemist's shop and ask for two hundred French letters. I turn on to Wapping High Street and halt, stopped by the distant sound of girls' laughter.

I can't do it.

Not on the High Street.

I stare, lost, the cold trapped inside my skin. A bus pulls up, headed north. *Good enough.* I join the short queue, enjoying the brief warmth of the bodies, and hop on.

Quartermaster is a bollocks. He's just making up jobs until work on the next building project starts at the docks. *He's just trying to make me miss dinner.* If only condoms were on the ration list – then I couldn't possibly order so many at once. *Will I need my ID card?*

But I can't quit. As much as I'd like to, I can't just stay on this bus for ever.

On my next holiday, I am getting as far away from the docks as I can get. I'd even go back to Disley, and spend the whole time with the barking-mad folk there. Dad dragged us to Disley after a direct hit on the Tower last year. Both him and Mum moved up to that forgotten village, and it was a terrible two weeks before I sneaked away on the train. Dad might've been angry but there's no doubt he was itching to get back to his armour and his old books. Mum, too, though you wouldn't have known it from her heavy looks.

Did that say 'Bethnal Green'? I fly out of my seat, push the stop button.

Of course we are in traffic and it is a bleeding long wait before I can get off the bus. *I will definitely be late for dinner.* I need to find a chemist's and hop straight back on the bus home.

The grim, broken street stares back at me. Many of the destroyed flats have stayed destroyed, the fires long burned out but the sites simply abandoned. I am a fool. It will take me an hour to get back. The sun is going down. Oh, Quarter is going to love this. At least I can see a chemist's, just across the road, and it looks like it's still open.

Maybe this will work out after all.

I march from the chemist's, my face bright red, as the door locks behind me. A huge bag of condoms in my hand.

I kept my voice as low as I could, but of course the man repeated it louder – 'you mean *condoms*?' – and of course the other worker was a young girl, and neither of them could hide their thoughts. *What does this boy need with two hundred condoms?*

Lightwood will never let this one go.

At least they don't know me here. I'll never come back to this chemist's. If I was still in Disley, everyone and their cat would know all about this by breakfast.

I wait at the bus stop as darkness settles. Next door, the cinema has just emptied, people filing out from the early show. *At least they are enjoying themselves.*

The bus pulls up, seizing to a halt. But just as the queue inches towards it, a low moan rises up all around us.

Air raid. My neck cranes upwards.

The siren wails. Any unidentified aircraft sets it off. And the Jerries are craftier than ever now; deliberately de-synchronizing their engines to fool the anti-aircraft sound detectors.

The bus driver ushers all of the passengers off. We all move as one, joined quickly by the still blinking cinema goers. A pub across the road sends a dozen more towards us. All of us headed in the same direction. Bethnal Green Tube Station.

My luck's not used up just yet. Bethnal Green, no longer

used as a station, is fitted to shelter 10,000 people, with beds for almost half of those. The safest place in the city.

People move together. Calm as things are these days, they all remember the nightly bombings. This was as much a part of their routine as getting up for work. Many still spend their nights in the shelter, just in case the bombing returns. They've basically taken to living underground.

Yesterday's wireless said we were planning a heavy raid on Berlin this morning. Hitler always wants revenge. *Those bloody V1 posters*. Self-propelled missiles are impossible, of course, but...

Other people would have heard the news, too. Even now, even after months without constant attacks on London, fear is never far away. They've seen too much to doubt even the wildest threat.

A crowd, mostly kids, rushes from the nearby arcade to join the growing queue. Others straggle behind, emptying out from offices, houses, pubs, cafés, the baked-potato stall. I step inside the shelter and immediately feel safer, even just in the ticketing area. The dull light of the single bulb shows the size of the crowd already inside. It will be busy once we get down there.

'Careful,' I say. A mother clutching her baby burrows into the crowd. The crowd bugles inward, and she is gone. *Where are the bloody wardens?*

I push in with them towards the stairs. If I had a uniform they would not be in such a panic. The stairs are ten feet wide. No rail in the centre, just a flood of people squeezing down the steps.

'Be calm, there is plenty of space for—'

People surge ahead. I give up, surrender to the tide. Once we're on the platform, I can help regain some order. *Oh yes, that is just what this situation needs – a builder out shopping for condoms.* Of course they'll all listen to me.

Bang. Bodies turn in alarm.

A man is yelling, blowing a whistle and yelling. I can see him when I twist back, just at the entrance. A policeman. *Thank Christ.*

'Be calm! Stay calm! It is not bombs. Not bombs!'

'Bombs!'

'Bombs!'

The whistle blows down the voices. 'It is the guns at Victoria Park. The Victoria Park guns! They are the new rocket guns. Our guns! Not bombs!'

'Bomb' seems to be the only word getting through. He is making things worse.

Bang.

Another heave, and I lose sight of the policeman in the mass of people. We are shoved again, gaining another stair, but then halt sharply. *We need to get to the escalator; to the tunnel.*

A blockage up front. Someone hits me, hard, in the lower back. I try to turn – 'watch yourself, mate' – but instantly another shoulder pushes me, into the body in front of me. Bodies are piling up, pressing close, forcing themselves inside. I am moving forward, and for a moment my feet are not touching the ground. A face twists back, a look of fear. More people are trying to enter the station.

I am squeezed, the bag falls from my hand. *The condoms.*

'Move right down along the stairs! Move down!' I call out, and others echo my cry, with increasing volume and desperation. The combined weight is heavy, crushing, like a bloody mountain falling on us.

Move!

Above the siren is still wailing. And people are still pushing down, more and more people, forcing their way on to the stairs, pushing towards the tunnel.

Again the rocket gun fires.

Too many people have tried to turn right to the platform. It has been blocked with stuck bodies. No one is getting inside the tunnel. We are just being pushed together, pushed down, pushed forward. Forward into what?

There is nothing ahead but a brick wall. I twist back to see the huge mass of people looming over us, tangled and toppling.

'Stop pushing! Stop it!'

'Bombs!'

Another huge push. There is nowhere to go. A man scrambling to get back to his feet is driven down by the weight of the others. The air turns slow, heavy.

'Move down! Move!'

'We can't – stop pushing!'

'Sod off, mate!'

It is becoming harder to breathe. Suddenly I am trying to push *back*, to escape the crush of people.

I am stuck. They keep coming, bodies building up, crushing. There is no air to breathe. A man falls, waving frantically – is gone. Arms and feet are thrashing. He is under us, under our feet, but the bodies heave to the left. Another falls – a child, his mother instantly reaches down – but can't get there. *Move!* I can't get anywhere.

'Bombs!'

I push back now, hard, as hard as I can. There is no air. The man might be right under my boots, or the child, I don't care, I have to get away. The dark thoughts, the bloody ravens, descend. *This is it.*

Something hits me, a blow across the cheek. Lights blaze in my vision. It is a man, a man has fallen on me. His weight slides off my shoulder and on to the ground. For a second, before it is covered by trampling feet, I see his face – a blue tongue sticking out of his mouth.

Crushed bodies block the stairwell. I thrust my elbows, throw wild punches, push ruthlessly back. I fumble, latch on to the guard rail. Grip it as hard as I can. I cannot move. I must get out. Dark thoughts, closing in.

'Help!'

'Bombs!'

'Move!'

The closing of a black wing.

6

Thursday, 4 March 1943

'Come in, Miss Cooper.'

A blonde woman, perhaps forty, waves me inside with a stern look. Instantly I notice the two thick bars of gold on her shoulder, the gold wings on her left breast.

The urge to salute comes from nowhere like a pang. I fight it off.

'I am Pauline Gower, the Head Flying Instructor.' She sits very casually on the edge of the table. Her voice is soft. 'You know why we gave you a chance?'

I shake my head. My final meeting with Queen Bee threatens to replay in my mind. This is Pauline Gower, Commander of the Women's ATA, holder of multiple international flying records, Britain's first female commercial pilot, the third in the world. *Not some nasty hag from the WAAF.*

'Desperation, Miss Cooper. It is clear that, aside from having absolutely no flying experience, you can't be a day over sixteen. When the ATA was established, there was frankly no chance that someone like you would ever be here.'

I nod, look away. *Why bring me here just to go off on me? What is wrong with these people? The uniforms must do something to their brains.*

'Times change,' she says, her voice still soft. She sounds nothing like the barking officers at Warmwell. 'We used to need ambassadors. Clean-cut, stable young women with vast gifts. Now, we need pilots. Every one we can get. I have sixteen planes that have to be in Scotland this afternoon.'

I blink in shock as I realize that I've seen Commander Gower before. She was in Leicester Square, at the film screening – standing next to Anna Neagle under the flash of cameras. *That night brought me here, and Gower was there, too.* Certainly an encouraging thought. I feel my breathing slow, relax.

'In addition to Ground School you will also learn all that we can teach you about aeronautics. And you'll have to get perfect results on every one of your exams. You come highly recommended, which is lucky for you. Word is you're a natural. Find it easy keeping your head up there, Cooper?'

I nod slowly. 'I think so, Commander.' Such compliments from Queen Bee are impossible to believe. *Highly recommended? A natural?* I apologize to her in my mind for calling her a hag. Why would she be nice? Or did she merely want to be rid of me so badly?

'Well, let's take you up and see.'

My heart judders. 'Commander Gower?'

'No point in teaching you if you don't have the stomach for it. I can't just take another pilot's word for it, however celebrated they are. We'll send you up with Joy, see how you do.'

I blink. Queen Bee was a famous pilot? *But I have more immediate concerns.* 'Now?'

'You have somewhere else to be?'

'No, ma'am.'

'Good. Now let's find you a helmet and a parachute.'

There hasn't been enough time, not nearly enough time.

Surely it is not required for a cadet to go up in a plane on her first day? No, this is definitely a test. I will merely sit in the cockpit, look as at ease as I can, and then Gower will wave the whole thing off. Won't she?

This is madness.

I close my locker with a bang. I don't feel one ounce as glamorous as the others. Instead of the sleek ATA flying uniform, I am in my full padded Sidcot suit – a huge, bulky one-piece suit for cold-weather flying. And there is no colder flying, Joy says, than a Tiger Moth in winter. The parachute straps bite my shoulders; my legs and back are stiff and heavy as I march out to the airfield.

A stale smell of tobacco hits me as I pass the crew room. One of the pilots – the Cold Front? – is curled asleep on the sofa in her uniform. The hallway seems to grow longer as I walk along it.

Joy is standing on the grass airfield in her flying kit. She is standing – grinning! – beside a yellow bi-plane. A Tiger Moth. With a steadying breath, I approach. The ground crew swarms by, everyone focused on their own tasks. The grass airfield has turned to mud, a vast mud pit. *Can the plane even take off out of that?*

In my heavy leather helmet and wide split-lens goggles, I feel like a giant bug.

I don't want to do this.

I worry for a moment I've left something in my locker. No, I have the scarf – tied around my neck. Should it be *this* cold? How cold will it be once we're up there?

I climb up the wing, squeeze into the front seat. I am almost between the two sets of wings; the lower wings spreading out past my arms, the top set just a few feet over my head. It is nothing like being in a Lancaster. I am crammed tightly in here. I try to adjust my feet and, looking down, I see the floor is made of wood.

It's just a box of plywood with wings.

Joy is at the controls in the Moth's rear seat. I can see her in the mirror, a wide smile on her face. *Can she actually fly? Oh, God, what have I done?*

I can hear Joy's voice clearly through the speaking tube attached to my helmet.

'Ready?'

'Yes,' I say, pressing the rubber mouthpiece closer. 'Yes.'

The speaking system is supposed to let me hear her

instructions even over the engine at full throttle. *And if I can't?*

Don't worry. She's the one flying the plane.

The fitter, a handsome man with a smirk instead of a smile, appears.

'Contact!' Joy yells out.

The man spins the propeller. A loud coughing noise and I realize where the engine is. The great hump in front of me. The propeller whirls dangerously just feet from my face. I can see next to nothing.

The whole plane vibrates. The instruments in front of me awake, dials rising and falling. On a trainer, all controls are duplicated and connected. *But I will not be touching a thing.*

'Not your first stooge ride, Cooper, if I've heard correctly.'

I can hear her smile through the microphone. *How does everyone know about that?*

'I'm ready,' I repeat. I will not die. I will *not* be sick.

'Then let's go.'

The engine is loud as we taxi away, to the east end of the muddy runway, rattling as we drag the tail behind us. Feels like the longest road I have ever been on, but at the same time it is too short. We reach the flight lines, slow to a muddy halt.

Huge barrage balloons, tethered to the earth with steel cables, hover threateningly. Built to stop German fighters from diving, they will just as easily stop us from rising. I look away.

The propellers are swinging. Louder, louder. *I've bent a*

few in my time. Unclenching my hands, I try to follow what is happening.

With a cough, the wooden plane shudders to life. There is a short window in front of me, but it does nothing to screen the wind. We are moving across the bumpy field, turning on to the deeper mud, the world vibrating and clattering. The feeling is nothing like the smooth glide into the air in the Lancaster. It is happening too fast – we are gathering speed, still bumping, still rattling, heading straight for the fence. I want to cry out, to stop, to get out and go back to the Mess. To go home.

The bumping stops and wind presses full in my face.

I know it has happened but I am too terrified to look.

We must have barely cleared the fence, and now we are staggering into the air, the wind hammering us, pushing us back to the earth. All around us, I know without looking, hang those damned barrage balloons. But we rise, higher and higher, climbing, and, in one gut-turning instant, level off.

The force of the wind is like an angry sea. It is freezing. The machine putters through the air. I am floating, the sky flowing past me, flowing through me. The only sound is the wind swishing across the wings.

I am flying.

This is nothing like when I went up with Cecil. When I was with him, it was as if we were sitting still – now, the sensation of movement forces me to grip the seat. Each drop, each shudder, sends waves through me.

How do these short little wings hold us up?

'How are you feeling, Cooper?'

She throttles back so I can hear her more clearly.

'Fine.' Too terrified to look down, I am filled with an aimless panic.

Joy seems to sense this. The whole machine tips, nudges me. *Look!* But I can't. My eyes are open, but all they see is gleaming blue and the black twirl of the propeller.

If you don't look down, how can you mark the check-points? How can you fly? I can't! I've picked the wrong job. This is all wrong.

When I flew with Cecil I was so calm I got up and *wandered around* in the Lancaster, picking the best view. *This* is completely different.

Joy knows what she's doing. I can still see the airfield, just on the edge of vision to the east. A very comforting sight, the vast sprawling space with its ugly lump of hangars and wavering barrage balloons. Much preferable to this huge, impersonal, featureless sky.

Again the aircraft leans, the nose drops, the left wing now in the corner of my eye, a longer moment before she rights it.

Look! With a sudden jerk we are again banking left.

Look!

And I look. The world is below. And I can see *all* of it. Huge, massive, spreading out in every direction. A patchwork of colours, rippled with hills. My eyes latch on to every tree, every person I can see walking down a narrow alley. *Much closer to the ground than with Cecil.* I am not sure if the thought makes me more or less nervous.

Now that we have so much height, and Joy has stopped tipping the wings, the sensation of movement has almost completely gone. We are floating. It is magic. No, it is not magic – it is this machine. It is the pilot.

'You ready up there?'

I freeze. 'Ready?'

'Follow me through on the stick and rudder.'

'Wait! Joy—'

'Just follow me.'

Which one is the stick? I calm my breathing. I am not in danger. Joy has control of the plane. And the stick is clearly here, and the rudder bar at my feet.

'Gently now, hold the stick in your right hand. Put your feet on the pedals – keep looking straight ahead, the horizon is just there, above the engine. See it? Keep the nose there. The nose of the aeroplane. Good, check the wings, make sure they're matched up. Now we're straight and level.'

My stomach heaves. *Moving the stick drops the wing, each right or left.*

'Bring the stick back – gently, even less than that – and the nose goes up. Feel how we're slowing down? So push the stick forward, get in back on the horizon. The nose on the horizon. Just relax, Cooper. Keep everything smooth. Good.'

That seems easy enough. Going along the bottom of the clouds, keeping the nose steady, keeping my breath calm. Smooth.

'Cooper, push the stick forward, more. Don't worry. The nose goes down, feel the air speed building up? The moment your nose drops, you're losing altitude. Now we're in a dive. So bring it back to level, bring the wings level. Relax the grip, hold it gently. There. Much better.'

Again my heart is racing. I didn't mean to put us in a dive! The stick is so sensitive. *Smooth*.

'See, the plane flies itself, Cooper, all you need to do is adjust every now and then. Keep the nose on the horizon, keep the wings level. Light on the stick.'

She is watching me in that little mirror, I can feel it. *Just relax. Breathe. Do not be sick.*

'All right, I'm taking the controls back. We're headed home now. Great work.'

We land smoothly and I get out, my eyes still ringing from the roar of the engine. It is good – astonishingly good – to be down again. But I know, somehow, that feeling won't last. Not enough to keep me here.

'See? You've got the knack for it, Cooper.'

'Joy – we shouldn't have – *I* shouldn't have—'

'Listen, the sooner you get comfortable, the better. Circuits and landings. A few more trips, then you're landing this thing.'

Saturday, 6 March 1943

When we finally got outside, as the policeman laid out the bodies on the pavement, we were told not to speak of what had happened. Not to mention it to anyone.

In that strange silence after the All Clear, many were carted off to Whitechapel Hospital, but too many were left on the pavement. In the dark they were just shapes, blue and twisted. But some shapes were small, too small.

There must have been a hundred – more. More than a hundred.

'An air raid,' I said blankly. 'In the chaos, I lost them.'

Quartermaster found my excuse wanting. As I was alive and seemingly fine, why did I not return to the chemist's and purchase the French letters required, at my own cost, seeing as I'd spent the division's money with nothing to show for it?

'Unless you've invented this whole disaster story as a way of covering up your larks?' he suggested with a hollow laugh. 'Though I doubt even you could make your way through two hundred condoms in a single night.'

I was too knackered to respond to this latest display of wit. I couldn't even muster a reply when the inevitable came.

'Well, Mr Squire. It seems finding a task for you here is quite impossible. Best of luck finding a job more suited to your... skills. Goodbye, Mr Squire.'

Monday, 8 March 1943

'The Ancient and Tattered Airmen, some call us. To be here, they have to be rejected from the RAF. Our pilots have bad eyes, poor coordination, nervous issues. We have eccentric millionaires, wounded veterans, retired bankers – anyone who holds a private licence to fly. We are a unit called into being by the war.

'Which is why we women are here today, too – some little more than girls. You come to us from all across the world, skilled and brave enough to help ferry each aircraft wherever it is needed. So if we're going to end this war, the Ancient and Tattered Airmen will have to co-exist with the Always Terrified Airwomen. Do your part by doing your best job.'

Pauline Gower is a serious woman, and we listen to her every word. Well, almost every word.

'Last year you would have all needed a private licence and at least fifty hours in your logbook. Now, we train you from the ground up. In three weeks you will all take a flight test, regardless of experience, and either make the grade or you will go home.'

There are fourteen ferry 'pools', or airfields, from Hamble in the south up to Lossiemouth in the far north of Scotland, and aircraft are shuffled between them as needed.

Before we can fly a plane, of course, there's Ground School, which focuses mainly on reading highly detailed RAF maps for use in cross-country flights, and rigorous testing on aircraft recognition.

We are each given a pocket-sized, ring-bound blue book, filled with four- by five-inch cards. The cover reads 'Ferry Pilot's Notes'. But everyone simply calls it the Blue Bible.

'This,' comes her voice, 'is the most important thing in your life. These pages have the flying and landing settings for every RAF aeroplane. Keep this on you at all times.'

The stiff pages explain which knobs to pull. I flip through the alphabetical listings, memorizing engine types, jet-tube pressures, oil temperatures, safety speed of a Master, then a Tempest, then a Hurricane, then a Spitfire.

I am a fool. Isn't living during the war dangerous enough without putting myself in a plane?

'I'd get that hair cut, too.' Pauline Gower smiles at me.

'My hair?'

'Do pilots wear helmets?'

So much for my new hairband. Trying not to think of the glamorous pilots in the crew room, flipping long blonde hair, I nod again. But Gower's smile fades as she continues.

'Every woman should learn to fly. The war has helped greatly in this regard, but once peace comes... my advice to all women will continue to be: learn to fly.

'When my parents sent me off to Paris for finishing school, I ran away. Learned to fly in secret – my father cut my allowance at the words "flying lessons". So I paid for the hours of training with violin lessons.

'I rented a Gipsy Moth, in a field near Sevenoaks. Charged half a crown per flight, fifteen shillings for two loops and a spin. For a year I slept in a hut beside the aeroplane.

'Adventure has its charms, as does danger. But this is more than that. This is an opportunity to earn your own money and make your own career. Aviation is a profession of the future. This is your future.

'We will train you as best we can – but this is a time of action. We need pilots, Miss Cooper. As many as we can get, and as soon as they are ready.'

I nod and try a smile. She does not appear convinced.

Tuesday, 9 March 1943

'From the west of the runway, look towards Shottesbrooke. If you can see the spire of St John's beyond the trees, you've got at least two miles' visibility. Get up there and use it.'

Gower has taken her usual position standing at the front of the hall, a great map on the wall behind her. All ten of us sit forward in our seats, straining to catch and copy down her every softly spoken word.

I run my hand through my short – *very* short – hair. Well, almost every word. I look even *younger*, but if it shows how serious I am, I'm happy to have done it. The hairdresser was nice enough, though I waited for almost an hour for her to be ready. White Waltham is not like the Dorchester depot.

I remember during the Blitz, when Nell took me to get my hair cut near St Katharine Docks. 'Looking snappy,' she said afterwards.

'If not, stay put. *Never* try to go over the top of clouds. Is that clear? Two pilots in the last week have met their end flying into a hillside. Bad visibility kills. You must develop a sound flying sense and take no chances whatsoever. *Never* fly over the top of cloud as a way out of trouble.'

It seems like she knows we've all seen *They Flew Alone*. Constantly she goes on about the dangers of a 'washout' and unflyable weather.

'I don't want to even hear the word "cloud". Think of it as "the concrete". You must never attempt to go over the top.'

The silence is loud. Gower, however, is not done. 'The ATA flies every type of RAF aircraft – and there are over two hundred. All aircraft have the same six-instrument panel: air-speed indicator, altimeter, gyroscopic compass, altitude indicator, turn indicator, artificial horizon.

'Now, knowledge of this equipment will save your life in bad weather. Which is why we won't be teaching you how to use any of it,' she says slowly, allowing another silence to fall. 'Because you are not to fly in foul weather. If reference to the ground is lost for even an instant, you're not likely to ever return to the earth alive. There is no purpose in teaching you how to fly blind, because you will never be flying blind. Is that clear?'

A weak cough from the back.

'You will fly without radio. There will be no check-ins with the nearest RAF station or incoming weather alerts. You will be alone. What you ladies will need to master, and what you can do quite safely and responsibly from the ground, is the engine. You will learn to dissect and reassemble these engines in the swiftest time possible.'

The noise in the hangar is deafening. Engines being tested, hammers ringing off steel, the wind pushing heavily against the metal hangar. And the smells – oil, petrol – harsh but not entirely unpleasant. The whole atmosphere makes me dizzy.

I mean to find and speak to Cam Westin, a flight engineer. A man is hard at work, covered in grime and oil. He looks up as I approach.

'Yes?'

'I'm called Anna.' I hurry closer. 'Can I help with anything? I've read up and know all about—'

'Tea,' comes the voice. 'Two sugars.'

'Oh, sure.'

I find the tea and cups, and put the kettle to boil. I stare around the hangar, seeing planes I recognize from the Blue Bible – Tiger Moths and light Trainers and, in the far corner, a Spitfire. For months we have permission only to fly Trainers. Then, if we are granted permission to carry on, we move on to faster planes, all the way up to twin-engine fighters like Hurricanes and Spitfires. *If I ever get that far.*

I add a lump of sugar and some powdered milk. I hold the hot cup towards him, but he doesn't look up from the engine.

'Your tea is here, Mr Westin.'

He grunts. I set it down beside him.

At the RAF base, the ground crew respects the pilots. I may not be a pilot yet, but surely I am something above the mechanics in the ground crew. *No, I am being awful. Treat everyone the same, that's what Mum always said.*

I struggle to imagine Mum having a chat with an engineer covered in grime.

The next hour is spent watching him, adjusting to the

chaos of noise and smells, and trying not to think too much about Gower's endless warnings. But it is impossible, and soon I am remembering Amy Johnson, caught in the clouds, stranded with no way down and her petrol almost gone. No idea where she was, she did the only thing she could, leaping from the plane and pulling her chute. It must have been several minutes of falling, tossed in the high winds, before she saw it – the Thames rushing towards her.

Amy Johnson drowned; and so did the officer of the warship, who, seeing her crash below the waves, dived in to try and save her. The waves, vicious from the storm, took them both to the bottom.

She should have stayed in the plane. Waited for an opening, some break in the cloud, and dived through. She should have waited, held her nerve.

Leap before you're pushed.

'Tea,' Westin says again. 'Sugar this time.'

Startled, I nod – he can't see me – and hurry away. Surely Gower didn't send me here to make tea? I heap sugar into the cup, adding less milk. How will any of this help me to fly?

'Your tea is here,' I say, steadying my breath. 'But actually, Mr Westin, I wasn't sent here to fetch your tea. I am to learn about engines from you. I already know all about engines from the Blue Bible, but I need to learn the basics of engine maintenance.'

The twisting wrench is still. He looks up at me. I am shocked for a moment by how young he is. Even coated in grime and oil, he could fit in with the kids at school.

'What's this then?'

'What—?'

'This, in my hands – what is it?'

I stare down at the engine, my mind turning furiously. Not a Merlin. Not a Vulture.

'A Hercules?'

'Didn't think so.' Westin smiles, the briefest twist of his lips. 'You'll only be on the Trainers, but it doesn't matter if it's a Moth or a Mosquito – a gummed-up spark plug will take it down. So it's worth your time to learn about spark plugs at least. I have a sneaking suspicion you don't know how to rivet either. That,' he coughs, catching my look as it falls on the flashy plane in the corner of the hangar, 'is a Spitfire. No need to worry about that, love.'

'So it is.' I force myself to meet his eyes. 'Sixteen hundred horsepower. Rolls-Royce Merlin-powered Mark IX in the nose. Ninety-gallon tanks.'

'That's it.' He blinks, half smiling. *I breathe a silent sigh of relief.* 'Everybody knows about Spitfires, and certainly anyone who dreams of becoming a pilot. A fighter and a high-altitude reconnaissance aircraft, His Majesty's deadliest warplane. And finally a match for the Messerschmitt 109. You don't fly a Spitfire. You move, it moves.'

I stare, silent, too overwhelmed by the great plane to be insulted by his tone. 'What's it like?'

'To sit in the cockpit of a Spit, with the power of the Merlin at your fingertips, is an exhilaration beyond anything else you can imagine. Controls so light you can manoeuvre with the slightest touch. This is the most exciting aeroplane ever built. At two hundred and fifty miles per hour, nowhere in England is more than an hour away.'

'Where did you go?'

'What?'

'In your Spitfire.' I try to imagine it, walking into the hangar with a chit for a Spitfire. 'Where did you fly to?'

'Me? I'm an engineer, love.'

I notice the sharpness of his tone, force myself to stop daydreaming. *I'm supposed to be learning from him.* 'Right. I know, sorry. But the ATA flies them?'

He gives a grudging nod. 'The RAF did not permit women to be attached to units. Physically and temperamentally unsound. Women were to fly only open-cockpit Trainers – Moths, Miles Magisters. All that's changed now, of course.'

I force a laugh, but my eyes are drawn back to the stunning aircraft. I remind myself that Gower was there, that night in Leicester Square. *I am meant to be here.* One day, I will fly one.

Westin, head down and carrying on in the same grumbling tone, doesn't seem to notice my new steely resolve.

'Not as fire-prone as the Hurricane, as the petrol tank is in front of the pilot, not in the wings,' he says. 'Still, once it catches, you're headed to three thousand degrees Celsius. You've got less than four seconds to get out – man or woman, there'll be nothing left of you. Now, love, some tea. With *sugar* this time.'

Wednesday, 10 March 1943

For weeks now I have not dreamed of Maida Vale, of Mum making cheese on toast, of the back garden and the soft grass under my toes. Even longer has passed since I last awoke, slick with sweat, certain I was back inside the shelter beneath the playing fields at school, or – worse – certain beyond doubt that I, too, was on the bus with Mum, and only I could hear the heavy whistle in the sky above...

I am not on a bus. Mum was never on that bus, either – still I cannot erase the image, the idea that Mum's death was an accident. That she wanted to stay here with me.

I know the truth, of course. She wrote a letter to Uncle at the Tower, telling him to take me in. Then she killed herself, using the gas from the oven. Everyone running around in gas masks, terrified that Hitler might drop a gas bomb, and she kills herself with gas. She asked Uncle to lie, until I was old enough. *Am I old enough now?*

There is no pain, Timothy Squire promised me – it's like falling asleep, he said.

She made a terrible mistake. She loved you.

I shake free of such thoughts – *bloody Cam Westin and his talk of exploding engines* – throwing aside the covers and shivering in the draught that courses through the window. Joy, as usual, is already downstairs, in uniform, her bed made up. I hurry to do the same. My short hair has freed me from hours of brushing, and I swiftly change into my uniform and slip out of the room.

After our morning toast and tea with Mrs Wells, Joy

and I bike down the road, passing through the fence. The wind is cold.

'Are there other black pilots?' I ask her.

She nods, her face unreadable. 'Sure. You guys have some Jamaicans, men from the West Indies – all the British colonies.'

'Any other women?'

She smiles now. 'Nope.'

'I'm only fifteen,' I blurt out. I don't know why, but it's too late anyway – the words are gone. 'But my birthday *is* coming up. In October.'

Joy only laughs. 'We'll make a fine team, Cooper.'

We pass the giant hangars as we reach the main entrance. I take out my books for today – map-reading, navigation, mechanics. *Mechanics is almost as bad as trigonometry.*

I need a break from all this studying. Now that I have to remember everything Westin grumbles at me, I feel like my head is going to burst. All around cadets bang their lockers shut. I squeeze my eyes closed, take a long breath.

'Was it the birds then?'

I blink in surprise to see Joy still standing there. She should be off collecting her chits. *And I should be in a quiet, dark room.* 'The birds?'

'The ravens, at your Tower. Are they what made you want to fly?'

The idea should be enough to make me cackle with glee – like Joy did when I first told her about life in the Tower as the Ravenmaster. But I don't; instead of the new birds, caged in their roost, flight wings clipped, I think of Mabel and Grip, who flew to their freedom. *Or death*.

'Yes,' I say. Joy is clearly worried about me – I must look as white as Mrs Morgan's old terrier. I try to raise a smile.

'Don't give up, Cooper.' Joy clasps my shoulder. 'The war is changing things – here in England as well as back home. Women in men's jobs, women in war. People are getting all bent out of shape – men and women both.'

'I know.' I nod, but I've said the wrong thing apparently, as Joy shakes her head.

'If my mother could have stopped me… It's all a bit over-whelming, it's all a bit too much. Sometimes there's nothing you can do to change people's minds. But there's something we can do, Cooper. The only thing we can do. Learn to fly.'

Everyone keeps telling me that.

'If I can make do in a land without soda fountains or proper ice cream, you can do this.' Joy smiles. Instinctively I clench my teeth at the mention of soda fountains. Flo's endless bragging still rankles me.

Joy looks truly happy to be headed off to the hangars instead of the classroom. I'm not so sure, myself. I'm only sure of one thing as I cross the freezing tarmac to learn about mechanics.

I am being watched. I've known it for days, but I am certain of it now.

You are mad. Who is watching you? Gower? She doesn't care. You think the German has returned and followed you here? *Get a hold of yourself.*

But I miss the presence of Joy as soon as she's gone.

163

Very few people are out among the hangars, the odd cadet racing off to navigation or mechanics. *What I wouldn't give for an hour alone in my old room.* I shrug into my coat and keep walking, not looking right or left until I am safely inside the classroom.

Mrs Wells fills my hot bottle each night and, despite my resistance, even does my washing. It is a wonder to have a bath each night. And the curtains on the windows are black and heavy, but wide open at night.

Meals with Joy are a laugh. For a moment I let myself imagine this is my real life – this is my real family, my real home.

But kind as Mrs Wells is, she is not Mum.

Through the opened window I can hear blackbirds singing, low and sad. I miss the Tower, too. The new ravens barely know me. I think of how they acted around Timothy Squire after he came back from Aberdeen. *Will they hop away from me, too?*

Joy tells me about her delivery yesterday – a Corsair to the Isle of Man (nineteen minutes), and home in a Gauntlet (thirty-three minutes). I would be terrified of an old bi-plane like that over the Irish Sea, but Joy said it handled good as new. Likely she was bringing it home for the wrecker's yard.

'Have you ever seen an enemy plane?'

'Nope. Saw some bad storms, though.'

'No 109s?'

The entire route is within range of the Luftwaffe. But we are a civilian crew, so weapons are removed from the gun turrets. No one is permitted, not even Commander Gower, to fly armed aircraft, no matter how many Nazi fighters might swarm the route.

'Why don't they let us have radios?'

Joy shrugs. 'Worried the Germans will intercept our lady signals.'

She laughs but there's little humour in it.

We have cleared away the dishes after the boiled potatoes and peas. Mrs Wells has retired to the sitting room by the fire. The cat, Francis, watches us absently then waddles off to join her. *He doesn't seem to be on rations.*

Hopefully the ravens are equally well fed.

'Here,' says Joy as we slump back into our chairs at the once again pristine kitchen. She pushes some candy across the table.

'What's this?'

'Candy. *American candy.*'

The taste is almost worth the fuss. Still, after a long day at Ground School, I could use something more substantial. Some meat, perhaps.

The mere idea of meat makes me think of the ravens again. They are always hungry. And Stackhouse clearly isn't up to the task of feeding them. Hopefully Timothy Squire is actually helping out at the roost. I can only imagine what it's like there if he's clean forgotten.

Timothy Squire, I hope you haven't forgotten your promise.

Thursday, 11 March 1943

The White Tower looms over me, shutting out the sky. At least I'll have something to tell Anna when she's on her leave. Something she hasn't seen – maybe even something Henry Reed had never seen.

The Tower ravens are nesting.

Well, two of them are, at any rate. Portia and Rogan have built a nest on the unused steps to the White Tower. Different from the straw nest inside their cage, this is a large stick nest made of mud and grass and bark – all sorts, even foil from cigarette packs.

It all started when I saw Rogan carrying two sticks in his beak. Portia followed him up the stairs. She watched as he left and came back with two more sticks, then a beak full. He was up to something. The next day he was at it again, lugging even more sticks – as many dropped as made it, but he kept at it. *I must be the only man in war-time Britain who's got the time to watch birds carry around sticks.*

Why did I get off at Bethnal Green? Of all places? Death is having a laugh.

You didn't die.

Not yet, but it's clear as sodding crystal that I am cursed.

The birds continued their nesting. Rogan, holding small branches with his feet, scraped the bark free with his beak.

Portia decided to help out. She tore up bark, helped carry it, and brought just as many beakfuls of grass as Rogan. Together they put in the lining. *It was a nest.*

And then Portia sat in it. After an hour, they switched, and Rogan sat, like he was frozen stiff, with Portia perched just next to him. Every few minutes, they swapped again. *What were they up to?* Then Rogan wandered off and Portia remained completely silent and still.

They can sense the coming spring. Anna said that they actually *change* with the new season, but I've no idea what that means. Maybe that's why they keep jumping in and out of the nest? Of course they'd have wanted to build their nest as high up as possible – the oak tree in the Green, or the tops of the White Tower – but as they can't reach more than a few feet with clipped wings, the back stairs will have to do. I've never seen a person use those steps.

I should have written to Anna to ask her advice. But it seemed like the two birds would only nest here – not inside their cage – so I got Stackhouse to agree not to lock them up again until the chicks have hatched. I made sure to clip their wings myself, to prevent any escape. Stackhouse can't be trusted. The man is so lazy it's a wonder he bothers to feed himself.

I remember Anna saying the ravens had never successfully bred at the Tower.

Well, won't she be surprised. I may not know a lot about ravens, but I know that I can expect to see some baby birds come spring. Brushing aside the quartermaster's mocking voice, I turn the corner towards the White Tower.

The steps are clear. Clearer than I've ever seen them in fact. My first thought is a fox. Easy enough for a fox to reach the nest – would Portia and Rogan scare it off? There's been a crafty-looking red fox down by the docks, with a great bushy tail and snowy fur at his throat – a real beauty. Had he found his way into the Tower?

I walk around to the cages and am shocked to see Portia and Rogan inside. Why are they locked up? They have to be with their nest – they won't lay eggs in here. I pull open the cage, peering around just in case. No sign of chicks – or a nest.

Perhaps it didn't work? Or the ravens simply abandoned it overnight. Maybe it's too early. Spring won't come – not truly – for another month. *Did someone clear away the ravens' nest?* Not the fox, who'd have left all the sticks and bark. *It must've been a Warder. Why?*

What is wrong with me? These bloody things are haunting me and I'm trying to help them breed.

'Yeoman Stackhouse!'

The man turns, his great cloak billowing around him. 'Private Squire.' He almost smiles. He knows the truth, that I am no soldier, that I am back to living at the Tower with my folks, but I don't give a toss what he thinks.

'Why are these birds locked up? They are meant to be out at night to protect their nest. You agreed not to lock them up, remember? They won't breed if we take them away from it.'

'As you can see, Private Squire, there is no nest.'

'Who cleared it away? I saw it two nights ago and now it's gone. On the White Tower steps.'

He looks me up and down. 'I am not the cleaner, here, Private Squire. If you have questions about the general maintenance of the Tower, perhaps you should ask your father? I am a Yeoman Warder, and it is my responsibility to look after the crows.'

'My father is the head curator, not some retired old soldier.' I say the last through clenched teeth. 'And you're about to get some help looking after the *ravens*, whether you like it or not.'

His eyebrows have climbed almost sheer over his head.

'Do *not* lock up the birds when they are nesting, Yeoman Stackhouse.'

The noises coming out of his mouth don't even sound like words. Just sounds, strange choking sounds like a duck that's swallowed a rock. I push past, leave him to his sputtering and gasping, wishing I'd had the guts to give Quarter such a farewell.

A plane flies over and I try to imagine being up there. One mistake on the landing and you'd bash your brains in. *Don't know how Anna does it.* She always was the bravest person I've met. A little mad, maybe, but not scared of anything.

I am trying to teach Oliver to speak again, but nothing. 'You *are* worse.'

The heavy gutters stream with melted snow. The truth is, I miss Anna. I should tell her as much, but it's not as though I ever get to see her. I know what I'll do. I'll write her another letter, tell her everything – how much I miss her, how I'm sorry I made a mess of everything. How I hope when the war's all over…

What? That you'll get married and live in the Tower together?

It's too mad. Anna wouldn't go for it, and neither would I. Still, I should write to her – and actually send the letter this time. *Tell her the truth.*

That I do nothing.

The horror of Bethnal Green flashes back for a moment before I can fight it off. I just have to do my job and get on with it. Anna needs me to be the Ravenmaster. I have to do it for her.

'Still haven't heard a peep from her, I'm afraid.'

Why am I talking like that? I sound like Oakes, or the posh Constable. Flo doesn't notice at any rate; she just looks up at me, her eyes wide and hurt. She came right up to Mr Thorne asking to see me. Now we're standing at the West Gate in the near freezing wind.

'Are you sure she's all right?' she asks.

'Anna? Of course. Awful busy up at the airfield, I hear. What about you, are you at the canteen?'

'I'm preparing for university entrance examinations,' she corrects me. 'University College London, I hope.'

'What? Like studying?'

'Yes.'

'Oh,' I say. 'That sounds interesting.'

'What about you? Will you go to university after the war?'

'Me?' I laugh. *Maybe talking like Oakes really works.* 'No, ma'am. Not the schooling type, I'm afraid.'

She smiles, a slow grin. 'Well, I think everyone's the schooling type. I'm certain you could do it if you put your mind to it. You could study more Shakespeare.'

I shake my head. *Me, go to university? Shakespeare? This is madness.*

'You want to see the birds?' I ask, triggering another smile.

Together we head over to the roost. I can feel her walking beside me, quite close, as if *we're* old friends from school.

'So what was it like, being here through it all?' She looks up at me, wide-eyed.

'Tough,' I say. 'Anna took it all well. She's a real trooper.'

'How about you?'

I pause, almost miss a step. I don't mean to, I don't mean to say a word, but it just comes pouring out.

'New guns were being tested, in Victoria Park. A new type of rocket gun. People had never heard the sound before. No bombs, no revenge attack. Just our own guns, being tested.'

We have both stopped walking, standing in the shadow of the White Tower. Flo is quiet, listening. I tell her; I tell her everything.

'We were told to be quiet. The policeman and fireman

171

and the wardens, everyone told us not to speak a word of it. Not to tell anyone what had happened.'

'For how long?' Flo has been away for long enough to sound truly shocked. *Morale is important. The illusion of safety is what keeps us safe.*

'A while.' *For ever.*

'But people will notice,' she protests. 'When parents don't come home, when kids don't show up for school. What will they say?'

'I don't know.'

'I am sorry, Timothy.'

I can see the faces, pressing in, the huge gulping mouths; the abandoned shoes, the clumps of hair.

Until I feel firm arms around me I don't even realize I am crying. My whole body wracks. My eyes run tears, my nose too, but I do nothing to stop it. I can do nothing. I can do nothing but cling to the arms around me.

7

Monday, 15 March 1943

Another washout day – a 'scrubbed day' they call it – though I'm not sure anyone has seen anything like this. No one will be in the skies for a day at least. British or German plane, the sky is off limits. I'm not certain I'll be able to get back to my billet tonight. The roads will be blocked thick with snow.

As long as it snows, I won't have to fly. *I hope it snows for ever.*

All morning was spent helping the ground crew shovel runways and broom planes free of snow, hunching against the icy, hissing wind. I stared up, dazed, as huge soft flakes came whirling down. We finally had to give it up for a lost cause. Not until we'd wasted the entire morning sliding around in a blizzard. *I have so much studying to do.*

As I stumble through the hall I exchange greetings with three other cadets by the lockers, with a stiffness that seems to come more with the uniforms than the cold.

A thousand miles better than the WAAFs at any rate.

The food at the Mess does not dispel the hunger. I need more, two or three times more. My fingers are frozen stiff enough that even holding the fork proves a challenge. I swear I can feel a swirl of cold air inside the room.

Joy got out before the storm. She's due to bounce around from airfield to airfield running deliveries over the next three days. With the bad weather, she won't be back for a week or more.

I wish she were here. I'm properly ashamed of my fascination with her skin, her hair – a black girl, a pilot, an American – she is all but impossible to me. And she is my only real friend in this place.

Through the windows the frozen wind booms. A pilot, finished with her meal, clears up and sees me sitting alone. There is only the slightest pause before she speaks.

'Beer-up in the crew room – you coming?'

It is Diana Gaines, the other American pilot.

'Ah, yes. Sure.'

'Well, come on.'

I hastily chew the last of my sprouts, clear up my stuff. My joints ache. I follow the pilot to the crew room – *I have so much studying to do* – and I am instantly hit by blue clouds of tobacco smoke.

Everyone is here, and Diana and I join a large group around the cards table, watching two women play. On the table are pound notes. *Lots* of pound notes. The small pilot must notice my staring because she laughs.

'More than a few gamblers in here,' Diana says.

'But, that must be – *hundreds* of pounds,' I whisper.

'Drop in the ocean to those two. Tall blonde is Barcsay, a horse-riding champion and Countess of some European place with a crazy name. One in the leopard-skin coat is Bella, a ballerina.'

I was surprised when Joy told me ATA pilots get a sub-sistence allowance on top of our pay. What are the living expenses for these kinds of women?

The pilots all chat away. I am used to hearing it as I walk past to the crew room, women talking and laughing, muted and loud at the same time. It seems they know each other from London flying clubs, and have an endless supply of hilarious tales from Heston or Brooklands. They lounge around, with their usual air of barely withheld disgust for everything around them. *Why did I cut my hair?* I feel like a silly girl.

No one talks to Diana either. The Americans are not so well liked. Their happiness and general health can't help but remind us that they've not been in the war – that they've left us to fight Hitler and survive on rations. *Well, they're here now.*

I wish Joy were here. Not that she likes the crew room any better than I do.

Westin, unsmiling as ever, suddenly enters, the lone man in a room of female pilots. I am surprised, given the contempt he seems to feel towards us. Still, he has to be better company than this lot.

'So you come here, too?' I instantly regret the question. Obviously he is here. 'Do you prefer this crew room?'

'It's the same, isn't it? Pilots and aircraft.' His smile does not match his words. 'Everyone here has successfully passed the rigorous testing required to become a pilot, haven't they?'

Well, I wasn't wrong about the contempt. 'Of course.'

'So.'

I cough. This man makes Malcolm seem like Timothy Squire. 'Cam – can I call you Cam? Is it possible that we could run into enemy aircraft on our routes?'

I have heard Gower tell me it is; I want Westin – someone, anyone – to tell me it's not. Even Jay said it could happen.

'You are referring to the possibility of encountering an on-going raid?'

'Yes. Or, I don't know, if a plane gets on your tail?'

He gives the worst impression of a smile I've ever seen. 'You think a Messerschmitt 109 is going to chase your Tiger Moth to the wrecker's yard? It won't happen.'

I liked him better when he said nothing. But I urge him on, with a question that has been sitting at the back of my mind, having spent too many nights watching the dogfights over the Tower. I know what's in the sky.

'If it does though?'

'A 109 on your tail?' A pause, as if he's genuinely considering my thoughts. 'Pray to whoever you pray to. Once they have sight, they'll never lose it.'

Well, I did ask him. 'But Commander Gower—'

'She is not my Commander. If you will excuse me.'

He pauses only briefly to observe the girls at the billiards table before sweeping out of the room. The air is immediately lighter all around me.

'British men are *so* charming.' Diana appears, grimacing towards the door. *Why did he bother to come at all?* 'Come on. I may be new here, but it can't be a beer-up if you're not drinking beer.'

It turns out Diana isn't so bad. Her father owns a diamond mine somewhere, and she told me she first took up flying to escape her mother – as the Trainers only had two seats, and prevented chaperones from tagging along.

We drink our beer and laugh.

Fall, snow, fall, I think, staring out at the massive bank of grey clouds. Amy Johnson and the officer – their bodies were never found. Did she surface on the other bank, the officer at her side, and decide that she needed to flee? Did they leave together, to start a new life in secret?

Oh, Timothy Squire. I must write to him, explain everything that's happened.

Diana and I play a game of darts with Tracy, a girl from Canada who everyone just calls 'Canada', and Margot, who came from Argentina and doesn't speak a word of English. *All sorts*, as Timothy Squire would say.

I throw my dart, miss wildly. Diana laughs, but her throw is just as bad. Margot makes *tsk, tsk* noises. *I have so much studying to do, but it is suddenly the farthest thing from my thoughts.*

'Another game?' Diana asks, after we are soundly beaten by Margot and Canada. I nod, going to the corner to pick up my lost dart. I freeze as I suddenly become aware of the music. Something about the violin is familiar. I know this music – somehow. What is it?

Mum used to play. I would hear it, from behind the closed brown door of the study. 'Your father was the truly gifted player,' she would always say, quickly putting the violin back in its case. I'm never certain that I remember hearing him play – and lately I've wondered if this was just another of Mum's lies about him. But, really, I know for certain that he played this piece.

Almost as soon as I recognize it, it changes and some brass band takes over.

'That song. What was it?'

Diana clinks her empty beer glass on the table. 'Who knows? "Screeching violin number 2"? Come on, Cooper, it's your toss.'

Wednesday, 17 March 1943

Our flight suits are new – creaky new. Across the airfield, looking very far from new, are seven Tiger Moths. The morning sun has cleared away the last of the snow. *The weather cannot put this off.* My hair is still long enough to blow across my face. I tuck it away, stare straight ahead at the waiting planes.

'All right, girls. Scramble.'

'Scramble?' repeats another cadet – someone obviously never enrolled in armed forces training.

'Pick up your parachutes and run to your aeroplane!'

I squeeze on the harness, already running. The parachute is *heavy* – thirty pounds at least – and needs both hands to keep it still on my back, but worse are the new fur-lined boots. With each step the stiff leather bites into my heel. I run – hobbling sideways – and reach my Tiger Moth.

'Come back!'

Panting, heaving, I drag my parachute and myself back to the starting point. Only one cadet beats me.

'Not nearly good enough. Do it again.'

This time no one hesitates. We are off, lumbering, and the Tiger Moths seemingly at the other end of a vast grass airfield. This time two girls – including a stout girl – beat me across. By the fourth time, I am last.

'Right, gather around, girls. Cooper, we can't wait all day. OK, so you can run around with the parachute. Now you need to learn how to use it. If you're four seconds late to pull the ripcord, you'll land heavy enough to break your ankles and possibly a leg. If you're five seconds late, there's really no point in pulling the ripcord at all.'

Four seconds to escape a burning Spitfire. Four seconds to pull the parachute. *This is all madness. I should return to the canteen, see if Mrs Barrett will take me back.*

The ATA motto is *Aetheris Avidi* – eager for the air. I am not certain that I am, not any more. *London is only an hour's train ride.*

In the Mess, pilots call to each other, chat about the day's deliveries, the deliveries to come. I finish my sandwich, wonder whether Joy has an overnight flight. No, she'll be home for dinner I am sure, or she would have told Mrs Wells. Mrs Wells always needs to know whether or not 'we'll be eating her out of house and home'.

Suddenly there is a call for full dress.

'Now?' many voices wonder.

'Imminent.'

A parade? I think of the pouring rain as I run to my locker for my parade uniform. A formal inspection – but why? The ATA has senior officers, but we are not a military organization. Most of these pilots won't have any experience with drilling. At least the lucky ones.

'Who is it?' voices ask excitedly.

'Churchill?'

I smile, thinking of how he came to the Tower two years ago. So much has changed. But not people's fears, evidently.

'This is bad. The Germans have spies everywhere. They will know. They will come.'

In the pouring rain we all inch in to stand under the Fairchild's wing. Joy, at the last minute, hurries from the east hangar to join our line.

'OK, pilots.' Gower herself walks up and down, inspecting the ranks. 'Here's how to make a proper salute. No, not like that. Yes, well done, Cooper,' she adds.

I almost smile. I guess the horrors of the WAAF may finally be paying off. I see the guest of honour approaching – who is it? – a woman in a fox fur and giant hat. She is very elegant, very impressive. She comes forward, an ATA fireman holding a huge black umbrella over her head.

'Welcome, please, Mrs Roosevelt, the First Lady of the United States.'

Instinctively, I almost turn to see Joy's face. *I am so happy she made it back for this.*

'The reluctant First Lady,' she says, acknowledging the salutes with a wave of her hand. 'I have no interest in being a backdrop for my husband. Nor, I imagine, do any of these fine women.' She beams a smile at us, but for a moment she is looking directly at me. 'So sorry for making you all stand out in the rain.'

'That's OK,' I blurt out.

She smiles, a gleam – of mischief? – in her eyes. It is not until moments later that I realize I am standing dry underneath one of the wings, while the pilots to my right are drenched to the bone. I can feel the angry glances from down the line.

'Wonderful to see all you pilots. Amelia Earhart was a dear friend of mine. The CAA in America says that women are psychologically not fitted to be pilots. It seems to me that, if women can pass the tests imposed upon men, they should have an equal opportunity for service.

'This isn't a time when women should be patient, waiting for opportunity to come knocking. We are in a war and we need to fight it with all our ability and every weapon possible.'

She stops in front of Joy. 'And what is your name, pilot?'

'Joy Brooks, Mrs Roosevelt. From New York City.'

'It is very good to see you here. Here in England, where the need is great. You are ferrying planes and freeing innumerable men for combat service. In America, women pilots are a weapon waiting to be used.

'Do your best, all of you. Be brave up there. Remember that a woman is like a tea bag. You never know how strong she is until she's in hot water.'

At that moment I recognize the figure under the umbrella at her side. Clementine Churchill – I have seen her before, two years ago, at the Tower. She is so graceful and dignified.

A siren cracks the air.

'It's an air raid, Mrs Roosevelt,' says the fireman, his voice unsteady.

'I can damn well tell that, can't I? Where are we going?'

'This way, ma'am,' he says, hurrying her away.

We all rush off to the White Waltham shelter, giddy with excitement despite the real danger. Mrs Roosevelt has been secreted away somewhere – she is not here now.

The First Lady has made a real impression on Joy. Even more than usual, Joy lets her hands do the talking. I lean forward, away from the stone wall of the shelter, listening in wonder. 'Mrs Roosevelt visited the Tuskegee Army Air Field – it was in all the papers. The First Lady visiting an all-black flying unit. People thought she was crazy. But she went up with Charles Anderson, the self-taught pilot who started the training programme himself. They flew for an hour over the skies of Alabama. The First Lady, flying with a black pilot.'

I nod, rebuking myself for thinking how easy Joy has it being done with the exams. She faced far more than I ever could in order to learn how to fly.

The bombs are not close. We are not the target; neither

is Mrs Roosevelt. *It is not the V1s.* But the Junkers still patrol the skies, and we'd better not forget it. *I shall tell Mrs Wells she must use the blackout curtains again.*

'Won't it be grand,' I say, 'when peace finally comes.'

In the silence that follows I cringe at how I sounded. (Around Joy, somehow I end up sounding like old Mrs Morgan next door.) All at once I am aware of how cramped the shelter is. *They are all listening.*

'I don't know,' Joy says, finally. 'I'd not live a year of my old life again.'

I say nothing. She was in a *circus* – she flew aircraft and laughed. She lived in America!

Things changed after the last war, I remember Mum talking about it. Women were allowed to vote – and to work at newspapers like Mum did.

What will happen when this war is over?

I lean back against the stone wall, and close my eyes, Mrs Roosevelt's words echoing in my head. *Remember that a woman is like a tea bag. You never know how strong it is until it's in hot water.*

Friday, 19 March 1943

'Sun's up and you're not.'

I pull inward, shield myself from the voice.

'Cooper, get up already. Or your toast is mine.'

I force my eyelids open, see exactly what I expect, and close them again.

'Up, Cooper. Or I'm drinking your tea, too.'

Is it three or four weeks that I've been at White Waltham? Three or four weeks of being woken up by Joy in the morning darkness. I shrug off the warm covers, pull myself to my feet. I fight back a wave of dizziness – you never quite adjust to the gnawing hunger.

'I'm awake.'

There is no light outside. Joy is wearing civilian dress – a white blouse and red skirt – and she looks different somehow, not so much older than me. I don't bother covering a yawn.

Ground School is over. The horrid exams, over. And my first leave is coming up. The next forty-eight, Joy calls it. I see what she means – it's two days, but I plan to enjoy every hour. Joy is staying at a hotel in the city, and wants to take me out. I feel bad; she is not from here.

I have money, too, as the ATA has paid my wages and reimbursed my uniform allowance. But I have to go to the Tower, see the ravens, find Timothy Squire. I have to go home.

Lately thoughts of Mum have become even stronger. I remember her, lying still on the bed, no sound or lights. I can see myself, tiptoeing into the room, holding folded brown paper.

'Mum?' My voice is barely a whisper. 'Is it… horrible?'

No response comes from the dark, unmoving form.

'Soaked in vinegar, like Dr Bishop said.'

'Come on, Cooper,' Joy laughs, and I blink away the memory.

I am still not quite awake. Joy is looking down at me

with her smiling brown eyes, and I see the friend – the only friend – I've made here. Maybe the only one I've got left.

'Get up. Show me you Brits know how to have a good time.'

Saturday, 20 March 1943

'You've got your uniform, the boys will love you,' Joy had said.

She'd insisted that we wear the full dress uniform – our Best Blues – skirts instead of trousers for tonight, silk stockings and forage caps. I insisted that we both wear some of my red lipstick – I *may* have said, 'good lippy is more essential than food' – and we both look rather striking. People are looking at us at any rate.

Or perhaps it's because I look too young, or the colour of Joy's skin, or because we're two women in pilots' uniforms. Joy doesn't seem to care, so I try not to, either. Plenty of other Americans here, and some of them black soldiers in uniforms. Maybe Joy wants to go and talk to them? She doesn't seem to notice them.

Everyone is laughing or grinning, and a band blasts out music. Joy had smiled when she said she would take me out and treat me to 'something stronger than ginger ale'. *Is this what she has in mind?*

'Are you sure?' I ask as we push through the crowds. I've heard of the Lansdowne, but never thought I'd be inside. *In a cadet uniform.* I wish Timothy Squire were here.

'My dad used to say, "You gotta live like your hair's on fire."'

I frown, absently reaching for my hair. I *did* live with hair on fire. And waited for ever for it to grow back.

'This is Colonel Clarke.' She points to a tall man, who nods in my direction. 'And a few WASP girls from back home. Opal!'

A sharp-featured girl staggers forward and locks Joy in a tight hug. Everyone is in their finest. Joy warned me with a story about Captain Billy Eugene being asked to leave the Lansdowne for violating the dress code.

'Opal, this is Anna Cooper, new girl at the airfield.'

'What I don't understand,' Opal says, turning from Joy to me, 'is why all you Brits are so prim and proper all the time. I know you're being bombed, but you're not *dead*, are you? Fat Tim and his Band! Let's go dance!'

I shake my head.

'Give us a few minutes,' Joy says, steering me away. 'Barely had time for a drink.'

We squeeze into the queue at the bar counter.

'What'll you have?' Joy calls over her shoulder.

I stare back blankly. Mum always had gin. 'Wine,' I say. 'Thank you.'

There is *something* about a pilot's wings. It is more than just a military badge; the golden wings topped with a crown, the letters RAF in the centre. And here, on almost every left breast pocket.

'Be careful now.' Joy hands me the glass. She is holding a pint. 'Nothing worse than a cockpit hangover.'

'Cockpit…? But I won't be flying soon – I mean, yet.'

'Bad habits are the easiest ones to learn, Cooper.'

Joy introduces me to other pilots – a copper-haired girl, a plump girl with a wide, smiley face – and brings me another wine when my glass is suddenly empty.

One of the girls leads us over to a new group, who are chatting loudly amid their drinks. Male pilots, all straight-backed and confident – officers. Eyes meet ours, glances are exchanged, and their group expands to accept ours. The conversation, however, carries on undisturbed.

'Bloody navy can't tell a Hurricane from a Messerschmitt.'

More laughing, not particularly good-natured. 'Fire at me every time. Everything they've got.'

'Hard enough to patrol the Channel without your own ships firing at you.'

A quiet voice speaks and the noise drops away. 'Don't be too hard on our navy boys,' he says. 'A sitting duck, in a tanker full of fuel.'

Rapidly all the heads are nodding in agreement. The speaker wears a small smile, but he is quite apart from the boisterous group.

'Cecil!' I cry out, louder than I mean to.

For a moment I'm not certain it is. He gives me a strange searching glance before a slow smile spreads across his face. *He doesn't recognize me. And I've just screamed his name across the Lansdowne. My face must be redder than my lipstick.*

'Well, Aircraftwoman Cooper. Fancy seeing you in that uniform.'

I try to smile. He *does* recognize me. Of course he does – he took me up in the Lancaster. *He also gives rings to every girl he meets.*

'You look so… you've grown up quite a bit, Miss Cooper. How are you?'

I remember Joy and glance back but she has vanished. The copper-haired girl is practically grinning. Cecil finally steps towards me, nodding goodbye to the group. His old smile returns.

'Sorry about the boys. This isn't strictly an officers' pub, not that I believe in keeping us all separate. They're a bit hard on the navy, and we get the same back. All I know is that I was very foolishly shot into the sea over Margate. And if it wasn't for the navy boys, I wouldn't be here now.' He laughs abruptly.

'You got shot down?' I say in surprise. 'In the Lancaster? Was anyone hurt?'

'I confess I did come within an appreciable distance of having my nose broken, but the crew is all spick and span. I have been moved off bombers for the time being. I'd say I've used up my good fortune. Unless, of course, you'll say yes to some dancing?'

My face must be a tomato. *I am unreasonably relieved that his nose is intact.* 'I have to be back. Back to the Tower before nightfall. Curfew…'

'You're going to be a pilot, Anna. One of the few female pilots in the world. A thoroughly dangerous job. You have to dance while you can.' He holds my gaze a fraction too long.

188

He's going to kiss me. The thought lunges into my head and my whole body tenses. What about Nell? What about Timothy Squire?

'What do you say, Miss Cooper?'

Unkissed, I blink my eyes open. *How could I not dance with him?* Nell would understand.

'Cecil—' The voice stops dead. An annoyingly beautiful girl has just appeared at Cecil's side. But she has eyes only for him. She is not in her uniform – in fact, I recognize her dress only too well. Now the green seems properly fashionable, and the wide padded shoulders create a flat shoulder line which makes her slim waist look like an hourglass. And in her heels she towers over me. *Perhaps she wouldn't understand.*

'Oh, hello, Nell. So nice to see you again.'

She is looking at me like I'm dirt. Like she did the first time we met. *And she is wearing his ring.*

'Imagine the odds,' Cecil says. 'Your old friend from the WAAF is here. And now she's a pilot!'

'Pilot?' She glances at the stripes on my shoulder. 'You mean "cadet", surely?'

She turns away from me. I no longer exist.

'Let us go and dance.' She starts to lead him away. He casts a look back at me, but lets himself be pulled into the crowd.

I stand still, awkwardly holding my wine. Well, she has won him from Isabella Pomeroy. I take a quick sip, let the cool liquid numb my throat. *You thought he was going to kiss you? Cecil Rafferty?*

I recognize some of the smiling faces out there. Westin,

for one, dancing with a full glass in his hand. He meets my eyes. My face lights up in recognition; his does not. If he notices me at all, it is with a small grimace. Joy, too, is out there, dancing up a storm and grinning wildly. I should finish this glass and slip out – Joy will understand. Cecil won't even notice I've gone.

I hesitate too long, as Cecil returns from the dance floor. Without Nell.

'What's the matter, Miss Cooper?' he asks. 'Not enjoying the company?'

'Well, ATA pilots can be quite… tiresome, if you didn't go to finishing school in Paris.' *I don't know where I got the courage to say that, but it certainly is true.*

'I heard from Nell that you recently took up residence in the Tower of London. How grand.'

'Well, yes,' I stammer. Nell is *not* my friend; not any more, if she ever was. 'I mean, I grew up in Maida Vale. I only moved to the Tower after the war started.'

'And you don't enjoy the company of the society girls.'

'They are hardly inviting.'

His smile softens. 'They are threatened, Miss Cooper.'

'By what?'

'By you, of course.'

I look up at him. He is not teasing. Is he? 'Stop it.'

'I mean it. By you, Miss Cooper, and by the hundred or so other girls to come to the ATA from scratch. To be a female pilot meant one was an elite – usually privately educated and well connected, definitely wealthy. And now… some ambulance driver can turn up and fly a Moth in a matter of weeks.'

I never thought of it like that. He is smiling and again I am glad he has his nose unbroken.

We settle quite nicely into chatting, discussing good and bad take-offs, and the problems of a sticky throttle.

'What do you want to do after the war, Anna?'

It is the first time he has used my name. 'After the war…?'

'It'll all be over some time,' he says.

'I don't know. What will you do?'

Cecil shrugs his wide shoulders. 'I was a tea taster before the war, believe it or not. I was told my job would be waiting for me. How it will compare to all this…'

'Hey, Rafferty!'

A pilot stumbles over, throws an arm around Cecil. 'What? Scouting out the local talent without me, Captain?'

'Ah, Duncan.' Cecil coughs. 'Dunk is my navigator, most important man in my crew.'

'Who's this then?'

Cecil suddenly looks as red as me. 'This is Anna Cooper, from the ATA.'

'Yeah? She ever been in the cockpit?' He sways forward, the beer spilling down Cecil's front.

'That's enough, Dunk.' He detangles from the drunken man.

'Enough? This is my eighth. Where's your eighth, Rafferty? Crew quota. No abandoning the quota because you met some new bird.'

'Dunk. You're a mess.' Cecil glances around, his eyes wide. 'Westin! West, can you give me a hand here? Duncan needs a hand getting down to a taxi.'

'Taxi? It's only – West, you bastard! What'ya doing? Rafferty won't meet the quota on account of this bird—'

With a grateful look from Cecil, Westin escorts the raving man towards the door. He gives me the briefest of nods in passing. *I will have to study up on riveting to win his approval.* By taking the screaming drunk away, he's already won mine.

'What do you say, darling? Time to be off?'

Nell has returned, shoulders raised and arms crossed. I am forcibly aware of just how beautiful she is. If only Westin would come back and take her away. *Darling?*

'Ah, I ought to stay a bit longer, I fear. The honour of my squadron is in question.'

'I am *knackered*, Cecil.'

'Go on without me.'

A very long moment passes. Nell does *not* look happy as she sways into the crowd. I am surprised that, having vanquished Isabella Pomeroy, she would give up so easily.

'We bombers get a good amount of attention, we know that.' He smiles, but his smile fades as he continues. 'But if this all goes wrong, if we lose this war, and Nazi Storm Troopers parade the battlements at the Tower of London, we will get the blame. Tea-tasting isn't looking so bad these days.'

I lower my head. *I have never thought of that either.*

'Well, Anna? Shall we have a dance?'

Wordlessly, I nod. Time slows. I am looking around, at the gleaming bottles, the hanging bunting, at everything but the man dancing in front of me. Joy is there, on the other side of the room, hands flashing. When the music turns slow, Cecil moves closer.

What will happen now? There is of course no question of simply shaking his hand, thanking him for the dance, and saying goodnight. *Then what are you doing?* Insistent questions rise up, but I have no answers.

Even after we move apart, I can still feel him. The warm imprint of his body against mine, his forearms firm around my sides, his hands on my back. I try not to look at him, my face turning hot. The next song brings us back together again. I glance up at him, for the first time, and just like that he kisses me.

Softer than I could have ever expected. And nice. Warm. Still, I pull away.

I step back, careful not to stumble. Suddenly I am conscious of my hair, my teeth, my body – and far too aware of him, his nearness, his smell, the heavy warmth of his hands. Some wild voice within me – not mine, not Flo's – is telling me to run.

Breath comes too fast. It is done. We have kissed. Something not unlike a bomb has raced from the sky and – what? Opened it up? Ruined everything?

'Well, Anna. There's a bar in my hotel, much quieter than this. What do you say?'

I don't know what to say. *What about Nell? What about Isabella Pomeroy?* All at once I am afraid that I have, in fact, ruined everything. *Oh, Timothy Squire. I am sorry.*

'Anna?'

'Oh no. I can't. I mean… the curfew.'

Another pilot saunters over, wearing a big grin. 'Headed down to the Kit Kat Club for a grog – you coming?'

Cecil shakes his head: 'no'. But he gazes back towards the door. He seems to regret letting Nell Singer go home alone. Flushed red and feeling the fool that I am, I extend my hand.

'Cecil. Thank you for the pleasant evening. Goodbye.'

The ravens will be the end of me.

Somehow they have heard my footsteps. I was nice enough to Mr Thorne – though his look told me this is my last abuse of curfew, permanent resident or not – and I have almost made it past the nest when the bloody birds start croaking. I fight off the ridiculous urge to walk on tiptoe. Timothy Squire has clearly done a bad job as Ravenmaster, and Stackhouse must not be feeding them properly.

Night presses down on the Tower. Not a single light on in the White Tower or the Jewel House. Like nobody lives here; like nobody's ever lived here. Even the most familiar routes become a little hazy, and these shoes aren't meant for the cobblestones. I stumble as I turn. A glass of wine too many, perhaps.

'I think they miss you.'

I freeze. Of course, it is him.

I grab his bony shoulders, crushing him in a hug. 'Timothy Squire. Are you – are you sneaking out?'

'Me?' Pulling free of my hug, he holds me at arm's length. 'No, I am a responsible member of His Majesty's armed forces. I certainly wouldn't risk my life and those of my allies by spending the night boozing it up with the lads.'

His tone is hard, and I am flooded with guilt. *More guilt.* I struggle for something – anything – to say, but suddenly his laughter fills the night.

'Good for you, Magpie. How can you do the job if you don't act the part, right? Come on, I'll make you a cup of tea. Trust me, it'll help.'

I nod weakly, following him to the Stone Kitchen. 'We just had – a group of us – a meet-up for planning…'

I mutter on as we cross the Ward. Timothy Squire says nothing as he ushers me in, closes the door behind us. He starts making the tea, the soothing hiss of the gas burner, the familiar clink of mugs. I feel terrible about my time with Cecil. But that's no use. 'You can't put honey back in the comb,' Flo's father would say. *Not that it was honey, exactly…*

'So,' Timothy Squire says, not turning around. 'Is it exciting?'

'The Lansdowne?'

'The training to be a pilot.'

'Oh,' I say, feeling as ridiculous as I sound. Luckily he is still intent on the tea-making. 'Sometimes, yeah.'

I notice a small portion of real milk – it must be his whole ration – and my heart leaps up. *Tea with real milk.* Now he turns around, carrying two steaming cups. He places one in front of me and it takes all my willpower not to reach out immediately.

'Are they strict?'

I shrug. 'About timetables and things. But it's not the WAAF – we're all civilians, so the worst they can do is send us home. And training a new pilot is not cheap.'

'They seem to pay well enough, anyway.' He laughs again. 'They say it's sixpence a pint at the Lansdowne.'

Eight, actually. 'They look after us.'

'What do you do?' he asks, taking a quick sip. 'Do you get to fly Hurricanes and things?'

'Well, some pilots collect fighters from factories and deliver them to aerodromes. Though some are needed at small airfields in the country, to be tested and armed. The grass airfields are camouflaged and can be a nightmare to find. So I hear, at any rate. I've never even sat in the second cockpit.'

'Some day that'll be you, Magpie. Flying a Spitfire to where it's needed most.'

I look down at my steaming cup. *Why is he being so nice?* 'Some people think women aren't strong enough to fly aircraft. But if you're relying on force, you're in trouble. The touch is really quite gentle.'

I finally take a sip. It *is* real milk. It is *heaven*. 'And what are you doing, Timothy Squire?'

'Eh? I'm still down at the docks. Building.'

'Are you on leave?'

He nods, suddenly flustered. 'A forty-eight, yeah. Here, you'll need this, right? I'm sure the time is pretty important up there. In the sky. This was my grampa's.' He hands me a beautiful silver watch.

196

'Timothy Squire – your grampa's watch? I can't take this.'

'Don't take it. Just borrow it. Until you come back, then I'll take it again, yeah? See, it fits perfectly.'

He's lying, of course. He's fussing to get it on my wrist, to show me it fits. Even on the tightest notch, it is loose. But I am sure of how important this is to him.

'Thank you.'

We sit together on the battlements wall, overlooking Tower Bridge. 'You've done a brilliant job looking after the ravens, Timothy Squire.'

'They've not been half-bad, to be honest. Well, Stan is always a bit of a—'

'Say, you haven't noticed Stackhouse hanging around Bloody Tower, have you?'

'Stackhouse?'

I watch Timothy Squire, staring fixedly out over the river. He is hiding something – that much is clear. 'Yeah. I know it sounds mad, but I think he might have been in my room. I don't know for certain, but someone left a letter on top of my diary.'

'A letter? What did it say?' Timothy Squire has gone white as a cloud.

'Nothing. It was one of the V1 leaflets. But it was meant as a message, I think.'

'It was me.'

'You?'

'Yes,' he adds weakly. 'Sorry. I know I shouldn't have gone into your room – especially after the last time – but I just wanted to leave you a letter. I thought it was better than posting it. But then I decided to post it anyway. And I forgot the leaflet on your desk. I'm sorry, Anna. I didn't touch anything or read anything and it was only that one mad time.'

'You posted me a letter?'

He holds my gaze for longer than normal. 'Eh? No. Not yet. I wanted to write it again. But I will post it, soon.'

'I can tell when you have a secret.' He has frozen, more than confirming my guess. Something he doesn't want to tell me. 'You said you weren't going to lie to me any more. Do you remember? Well, what is it that you're keeping from me? This letter?'

He sighs, a heavy, elaborate sigh. 'I can't tell you.'

'Timothy Squire…'

All at once his face crumbles. 'I'm not a sapper, Anna. I was kicked out of training. That's why I came home early – that's why I'm stuck down at the docks. And now that's over, and I've got nothing to do but mope around the Tower with these blasted ravens. The bloody Ravenmaster.'

He looks relieved again – the weight of holding back the truth must have been taking its toll. *I knew it.* Timothy Squire can't keep a secret for more than a second. *He's not a sapper?*

'I – well, Lightwood and I – we messed around with

the fuse. I mean, we were supposed to blow up this bridge, right, but we messed around with the fuse, just testing it out, just before and... nothing. The explosion was meant to be massive, but nothing happened. Just a tiny click, and silence. Major sent us straightaway to work at the docks.'

I am as shocked as he is by the laughter that rings through me. I can't stop, I just keep laughing. Loud enough to wake the Inner Ward residents, birds and humans both. He stares back, at first annoyed, then a bit worried. Soon, though, a little smile cracks his lips.

'I really thought it was going to work,' he mutters.

Now we are both laughing, loud enough to wake the whole Tower of London.

Moonlight shines down on the turrets. It is no longer the wine, but the sheer exhaustion that has me light-headed. Timothy Squire is not the quiet, distant boy that came back from Aberdeen. He is his old self, laughing and talking rubbish, tapping his palms on the stone, looking out over the Thames, over the city. Laughter makes him handsome – maybe not as handsome as Cecil, but still handsome.

Across the battlements warm wind sweeps up, and we sit, silent, but in complete awareness of each other. Even as my eyes look around – at the turrets, Tower Bridge, the new stars piercing out – they always come back to him.

'This place kicks.' He catches my glance, smiles, peers up at the sky.

'That's Ursa Major.' I point up into the blackness. It is the deepest, stillest part of night. 'The Great Bear. Can you see her – just across from the moon? One of the largest constellations in the night sky.'

'Oh,' he says.

Yeoman Oakes taught me that. When I first asked him to take me to Salt Tower to look at Hew Draper's carving, an astrological chart, I was only trying to be nice. But to stand before it is to understand how complex it is, how fascinating a map of the stars can be. After Uncle died, though, we never went back.

'Aren't you scared?' Timothy Squire says. 'Of being... up there?'

'I was...' I sigh. 'I wanted to volunteer, to help, but I didn't mean to join the ATA. I didn't know I *could* join up. I'm still not sure quite how it all happened.'

He laughs. 'Rules aren't what they used to be.'

'I'm sure you'll get another chance, Timothy Squire.'

'Nah. But I'm done whinging about it, at any rate. I've got these birds to look after. And I'm proud of you, Anna.'

'Thank you.'

Moonlight shifts across the towers, disappears over the battlements.

'So what's really happening down there? The docks, I mean.'

'It's meant to be a secret, Magpie.'

'The invasion.'

He nods. 'We were building some sort of great floating city.'

'Will it work?'

'I don't know. Armed forces business, isn't it? But it didn't work when we tried to land at Dieppe. It's never worked before, Lightwood tells me. And the Germans will be expecting it. Rommel will be there, waiting for us.'

'But there is a chance? This time?'

He grunts. 'The only way our invasion could ever work is if we throw everything at them – every plane, every tank, every soldier. And then we're going to need some proper bloody luck.'

'We have to get over there soon,' I say. 'Before the V1s.'

He coughs. I am aware of what he doesn't say. *That the V1s are impossible. That I shouldn't worry.*

We watch the pale disc of the moon, thinning as it rises. Darkness begins to fade from the sky.

Finally, he says, 'We'll be all right, Magpie. I promise.'

I reach out, take his hand, hardened by his months at the docks. *Sapper, labourer, Ravenmaster – I don't care.* After an impossibly long instant, he squeezes back. Birds – robins, blackbirds, the returned starlings – chirp and sing up the sun. The dawn chorus, Uncle said. 'A daily miracle', he called it, and I can believe it. The ravens are still silent in their cages.

Thin rays of orange creep up Tower Bridge and I realize I have never seen the sunrise from here. I had no idea that it could rise, almost perfectly, between the two towers of the bridge. This new light is a new day, and Timothy Squire and I watch it together.

When he kisses me, his lips are as soft as I remember. Hesitantly, a little quicker than Cecil; after another moment, all thoughts of Cecil are gone for ever.

'Timothy Squire. We should talk. About what happened two years ago. With my father.'

He smiles. 'Doesn't seem the right time, does it?'

I shake my head. Now feels the best time to talk about it. So many things that I want to say, that I've wanted to say but didn't even realize, come flooding out.

'You were the only one – you know that? When I first came here. The only one who wanted to help me, who cared about me. You were a great friend. I know – all your stealing wasn't meant to hurt anyone. You're just dumb as a brick sometimes. And you help with the ravens, and I know you don't really like them. In the beginning I think you were actually scared of them—'

'Anna—'

'And when my father came – when that *man* came here, you were so brave. And you chased him away. You chased the bastard away for ever.'

His voice is different, softer. 'Anna.'

I keep talking, terrified that if I stop now I will never say it, never tell him the truth. He is trying to stop me, he thinks it is the wine – can it be, after all this time? – but I must keep going.

'Anna.'

I look up at him, forcing myself to stop. 'Yes, Timothy Squire?'

His eyes are soft, kind. 'I think it's time to feed the birds.'

Sunday, 21 March 1943

I didn't even try to sleep. I sat on the bed, writing in my notebook, staring out of the window, listening to the whistle and click of starlings. Anything but sleep. Walking down the stairs of Bloody Tower, my head feels stuffed. Even the stairwell is too loud and bright. All I can think of is breakfast. I almost miss a step – music comes from Yeoman Oakes's room. Loud music.

Carefully, I knock. The voice at the other end is so loud it is startling. Usually Oakes is listening to the radio – 'Life with the Lyons' or 'Workers' Playtime' – but this is something else. Screaming trumpets and banging drums. It is 7 a.m.

'Come!'

I push open the door. Music hits me like a rush of wind. Oakes is standing in the middle of the room, looking almost flushed. He is in his shirtsleeves. He seems surprised to see me, but his face soon changes and he laughs. With a great hug, he lifts me off the floor.

'It's not English, I know,' he says, letting me down and smiling at the Victrola. 'Don't tell Churchill, OK?'

My head throbs in protest at the trumpets and drums. For days I have been thinking – well, I've been thinking about it for much longer – that I must ask Oakes about Father, but, now that I am here it no longer seems such a good idea. I put it from my mind.

'Your uncle loved this music, as you must know.'

Letting the door close, I enter the room, standing awkwardly amid the noise. I think of the ravens, how surprised they were to be let out so early by Timothy Squire and me. Especially Portia – she seemed *strange* somehow. She made all sorts of knocking sounds I've never heard her make before. And Rogan, too, was all puffed up, making his dominance displays and calling loudly.

Timothy Squire muttered that Stackhouse promised to leave them out. *Leave them out?* I decided not to ask. He's meant to be the Ravenmaster now.

Timothy Squire didn't say anything about the ravens' odd behaviour, but I felt like he was... sad. Something is going on. But truth be told, the ravens weren't the first thing on my mind at the time. Of course I won't see Cecil again – but if I do, I will just tell him the truth about Timothy Squire and me.

Which is?

'Listen, listen.' Oakes is doing his thing where he is talking, but not really *to* anyone. Uncle *always* did that. 'This part... here.'

And, after a moment, 'Oh, he *loved* this piece.'

Oakes is too far away to notice my sour look. He is lost in his music. Or something. I glance around, worried I will see an empty glass of whisky and water. But there is nothing, only a tie lying across the chair.

A quick scurry of strings and then the sound of horns hangs in the narrow room, which is neatly stacked with books and papers. I'm sure Uncle did like this – he once took me to the longest concert I've ever heard at the Queen's Hall, the night before it was bombed – but breakfast, and relief from this headache, awaits.

'Tell me, Anna. Is *this* what it feels like to fly?'

I nod, trying to adopt a listening face. *How can music sound like flying?* This is just loud, swaying trumpets and horns. My eyes hover again to the shelves, yet no empty glasses can be seen. But as the music grows, it floods out, becomes somehow purifying, proud, the joyful horns reaching and ascending.

'Do you hear it? The swan theme.'

The sound is – well, like being suspended, weightless, hovering, free and alone. Like great swans pounding their wings, soaring. Flying. It is remarkable. It is *extraordinary*. For a brief moment I forget all about my pounding head.

Oakes is smiling at me like a fiend. 'You see?'

I am smiling too as the music crashes around us.

'Sibelius,' Oakes says, as the piece finally ends. He carefully takes the needle off the record and then lifts his tie, slides it over his head and pulls it tight. 'His Fifth Symphony. Marvellous. Now, how can I help you, Anna? Not another faked birth certificate, I hope?'

I shake my head dumbly, unsure what to make of his transformation. 'I was hoping for some real eggs.'

'Sorry,' he says, as we take our usual seats in the Stone Kitchen. 'I have all your uncle's old records. Sometimes it's nice to listen to them. Sorry about the breakfast.'

Oakes shrugs at me from across yet another bowl of

dregs. *At least they're not burned.* Sometimes Mum burned the pan. I don't know why, but the eggs would be black and ruined, and Mum would curse – curse the pan, the eggs, herself. On burned-pan mornings I would just tell her I wasn't that hungry, and anyway I didn't really like eggs so much, but that I couldn't wait to come home from school for cheese on toast. The cheese on toast was never burned.

'Yeoman Oakes?'

'Yes, Anna?'

'I really miss Uncle, too.'

He squares his jaw. There *is* a smell of whisky I notice, but it is only slight. 'Your uncle was a good man, Anna. The Tower is not quite the same place without him. We miss him here every day.'

I want to reach out, take his hand. 'It's only you and me now, Yeoman Oakes. We'll just have to do our best.'

Oakes gives a sad smile. I feel terrible for bringing up the whole mess. The smell of whisky is not as slight as I first thought.

'Did Uncle ever tell you the story of Bran the Blessed?'

Oakes draws a deep breath and lets it out slowly. 'I'd love to hear you tell me.'

'"Bran" means raven in Welsh. Bran was the King of the Britons, and after a great victory, he was wounded and dying. He had his men cut off his head, and bury it under White Hill, so he would always be there to protect Britain. Even after he had gone. And the Tower is built over White Hill. So we will always be safe here.'

Oakes is nodding to himself, his eyes far away. 'That is the kind of story your uncle loved to tell.'

Uncle *did* tell me that story, and so many others – about ravens, and Tower history. About hope. I must not remember him for the secrets he kept. *We all have secrets. We all try to do what is best.*

'Yeoman Oakes, have you finished your book? The one about the Tower prisoners?'

He comes back to the present with a wistful smile. 'Almost. Almost.'

We eat the rest of our breakfast in silence, though Oakes seems to have cheered up considerably since my story of Bran.

I know that I shouldn't ask him, not now, but I can't stop myself. I have to know the truth. 'Yeoman Oakes,' I say, handing him a washed bowl to dry.

'Yes, Anna?'

'My father. What is his name? His real name.'

'I can't think there's any harm in knowing that.' He sighs. 'His name is Will Esser. But don't waste your thoughts on him, dear.'

That doesn't even sound that German. Will is likely short for Wilhelm. He was hiding even then. I have to be careful – ask too many questions and I'll never get another word out of Oakes. He seems to be aware that he's said too much already. But there is one more thing I have to know.

'Mr Oakes – why did my father leave? Why did he leave me and Mum?'

The new life seems to drain from his face. 'I know very little, Anna. They fought – apparently they were not very happy. Nothing too unusual. He headed back to Germany, where he found a scientific post as I understand. A smart man, everyone said. When trouble began, she changed her name – and yours – to Cooper, and became a fervent anti-war journalist.'

A scientist? Uncle never mentioned that. I thought Father was a sailor. Or… I don't know – maybe he was simply a violinist. *But why lie about it? There's nothing wrong with being a scientist – nothing worth keeping secret.*

'Thank you, Yeoman Oakes.'

The washing up finished, I turn to leave.

'And, Anna,' he calls as I reach the door, 'my name is Gregory.'

'Go on, Flo. Order what you like.'

She pauses, looks at the menu again. I will make up with her, too. I feel light, happy. *Then I will make up with Nell, and we can all be friends again.*

'Tea with milk, please,' she tells the waiter.

'I will be paid quite well,' I say, after ordering the whole-meal bread and raspberry jam and clotted cream.

'But you haven't been paid yet.'

'Soon enough. But suit yourself.'

The idea of me paying for us doesn't sit well with her. *Well, if you're going to stay on in school, you can't expect to collect proper wages too.*

'Another bombing raid.' She sighs into her freshly delivered tea.

I have eyes only for the clotted cream, of which my bread has already received several lashings.

'There has to be another way, Anna.'

'Another way for what?' I say around mouthfuls.

She is giving me *that* look. *We can't all be as delicate as Florence Swift, with her little bites.*

'To end this mess. War just leads to more wars.'

I say nothing but glance up at her serious face. *She sounds like Mum.* An end to the war. What happens when the war *does* end? I try to think of it and my mind keeps going back to Timothy Squire and me holding hands on the battlements.

'I will not take part,' she says.

'You're fifteen, Flo.'

The moonlight on the Tower, the quiet peaceful night. Is it possible to ever have such a night again? To have a future of peaceful nights?

'Yes. And I don't believe in killing. In murder.'

'Murder?' I repeat, finally looking at her. *What is she going on about?*

'What else? Trained to kill, our gallant boys. What is it all for?'

I shake my head. 'The Germans bombed us, Flo—'

'So now we bomb them?'

I nod, happy at least that she's admitting there's a war on. I wonder what finally changed her mind. Not Mr Swift, that's for certain.

209

'And then?' Her voice has a sharp edge.

'We force them to surrender.'

'Or they force us. So, in the end, the side with the biggest army wins? What does that mean?'

'Flo,' I say, trying a lighter tone, 'they aren't going to make you kill anyone.'

'No. Only to help the war effort.'

'I know that you've been away in Montreal, but our bravest men are out there, right now, risking everything to keep us safe.'

Her face turns angry, cruel. 'Don't fight for me. Don't die for me. Don't make me a victim.'

'Flo, our men will keep fighting until we win.'

'Not in my name.'

'So you'll go to gaol then?'

'If I have to.'

'You sound like a conchie.'

I spent my mornings at the canteen listening to them – *Germany has lost its dignity, what will England lose? There are no winners in war* – and even Oakes says similar things. But I never imagined hearing such things from Flo. What has happened?

It was Flo's voice, her encouragement, that gave me the courage to race towards the bomb and save Malcolm during that Tower raid two years ago. She was always so brave, so strong. She barely *looks* like herself, staring at me with red eyes.

'You work with the air force, don't you? I mean, you're one of them, Anna. You and that friend of yours – Nell.

210

So you both must know. These "firestorms", like the one created in Hamburg. They say forty thousand people suffocated in the cyclone. Most were roasted alive in bomb shelters.'

'Flo, that's not true.'

'You don't even ask, do you? You don't care.'

'Where did you hear that? Your dad? What do you know about living through bombing?'

'Timothy told me. Timothy Squire.'

I stare in silence, even the clotted cream a distant memory. *Timothy?* 'Timothy Squire told you?'

'Yes. I came to see you. You didn't write, you didn't tell me you'd run off to join the air force.'

'I couldn't, Flo. I have a proper job, a serious job, helping our country win this war. I'm sorry I don't have time to go on play dates with you and Timothy Squire.'

Timothy Squire never mentioned that Flo came to the Tower.

'I do know what it's like, Anna, so don't give me that look. I know what it's like in the hospitals. I know what it was like for Timothy when he was nearly crushed to death in Bethnal Green Station. What? He didn't tell you? Well, no wonder. You're never around, and you don't write to anyone. It's clear enough that you don't care. You just want your revenge, same as the Germans do.'

I am almost too shocked to say anything. *Timothy Squire, why didn't you tell me?* But I can't sit in silence across from her – I can't let her know she's right. *Why didn't you tell me?* And now I am going back to White

211

Waltham and it will be weeks before I can see him again. *If I even want to, now.*

'Goodbye, Flo. Good luck praying Hitler just goes away.'

'Goodbye, Anna. Good luck trying to bomb more civilians than the other side.'

My half-finished bread and jam is like an accusation as I pay the bill and leave.

Tuesday, 23 March 1943

I bring down the hammer, nailing into the wood. Heat makes the sound louder. Holding still another nail, I hammer the planks together, lost in the task. Over the bronze sounds of a bell and the insistent croaking of ravens, I focus on the box. People are getting married all over the city, and the birds are always a distraction; I can block them out.

'What is that?'

The voice startles me and the swinging hammer almost catches my thumb.

'All right, Malcolm?' I say, turning back to the box. Malcolm, Yeoman Brodie's kid, is a right pain. He never speaks to me – only to Dad, who shares his fascination with the Crown jewels and old bits of kings' clothing. He walked right past me the other day, like we haven't both lived in the same bloody Tower for fifteen years.

Better he walks past than any of that 'Timothy Squire is a rotten liar' *rubbish.* One more person talks, sings, or coughs those words and I'll use their femur bones to build this nesting box.

I have to tell Anna about her father.

I knew about her mum's death – or the way of it, rather. After a few hints about being friendly to the new girl, Mum told me the truth when we were in Disley, but I was told not to speak a word of it to Anna, as her uncle would when the time was right. Well, Henry Reed must've lost his nerve, because Anna ended up finding out on her own, and all of us who'd kept it secret from her came away looking like devils.

The lie clings to me. I will not lie to her again; I promised her as much, before I left for training. *A dozen times or more.* You'd think from how she goes on about it that it was all the stuff I nicked that made her mad – but really it was because I hadn't told her I knew the truth about what had happened.

During a second-form history test, after I was caught looking at Vera Rowe's answers, Headmaster Brownbill made me sweep the classroom. When I didn't do a 'sufficient' job of it, he thought I was taking the piss, and he made me sweep it again and *then* sweep the library. *Penitence*, Dad called it as he happily agreed to let me into the library at dawn, and to keep a careful eye on me as I set to work.

Helping the ravens breed doesn't feel quite the same as pushing a broom across the endless stone floor of the library. But it doesn't feel *so* different, either.

'What is that?' Malcolm says again, coming to stand

213

right beside me. He throws a skinny shadow across the box and keeps standing there, oblivious as a fish in water.

I sigh. 'It's for the birds, Malcolm.'

'But the birds already have those big cages. What's the box for?'

'Ask your dad,' I say with a smile.

No, I am being mean. Malcolm is just odd. And the memory of Quartermaster carrying on about the French letters still stings. 'It's a nesting box. So then birds'll lay eggs and all that.'

'More birds?' He sounds horrified.

'They won't hurt you.' I remember that Anna told me that one had bitten Malcolm. Stan, I'd wager it was. 'Just don't go touching them.'

These beaks could do some damage; the talons could shred the skin off your arm.

And Rogan seems about ready to attack anything that moves. He lunges at me when I try to feed him now. They are always together, Rogan and Portia, but they are not acting as usual – no preening each other's feathers, no soft cooing. Just angry ravens, snapping bills and loud *kraas*. I need to get this box ready before I lose an eye. I wish Anna were still here, to help me keep a watch on them.

'You are a sapper,' Malcolm says. 'Aren't you? And Anna has gone off to join the ATA.' He pauses, then looks up at me. 'I want to help, too.'

'Then pass me some nails.'

Malcolm does not move. He is standing there, between me and the box of nails, staring like a stunned fool.

214

'Right, Malcolm. Go and join up somewhere next year.'

'I want to join up now.'

I squint up at him. 'You're fifteen.'

'So are you.'

'There's no job looking after jewels in the war, Malcolm.'

He doesn't seem offended, or even seem to have heard. 'I read about the Meteorological Centres. Helping to forecast the weather.'

He can't be serious. 'You want to work at the Met? To help the war?'

'I'm very good at maths.'

'Well, good luck, Malcolm.'

'I remember all sorts of things, details and notes. Ask your father. I am very good at details. I don't fancy going all the way to Bristol for the interview though. Say, why aren't you at work right now?'

I let the hammer fall. 'This is my work now, Malcolm. All right? Be a good lad and leave me to it.'

Tuesday, 23 March 1943

Diana Gaines is dead. I almost didn't know her – she was very kind to me that day of the snow storm. No one seems to have known her well. No one is likely to forget her now. Diana's engine shut down, and she plummeted like a stone from the sky.

'Bumped off,' they all say.

Now we are all standing around in the cold for her

funeral. The whole group is here, under the great spire of the Shottesbrooke church, including the officers and Commander Gower herself. Letters were written to her family in America, but no response has come yet. The ATA clearly wants to get this over and done with.

'Sabotage,' Joy says as the service ends and we file out side by side. The pale sun is still inching up the sky. 'It's the only possible explanation.'

I nod wearily, glad she's keeping her voice down. Unfortunately, spy mania still has a hold, even here. 'You think a Nazi spy damaged her engine?'

'No.'

'What? Who then?'

She leans close, looks around. 'Don't you know anything, Cooper? You think the RAF wants us to exist, a unit of women flying the same ships as they do? You've seen how they are.'

'The RAF...?'

What is she even talking about? Surely not – I mean, the very idea is impossible to imagine. The only RAF man I really know is Cecil – and he would never consider such a thing. But Joy is not done trying to convince me.

'One of the girls had her engine catch fire while she was taking off. She landed, managed to douse the fire. What did she find in the engine? Rolled-up oil rags.'

'Joy, that's a mistake, surely.'

It doesn't seem possible that Westin could make a mistake – especially not one of that magnitude – but mistakes do happen. *I once hid in a petrol depot during an air raid.*

216

I hope Westin does not feel guilty about it. He may be grumpy and arrogant, but he's a great engineer, and he's Cecil's friend. I cast around to see if I can spot him, but he's nowhere to be seen. Joy is still banging on.

'The RAF, Cooper. They want this place shut down. Get the girls away from aircraft and back in the kitchens where they belong.'

Stunned into silence, I say nothing. An RAF man would *never* do such a horrible, murderous thing. It is *treason* to even suggest such a thing. Joy is merely tired – sick with grief. She doesn't know the RAF, the British people. She has heard too many American stories.

'Joy, you told me the boys just need some time to adjust. That they'll be cheering me on…'

'It's gotten worse, not better. They want us *gone*, any way they can.'

I can't even think of any of this right now. The RAF involved in sabotage? It is too much. It is impossible. And I need my head to be clear.

Tomorrow is my biggest test – my first solo flight.

Joy is looking at me with narrowed eyes. 'Just be careful, Cooper. Always be the last one to check your ship before you take off. Got it?'

IV

THE SKY
BETWEEN US

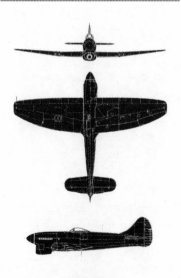

"TEMPEST"

'Should the Allies turn invaders, we will throw them back into the sea.'

Hitler, Führer Directive no. 51, 3 November 1943

8

Thursday, 25 March 1943

I never want to see the pesky sun come up again. I drag out the ladder I stashed behind the garden hedge, and position it on the King's House. The cold dawn laughs at me. *I'll just add it to the list. Bleeding world is laughing at me.*

I climb the ladder, up to the joint where the two high roofs meet. No prisoners in here now. I remember what Anna told me about Rudolf Hess – how the Warders kept him in this house like some honoured guest. Should've shot the mad bastard as soon as they spotted him.

The nest box looks on the Green, so the ravens can keep a beady eye on each other. Everyone knows where everyone is and all that. *Should work out just fine.* I reach the top step, and not a single croak greets me. I know before I can even see it.

'*Wizard* show Portia. You've done it.'

And she has. Portia has laid four eggs – small, pear-shaped things, almost green, with tiny black spots. Even less appetizing than the hens' sad eggs before they stopped laying.

Time was when eggs were big and white and delicious with some buttered toast. The new mum, who is not looking any worse for wear perched on the side of the box, swiftly sits back on the eggs. She doesn't seem *thrilled* to see me – my stomach might have rumbled – and within moments Rogan appears in a flap of unbalanced wings, bringing up an offering of food. No chance my stomach's rumbling at this.

A mouse, it seems to have once been. Rogan drops it on the side of the box, nudging the ruined ball of fur towards Portia, who hops off the eggs to tear it up some more. I only get a brief glance at the eggs – so small – before Rogan hops on to keep them warm.

Portia barely finishes eating before she turns her attention to me – and one thing is clear, I am not wanted up here. Even after I built them a nesting box *and* let their wings grow long enough to fly up here. And hopefully not too much further, though I doubt they'll be off anywhere in a hurry. Not until these chicks have grown at any rate.

Here come the croaks, from both mum and dad. *Rack. Rack. Rack.*

'Yes, fine. I'm off. You're welcome, the lot of you.'

I slide down the ladder with loud croaks still filling my ears.

Sunday, 11 April 1943

More than two weeks have come and gone. A proper sad few days, as I've had the job of clearing out the dead eggs, which

Portia rolled from the nest into the gutter. She must have known they weren't going to hatch. The little things were cold to the touch despite all of their sitting on them, and the thin shell squeezed under the gentle pressure of my fingers.

But one nestling survived. I watched the egg, the last one, trembling and shaking, threatening to crack. *How did the little lad breathe in there?*

He is out now. No feathers, eyes closed, raspy voice. Seems to be one giant pink mouth, begging for food. Both parents take turns feeding him. At first Portia scolded me for coming too close – *Rack! Rack!* – but once I proved willing to bring presents of extra food, she now suffers my presence. Still more than a sight irritable, though. *Definitely Anna's raven.*

I don't know how many of the eggs usually make it, but we've got one and I'm counting us lucky for it. Not an easy road ahead, mate, even with all three of us looking out for you. You have to be strong to live in the Tower. This little guy will have to be more than strong to survive in the Tower now: rationed food, possible air raid at any time, the world's laziest Warder.

I remember Dad talking about some display of Japanese armour – samurai armour. I saw it once, a long time ago, when he was dusting off a bunch of old pieces. I remember how it looked – black, fierce, horned. *Kind of like you, little guy.*

Dad had gone on and on about some warrior – one of the last samurais – who had been a great swordmaster. Yugoro Something-or-other. But that doesn't sound quite right for a Tower raven.

'Hey.' I lean in, watching the new bird, its beak already sharp. 'What do you make of "Yugo"? It's a fighter's name – and you'll have to be a fighter, yeah?'

The raven's head turns, as if meeting my gaze like a challenge.

Yugo it is.

The clock-tower bell chimes behind me. As quick as I can, I scurry down the ladder, release the other birds for the morning, leaving Portia, Rogan, and Yugo in the nest box.

I feel a strange sense of lightness. Yugo is born. The ravens are happy.

My penitence is almost over.

'Yeoman Stackhouse. The chick will be in the nest box for six to ten weeks. You can reach the box by climbing and peeking in. Portia will croak at you but just ignore her and check that the baby is doing all right. Once a day. Some extra food for the parents – they'll make sure Yugo gets it. Do you understand?'

'No.'

Truth be told, my penitence may never be over. Not until Anna learns about her father still being over here. But there'll be a time for all that, and it's not now. The past few weeks I haven't slept more than a wink before the nightmare of Bethnal Green roars into my head. Screaming women and children, mouths hanging open, trampling each other in fear. I can't stay here, raising Anna's birds, no matter how much I owe it to her. People need their proper lives back. I have to do what I can to end this bleeding war.

'Here's the deal, Yeoman Stackhouse. When I come back to check, which I will, and if Yugo is a healthy weight, you will find, just inside the cage, a bottle of single malt whisky.'

He narrows his eyes at me. 'Is that a bribe, boy?'

'Certainly. And a fair one, I wager. I can rest easy knowing that the birds are well looked after, and you'll be getting paid twice to do one job.'

'I already look after them.' He indicates the ravens with a flick of his wrist.

'And we're a sight more than grateful.'

'No one said anything about climbing way up there.'

'No one said anything about whisky either.'

I hold out my hand, which he inspects with great suspicion. 'Single malt you say?'

'Highland's finest.'

'Just once a day?'

'Ladder's behind the hedge.'

Still frowning, he reaches out and clasps my hand. 'Deal.'

Now that the ravens are in good hands – good enough, at any rate – and Anna's father has cleared out, I have an appointment to schedule. And a bleeding war to put a stop to.

I've no clue when I decided this – surely not because of what Malcolm said about being useful. My thoughts are all jammed together. I just know that I can't stay here at the Tower. And being around Stackhouse makes me *more* certain of it.

Quarter's threats for secrecy about the Phoenix units could hardly be clearer. I know what's coming, and I know just who to talk to. I remember from his letter that his office is in London.

It's time to take my place again.

Wednesday, 14 April 1943

In the hangars no one is in sight but Westin, working expertly away. I feel his eyes on me as I speed past, desperate to be away from aircraft and engines. I can't study for another second. Perhaps I can find a magazine to read. Anything, so long as I don't have to memorize it. Luckily I have an aspirin. My head *aches*.

There is always laughter from the crew room. Despite the weather and the gruelling flight schedules, the pilots are determined to enjoy themselves. Even if they spend the whole time bragging about their London flying clubs, it beats studying. For a brief moment I am reminded of my life at WAAF. *And anything beats mucking out toilets.*

'You want in?'

I blink at the voice. Lost in thought, I have wandered right into the crew room. One of the girls – glamorous – stares at me with a flat look. She's holding cards. No one else is here. *So much for the laughter and celebration of the crew room.*

'Oh – sorry, I don't know how,' I say.

'It's blackjack.' The same flat look says, *Only an idiot doesn't understand blackjack*. I don't how to play *any* card games. The only game I know how to play is Monopoly, and I'm terrible at that. *Though I suspect Timothy Squire was cheating all along.*

All I can think of is Flo's grinning face. *I cannot believe her*. And Timothy Squire. He is the most rotten boy in the world. They deserve each other.

'You playing or not?'

'Yes. OK.'

I walk over, slip into the chair across the table. *What am I doing?* I am a pilot and I, too, am determined to enjoy myself.

'Megan, isn't it?' she says.

'Anna,' I mutter. 'Anna Cooper.'

'Right.'

'You're Bella. The ballerina.'

She stands to give a short, theatrical bow. I look at my cards. *Do the suits have to match? I have two red cards already. Or is this the game where I have to get to twenty-one?*

'The British sky is so tiresome,' Bella says, pressing down a card. She smiles and I am surprised to see she has a gap in her teeth. *I thought all these girls were perfect.* 'Slate and grey, boring and damp. A summer morning in Kashmir, the dizzy colours and biting air – that is a proper sky.'

'I've never been to Kashmir,' I answer.

The only sound is the crisp flip of cards. I lose – *it is the game to twenty-one* – and Bella shuffles for a new game.

227

'That was so horrible,' I say, striving to find some common ground, 'what happened to Diana.'

Bella shrugs. 'A dangerous business, flying aircraft.'

She wasn't knocked from the sky by the dizzy colours of the Kashmir morning.

'Well, Joy said – she said the engine might have been sabotaged.'

'Joy? Is that the coloured girl?'

I'm not sure I like the way she says that, but who knows what relationship the British and the Americans have these days. *They did wait a long time to join in.* If Japan hadn't bombed America, they might never have come at all. Some people feel like we don't need them.

I'm sure that's all she means. I decide to focus on the game. *I only have fourteen, but if I draw anything over a seven...*

'So you're going to the midsummer party then?'

I purse my lips. *Do I want another card?* 'Not sure.'

An eyebrow rises. 'That's the way, my dear. Don't let him know too much. But I'd be a little careful with that one. All the other girls jump for Cecil Rafferty. And I reckon he's grown used to it.'

Cards flee from my thoughts. 'Cecil... midsummer party?'

'Oakley Park, the family estate in Yorkshire. Minx figures Cornwall would be better. Though what's so exciting about bonfires on hilltops, I couldn't say.'

The family estate in Yorkshire? All these snobby girls will go, I'm sure – Isabella Pomeroy will surely be there. Will Nell go? I control a shiver at the thought. I can see the two of them fighting; Isabella Pomeroy, her mouth always open. *To show us her perfect white teeth.* And Bella thinks I'd be invited?

'It's your play, Megan.'

Her words bring me crashing back to earth. I don't have time to be daydreaming and playing cards with famous ballerinas who can't be bothered to remember my name. She presses down my next card – a seven – and I receive another raised eyebrow. *I win.*

'I'm sorry, Bella. I have a flying exam tomorrow. I have to go.'

9

Thursday, 15 April 1943

I am in the cockpit but my mind is somewhere else. In Maida Vale, in the Tower, in some long-forgotten daydream. Timothy Squire. Flo must think he is *so* fascinating. He's probably telling her some great story of his sapper training. Some great lie. She calls him *Timothy*.

Again I picture Flo's face when I saw her last. Smooth and composed – so sure of herself. *It's easy to be sure when you have no idea what you're talking about.* No, I must focus. *I can do this.* It's only a Moth.

'You alive back there, Cooper?'

Last time I looked up, Gower was strapping herself into the front cockpit. *How long have I been staring off into space?* I adjust my goggles, reach out and switch the ignition on with a hasty, 'Yes, Commander Gower.'

This is my first flight in the rear cockpit. I peer over her helmet, down the long runway. *I am the pilot.* I feel for the harness – it is buckled. My parachute feels heavy but at least I am sure it is there.

The flight engineer removes the wheel chocks and spins the propeller into life. Miraculously, the ever-present Westin is not here; he must have caught wind of Gower's mood. *Smart man.*

Squeezed in my seat, my leather helmet a size or more too tight, my mind goes dangerously blank. No, just remember the lessons. *I've copied them out again and again.* I've flown with Joy four times. This is a simple aircraft to handle: no breaks, no flaps, no instruments. No roof. And a simple task to perform: go up and come down. That's all.

Will this tiny yellow aeroplane really lift off the ground?

'Cooper?'

Taxi into position to take off. We taxi off, dragging the tail behind us. No instructions from the speaking tube. Well, I know the instructions.

I reach the take-off point. Take-off is always made into wind. Well, we've got plenty of that. I can feel it full in the face without seeing the windsock flailing in the gusting breeze. A queue of aircraft, two in front, one behind. I wish there wasn't an aircraft behind, watching. *Everyone is watching.*

Clouds dot the sky, but it is mostly clear and blue. As if to confirm how safe it is, a green flare soars above the control tower. *Red*: unsafe. *Green*: proceed.

I have done Joy's laborious pre-flight routine. I am ready. The flight engineer gives me a thumbs up.

Yes, I can think of the steps now. *I pray I've remembered them correctly.*

Engine speed controlled by the throttle. Yes, that is

easy enough. I push open the throttle. Speed and nausea come quickly and together. It *is* a plywood box with wings – and it's creaking like its flying days are over. Just one more, please.

The left wheel hits a bump. Another. I pull gently back on the throttle but hit a ridge, and again, until the plane is pitching back and forth like we're at sea. Why can't White Waltham have tarmac? I push forward on the throttle, full power, and I feel the tail lift off the ground, with only mild protest.

Gower says nothing but I fear her silence even more. She must doubt that I can even get this thing in the air. *Can I? Can I truly take off in this plane?* All I can imagine is the plane skidding off the runway and smashing into the hut. And then a taxi taking me directly from the hospital to home.

Stay straight; stay focused on what's in front of you.

A Tiger Moth leaves the ground at 50 mph. We must be close.

Gaining speed, I open the throttle. Wheels push off and the ground lurches away. This flimsy little plane, holding its place in the sky. The world unfolds itself beneath us.

I shift my left hand to the stick and take my first breath in what seems like hours. *Stick controls the wings; pedals at my feet control the rudder.* I know how to do this.

I start the climbing turn. Moving upwards into the now familiar sky I circle, gaining height. And then I hear them – Sibelius's bloody trumpets. *I am flying.*

A fairly strong cross-wind from the left pushes up my tail.

Blocking out the swiftly returning fear, I focus on the small movements until it becomes an almost mechanical process.

My first turn is decent – decent enough to avoid reprimand anyway. Hold the plane steady, level and straight. The sun is behind me and the day is bright. The clouds to my port side keep gathering, but I am well clear. For now.

I hope.

Suddenly I hear Mum's stern warning. *Hope is a good breakfast but a bad supper.*

One 180-degree turn to bring us parallel. *Always land into wind. Engine throttle back, glide towards the ground.* A wide descending turn as the airfield hardens into shape beneath us.

I line up the runway, directly into the wind. At 1,000 feet, you don't have a real sense of speed. At 100 feet, you notice the slight blurring of the landscape around you, like speeding on the Underground when it pops up for air. At 50 feet, you feel the surge of wind, even in a Moth.

'Speed of approach,' comes a voice.

What does that mean? I am too slow? Or too fast?

The answer is clear as we descend steeply. Just before we reach the runway, at around 30 feet, the angle of the ground seems to shift. It is sudden, and disorientating. But I've had enough landings with Joy and know what to expect. I ignore the strange upside-down feeling, and focus. I'm supposed to approach at 60 mph and lose speed by throttling back, gliding in until the moment 'you can see the blades of grass', as Joy says, and then put the stick back gently and shut off the throttle.

We are going *fast*, though, faster than Joy would ever try to land. Gower can take over the controls at any time. Will she? Already I am over the middle of the runway. Then I feel the two wheels touch – a slight hop – and we are speeding across the field. No brakes to slow down, and we are swiftly taxiing back to the flight line.

Silence from the front cock pit.

'Not terrible,' Gower says finally. 'Well, the landing was clumsy – the definition of clumsy – but your turns were good and the take-off was satisfactory.'

'Thank you, Commander Gower.'

I did it. I have never been happier to be on solid ground.

As Gower gets out I hang my head, trying to catch my breath. *I made it.* Taking this sweaty helmet off will be bliss.

'Cooper.' Gower knocks the side of the plane with her hand. 'One on your own, a little cleaner, and then come and pick me up.'

I expected to feel lonely – up here, by myself. *Lonely and terrified.* But I don't at all. In fact, the feeling is quite glorious, being up here, encased in blue; glorious, even in my sweaty helmet.

A little cleaner, she said. I can do that, throttling smoothly to cruising speed. So long as I avoid these clouds. I force myself to focus, to be vigilant.

The constant threat of clouds, forming from nothing to throw up a wall or gathering with incredible speed to push you down the sky, is an altogether new fear. I remember thinking of bright cumulus clouds as friendly, almost happy – here they are mindless, restless obstacles, as terrible as cement walls. *Especially if I lose sight of the base.*

And I can get properly lost even without any clouds. The sky is impossibly huge, and my plane is so small. I could follow the wrong landmark and end up somewhere over the sea, and never find my way back to solid ground.

I must relax or I will give myself a heart attack. Close the throttle, trim for the glide. Keep the airfield just beneath the nose. The feeling grabs me, clenches my stomach. But I am not afraid. I refuse to be afraid.

I am smiling as I swoop down to pick up Commander Gower again.

Monday, 19 April 1943

Major Jack Roland's office is large and largely empty, with the man himself seated at a wide wooden desk scattered with papers. He looks even older, his hair thinning to the back, his moustache long and streaked with grey. But his dark eyes are alert. *He recognizes me.*

'And what can I do for you,' his eyes skip down to the paper, 'Timothy Edward Squire?'

Well, he almost recognizes me.

He's offered me a second chance once already. Must

be something he likes in me; or he's that desperate. Either way…

'I attended sapper training in Aberdeen, sir. You tasked us with demolishing a bridge using a time-delay bomb – two hundred and twenty-five grams of TNT, it was, sir. Lethal to anyone within a twenty-five-mile radius, with the possibility of injury within a hundred and fifty miles.'

He watches me, silent, his fingers tented. *I am rambling.*

'We were using Type 70 clockwork fuses. But it was a horrid rainy day, sir, and a Type 67 is a much quicker fuse, so I – it was bucketing down, sir – I switched them out, sir. It failed. The bomb didn't blow.'

Major squints his eyes at me. 'And?'

'Well, sir… I could do it again.'

He pauses, glancing back down at his sheet in confusion. 'You want to join bomb disposal? You have come to the wrong place, I fear.'

Right. He has no idea who I am. Just get to the point already.

'Clockwork fuses are tricky, sir. I know how to remove them, quick and safe. If there were bridges wired to blow, I could stop them.'

Major Roland looks at me, serious, eyes narrowed through his spectacles. 'What is it that you're talking about, lad?'

'I helped build the Phoenix units, sir, down at the docks. I know what's coming.' *No sense in walking it back now.* 'We'll have to seize the bridges intact. No doubt they'll be wired for demolition, and those bombs will be set with clockwork fuses. They'll be set to explode the moment the first shot is fired. So what you'll need is a sapper who can stop the bombs going off.'

A huge, guffawing laugh, like the bursting of a paper drum. I freeze, uncertain if my gamble has paid off. *I've got nothing to lose. Quarter has seen to that.*

Major takes off his glasses, rubs his eyes with the back of his hands. 'Well, now. You seem a bold enough lad. I might just have a spot in my camp that needs filling.'

In for a penny, in for a pound.

'Two spots, sir. There's another sapper, who trained with me in Aberdeen.'

A trace of caution enters his voice. *I'm going to muck up the whole thing.* 'Another gifted sapper who failed basic training?'

'Afraid so, sir. He helped me, ah, not blow up the bridge. Knows how to cock it up... how to stop a detonation, that is, better than anyone. He's been down at the docks, too. Arthur Lightwood, sir.'

I can feel his eyes, measuring me like a fish at Billings-gate market. 'Fine. But you'll both be required to finish your sapper training and pass the test properly. You can do that with my unit. The men are assembling in Tarrant Rushton, in Dorset.'

My first thought – not Aberdeen? – is instantly cancelled by my second. 'But that's an RAF base, sir.'

'Yes, Mr Squire, so it is. I thought you knew all of Churchill's plans?' The dark eyes gleam. *This is a dangerous* man. *Don't forget it.* 'You'll need the RAF to get where you're going.'

I'm as wide-eyed as a posh kid lost in the East End. I'd assumed we would cross the Channel in a minesweeper, or a fishing trawler. But a plane – like Anna flies – *that would be kicks.*

I feel my face turning hot. 'I've never even been in an aircraft, sir.'

'No aircraft. They'd hear you coming, and that would decimate years of careful planning, assuming you haven't done that already down at the pub. No, we need you to land swiftly and silently, and begin operations immediately.'

Flying without aircraft? What is going on?

'You and your friend can find your way to Dorset, I trust? And refrain from sharing any of your knowledge with your mates?' His look says he very much doubts it.

'Yes, sir. Thank you, sir.'

I salute – twice – and slip out before he can change his mind. *My luck is back.*

Monday, 19 April 1943

My first day of leave since the test, and the sun looks ready to give me a glorious show. It feels strange to be walking around in civilian clothes. Clothes that barely fit – I seem to have grown taller since January. I must be as tall as Timothy Squire now.

At least I have money to buy new clothes. If only I still had Nell as a friend; I remember with a sad smile when the two of us went to fetch the goose for Christmas during the Blitz. I was almost too scared to even speak to her. She said so many shocking things that it was impossible to know what to say. *How I would love to talk to her now.*

But I have not come to the Tower on the off chance I might run into Nell. I must speak to Oakes, tell him I have passed my solo flight test. And of course I would like to talk to Timothy Squire, if he's not off somewhere with Flo.

But the real reason I am here, the reason I *need* to be here, is the ravens.

As I reach the roost I see Yeoman Stackhouse has beaten me to it. *Not that he has put them to bed.* I spot Oliver, frolicking, and guide him into the cage. He moves a little too quickly for a bird that's supposed to have just finished his biggest meal of the day. I add Stackhouse to the list of Warders I have to talk to.

'Good day to you, Oliver. Do you remember me? You do?'

Oliver croaks as I usher him to bed, adding a high-pitched whistle I've never heard a raven make before. A clever bird.

'Timothy Squire tells me he's teaching you how to speak. What have you learned so far?'

Oliver looks back at me. Not even a croak. What would Timothy Squire teach a raven to say anyhow? *That was kicks?* Some fact about bombs? I close the gate tight. For a blissful minute, I simply breathe in the air – the smell of the Tower, of stone, of the river. Of home.

'Good night, Oliver.'

Now where is Portia? And Rogan, for that matter?

In the moment before I turn, the moment before I walk away to find them, I see Oliver's beak open. It is the raven's beak, but it is Timothy Squire's voice. The word he has been teaching him, the one word the raven can speak, is perfectly mimicked. Clear as a bell I hear it, and it rings through me with fear and wonder.

Anna.

A rustling sound behind me makes me turn. Out of the shadows walks Timothy Squire.

'Magpie.'

I stare at him in shock. He remains quiet, hands bolted to his sides, bag slung over his shoulder. 'What are you doing here?' I ask.

'Taking care of the birds, aren't I?'

'I've seen the wonders of your work.'

'You think? Follow me.'

It's only been a few weeks – less than a month – since I last saw him. But he does look different somehow. *How do I look?* After that night on the battlements – on *these* battlements – has everything changed? Or does he only care about Flo now?

'I've just put them in their cages,' I say.

'Not all of them.'

He gestures for me to follow. We cross the Green to the King's House. He ducks around the corner into a little garden – *I never knew that was there* – and comes back dragging a great ladder behind him.

He sets the ladder just between the two high windows, where the slopes of the two roofs sink and meet. That must be as high as the ravens can fly with their clipped wings. It's also smack in the middle of one of the most important buildings in the Tower.

Timothy Squire guesses my thoughts before I speak them.

'Don't worry, if the King turns up, we'll move off.'

Holding the ladder firm, he gestures for me to go up. I can't help but glance around first, looking for Warders or Wives, but see only a distant Scots Guard, intent on his own business. I climb.

At the top is a wooden box, filled with grass and sticks and mud – a nest. Portia and Rogan are here. And there is a nestling in the box.

'Oh, Timothy Squire. This is wonderful.'

He squeezes up beside me on the ladder.

'This is Yugo.'

I was greeted with a harsh *quork*, but Yugo makes a soft sound as Timothy Squire's face looms over the nest.

'It's been near a month. Opens his eyes now and every-thing.'

The nestling's eyes *are* open – a startling bright blue that will in time turn a deep brown like the others. Feathers are coming in, too, shiny and black on his head and wings.

'Spends most of the time lying with his beak tucked on his wing, or begging loudly to be fed. Might've fed him a bit too often.'

The young bird sidles up to the edge of the nest, and

Timothy Squire pinches some food into the waiting mouth. *I'd wager it*: the bird only has eyes for him. It looks like the two have bonded, whether Timothy Squire realizes it or not. Portia can certainly tell, letting him up here without a scolding. That harsh treatment is reserved for me. She still recognizes my face, but my importance around here has clearly been usurped.

Yugo now stands at the edge of the box, flapping his wings. Does Timothy Squire know anything about bonding? Well, he knows enough to hatch a nestling at the Tower, something even Uncle couldn't do. And that's not including Oliver, the bird he taught to *speak*.

Junior Ravenmaster, indeed.

'Can't be doing such a crap job then,' he says, with his unnerving habit of reading my thoughts. 'Corax still hates me, though.'

'Thank you, Timothy Squire.'

'I'm glad you're here,' he says, helping me down the ladder.

'You are?'

We wander over to the hard bench – our old bench – and his face takes on a stiff, serious look. ''Course. Thing is, I am going off for training in Dorset. Properly this time – to become a real sapper. God's honest truth. Major's agreed to take me and Lightwood back on. I've never been brilliant with letters – and I wanted to say goodbye.'

'Oh. That's great news. I just thought… on account of your guest.' My attempt at a casual tone is an utter failure.

'My what?'

I force myself to look up at him. 'I know about your visitor.'

For a moment he stares at me, white as a sheet. It's all I need to see. *Oh, Timothy Squire.* My stomach drops like a shoddy take-off.

I laugh, a harsh, grating sound in my own ears. 'She's so great, isn't she?'

His face changes again. For a second he looks – *what?* Relieved? But then the same wide-eyed shock.

'Anna. What? Flo? Are you talking about Flo?'

'Oh, *Flo*, is it? You two got to know each other pretty well.'

'What? Barely. She came to the Tower – she didn't know you'd left. She didn't know anything.'

'She came to see you?'

'She came to see *you*.' He takes a blue mug from his bag, holds it out. 'She wanted to surprise you.'

'She has.' I don't move to take it.

'What? You're mad at her? At me?'

'She came back though, didn't she? Why do you think she keeps coming here, Timothy Squire?'

'I don't know.' His voice is heated. He puts the mug back in his bag. 'To see the ravens? She's read all about them in the bloody papers.'

He stands, and I'm only an instant behind him.

'Does she help you feed them, too?'

'I *wish* she'd help me feed them. No one else does. *You* don't. Every morning I go up there and feed them. Did you even know that? Yeoman Bloody Stackhouse is

243

happy to let them all starve and die. They likely would be dead if it wasn't for me. What would the papers make of *that* story.'

He starts walking away, but I refuse to let him just run off. Together we stomp at a hurried pace across the Parade Grounds. A passing Scots Guard gives us a wide berth. The wind seems to push us faster.

'Don't make yourself a hero. Clearly you had the time to hang around building boxes. I have to help win the war.'

A dangerous moment of silence. His pupils are enormous, his face too pale. *Well, it annoys me to no end.* This little conversation he had with Flo – he's going to tell me everything he told her and more.

We are climbing the steps to the battlements, directionless and at speed. His bag scrapes on the stone wall as he climbs. On the top stair I pull up, stopping dead. After the briefest hesitation, Timothy Squire stops too and turns back to face me. He frowns, not quite meeting my eyes.

'Why didn't you tell me about Bethnal Green?'

'You weren't here.'

I flinch, hearing the thought behind the words. *You don't care.* 'Well, I'm here now. Are you OK?'

''Course.'

'You shouldn't have told Flo about firestorms.'

'She asked,' he says quietly. 'She likes talking about bombs.'

For a moment my heart breaks for him, the boy who loved bombs and adventure, and then joined the sappers and got thrown out.

'You scared her, Timothy Squire.'

'Why? It's the same as they did to us,' he says. Then when I don't answer, he adds, 'They're Nazis, Anna.'

'Not all Germans.' *I don't know why I said that, but it's too late to take it back.*

He takes a step towards me. The wind pauses, draws breath.

'Anna, he's not there.'

'What?'

Now he is looking directly into my eyes. 'Your father. He's not there. You can't worry about him, that he'll be in Hamburg or Cologne or wherever.'

Why is he saying this? But I know why. *Because I lost Mum and he thinks I'm scared to lose Father, too. Even if he is a Nazi.*

'He's not in danger from firestorms or any kind of bomb, OK?'

'How do you know?' I ask.

One last look before he turns and marches off. 'I just know, all right?'

This time I do not follow.

Another meal with Oakes in this cold kitchen. A thin potato soup and weak tea. But for once I am not thinking about food.

'Is it truly a crime,' I say, trying to keep my voice soft,

'for my father to be German? I mean, what if he isn't... isn't a Nazi?'

Oakes's spoon slides gently down his bowl. He is staring into his soup as if it has something to tell him. 'I have resumed my research, for my book on the history of prisoners in the Tower. So far, I've recorded one thousand, eight hundred and thirteen names. One of these many prisoners was a man named Fernando Buschman, who was held here during the Great War. He was born in Paris, and his mother was Brazilian. But his father was a German.'

Oakes looks up at me now, and I almost wish he'd go back to his soup. Something is stirring behind his eyes. *Fear*?

'Fernando Buschman was in London on behalf of his family business, importing musical instruments, and he sent several telegrams to a man in the Netherlands. Mr Buschman claimed it was business, but Scotland Yard suspected otherwise. This Dutch contact could be a spy; Mr Buschman could be a spy.'

With a great creak, Oakes leans back in his chair, our meagre supper abandoned.

'He was arrested and brought here, to be executed at the rifle range set up behind Constable Tower. Mr Buschman was an exceedingly gifted violinist, and he requested his violin, to give him solace during his final night. It was granted. He played all through the night, and the other prisoners stayed awake, listening. The last piece he played was Vesti, "La Giubba by Pagliacci", the saddest song in the world.'

Thursday, 22 April 1943

I return to the crew room, helmet in my hand. A solid day of flying today; but one thing still niggles in my thoughts. On my third approach, happy as a bird, Gower suddenly took over the controls and landed the plane herself. *Why?* Had I done something wrong?

If anything, I thought my previous landing had been my best. She certainly hadn't said anything – no more talk of being clumsy. She seemed quite impressed, in fact. Then why steal back the controls? And without a word, without any explanation at all?

No sense getting cross with Gower. She doesn't seem like the type to try such tricks, but one never knows. Maybe it is important somehow. Maybe I was growing too confident too fast? When I saw Westin yesterday, I lied and said I was going solo already. Not that he seemed impressed. And Westin certainly wouldn't go to Gower, no matter how much I was bragging. *He doesn't talk to a female pilot unless he has to.* I put it from my thoughts like Timothy Squire and Flo.

My knees ache. My eyes, too, from the glare through the cockpit. The goggles only do so much. I march down the corridor, keeping to myself. I check the pigeonhole for any letters, but the box is empty. Timothy Squire could find some time to write; at least offer an apology. Sometimes, when I am too knackered to keep studying, I think of how he braved the air raid to switch shelters and be with me. Foolish, mad thing to do, but I remember how it felt when he gripped my hand in the darkness – how it helped.

Well, no one's coming to help me now.

'Someone asking for you, Cooper. A boy, can't be a day over sixteen. Says he's from the Tower.'

Now *that* is lucky. All I had to do was think of him making a great gesture, and he goes and turns up at White Waltham. Come to explain himself, tell me it's all a mistake – he doesn't even like Flo. She is so annoying, so perfect all the time, with her stories about ice hockey and Canada and ending the war by reading poems to the Germans. I rush to see him.

But it isn't Timothy Squire. In fact, it's the last person I expect to see.

'Malcolm.' I breathe in sharply. 'What are you doing here?'

'Working.' He smiles as if this was the commonest thing in the world. Malcolm Brodie, the most boring human I have ever met, is here at the airfield.

'I don't understand.'

'I've joined the Met Office centre here at White Waltham. I'm training to become a meteorological adviser. It's really quite fascinating. Did you know that our weather here, today, is affected by the pressure which has travelled thousands of miles from the Arctic?'

I can say nothing. Malcolm never says more than three words at a time. And none to me. *What is he doing* here?

'Well, it's great that you're helping, Malcolm. But I have lots to do today.'

He nods, still smiling, as I leave. *What on earth is Malcolm doing at White Waltham? Meteorological adviser?*

I shake my head to clear it. I have too much studying to do – and something I want to do even less. Something we are *forbidden* to do.

But apparently I can't say no to Joy.

I slump on the corner of my bed, frowning at nothing. Frowning at everything. Joy carries on trying to teach me to use the instruments, pacing up and down the cramped room. She seems to have smuggled some books from an RAF pilot. *Maybe one of the men she was dancing with at the Lansdowne.*

And here I was thinking they all wanted us dead.

'But we're not allowed,' I say, once again, my voice calm as I repeat the familiar mantra. 'ATA pilots are only permitted to fly under visual contact conditions: two thousand yards visibility and an eight-hundred-foot ceiling.'

Joy shrugs me off, pushing the book under my nose. 'Tell that to a thunderstorm.'

I take the heavy book but leave it closed.

Joy insists that I must learn. But I can't risk being kicked out – which I will be if I don't pass my cross-country exam. I must forget about the instruments and focus on avoiding situations when I'd need them. *I must focus on studying my map.*

'Joy, I understand what you mean. But at the ATA pilots must endeavour to make a safe landing to avoid being caught in instrument conditions. You know this better than I do.'

'But, Cooper, it's crazy, don't you see? Not letting us learn the instruments? How in the world – *why* in the world—'

'It's the rules, Joy.'

'It's the RAF's rules.'

Not this again. Maybe she didn't borrow the book from an obliging RAF pilot.

'Cooper, just think about it, OK? We are being sent up there to die if it's cloudy. If it's cloudy – in England! We're lucky any of us ever comes back. There's no excuse for sending us up there blind. No excuse but what the RAF says.'

I shake my head, but remember the fear during my solo flight as the heavy clouds threatened to surround me.

'Joy, it's absurd, of course, I agree. But there is no conspiracy. It's just, well – it is what it is, all right? We've made it this far, haven't we?'

'Diana Gaines didn't.'

'*She* had a faulty engine. Something even male pilots can have.' I glance down at Timothy Squire's watch. 'Fine. I will look into it as soon I've passed my May the first test. Once I have my wings – once I'm a real pilot – I will study the instruments. OK?'

She gives an irritated sigh, which I am meant to hear, before collecting her books and leaving me to mine.

I have too much to do; too much to learn, too much that I already can't figure out, to try to master a far more difficult set of skills which I will never need. And the constant ringing in my ears – planes are *loud* – is horribly distracting.

For this to even conceivably happen, I must study the map, carefully marked up and measured, committing the landscape to memory until I see the rivers and steeples as clear in my mind as the room around me. *The pinpoints.* I must know them all and memorize each and every turning point.

No more beer-ups in the crew room, and no more of Joy's ridiculous lectures about the instrument panel, or gauges and levels – none of that is needed for my exam. I may as well be spending an hour a day learning the periodic table or memorizing all of *King Lear. There are real things I have to know.*

I unroll the map across the blankets.

And if I don't know them, I will be sent home.

Friday, 23 April 1943

Malcolm visits the crew room, his gaze wandering from the pilots and back to his feet. It is strange to check the board in the Met Office, and to see him at the corner desk, hard at work with his charts. It is far stranger to see him here.

He has, he manages to say, come to talk to me. He's very curious as to why I've joined the ATA.

'Is it because of the ravens?'

Why does everyone ask that?

Sinking lower in my chair, I try to hide from the sharp eyes of the other pilots. If Bella and the others actually think me capable of… attracting… Cecil Rafferty, how quickly they will change their minds when they see me chatting with Malcolm.

'Why *are* you here, Malcolm? I didn't know you were interested in… Meteorological Centres.'

No need to be mean. He's doing what he can, same as me. I should be helping him, encouraging him. Just not in the crew room.

'It is quite fascinating, truly,' he says, leaning forward and speaking far too loud. 'Did you know that nine out of ten lightning bolts strike land rather than the sea?'

His wide eyes are too much, and I crack under his eagerness. Sitting up straight, I lean forward, meeting him halfway.

'Well, I'm glad you found something you're good at, Malcolm. I'm not so sure I did, to be honest. I find the whole thing slightly terrifying, as it turns out.'

It feels good to say it out loud. To say it to someone I – sort of – know. I remember with a smile how Yeoman Brodie used to claim Malcolm and I were best mates at school, and he never once looked in my direction. *He's still the same odd boy.*

And I'm the same odd girl.

I notice now that he is smiling, too. Positively grinning, in fact. 'Well, that's the real reason why I'm here, Anna.'

'What do you mean?' I ask, suddenly wary. That look on his face is not comforting. *Maybe I should have kept my distance. Maybe I should have learned from these snobby pilots and simply ignored him. What have I got myself into?*

'This is why I wanted to become a meteorological adviser,' he says. 'Why I came to White Waltham.'

'Malcolm, what are you talking about?'

He lowers his eyes, his grin fading. 'I thought about it, for weeks I couldn't really sleep, and when I did, I dreamed about it. The bomb, it was so close. It was two years ago but I can feel the heat, right now, if I think about it. It was *petrifying*. You saved my life, Anna. That is why I am here.'

My voice falters. 'I don't understand.' I search my mind for something to say – *Malcolm, do you have the weather for tomorrow?* – but nothing comes out.

'I heard you were becoming a pilot, and I knew how important weather is. I thought, if I studied hard and learned enough, I could come here – come here and help. Come to White Waltham and keep you safe.'

Friday, 30 *April* 1943

My last landing was awful. Memorably awful. Joy had to take over or neither of us would be here. I couldn't keep the swerve under control, and I kept thinking that I had no idea what I was doing and that I could never possibly learn how to do this, and I cursed Oakes for signing the forms, and I cursed Nell for convincing me to join the WAAF; I'm too young and too inexperienced, and I should just be at school, what am I even doing here...

That only made it worse. Even Joy couldn't muster a smile after she saved us and bought the plane down.

'You'll get there,' she said.

Her face said something else: *I made a mistake with this girl. She'll never be a pilot. She's only a child.*

I cannot give up. I would miss it all too much – the noise of the hangar, the smell of the petrol as you taxi out, the feel of the wind as you lift into the sky. The rush of life. The terrifying thump as the plane returns to earth.

I can't go back to the Tower, to Oakes and the Warders, as just a regular civilian. I would be no different from Flo, no more useful – a spoiled conchie. The prospect is too disturbing to even consider. *And now Timothy Squire is off with the Sappers.*

Timothy Squire and Flo. I can't believe it. He's probably dreaming about her right now, chewing on his fingernails. It is disgusting. Forget them both. My final test is tomorrow, and then I am a proper pilot.

I must go home and get some sleep.

On the way through the corridor I reach a hand into my pigeonhole and stiffen with shock. A letter. I yank it free.

Miss Anna Cooper.

'*Miss?*' Not Timothy Squire. I tear it open there and then:

You are no doubt very busy showing those society girls just how suited you are to becoming a pilot. But if you can spare one evening, why not show them that you belong equally in their society.

It is my deepest wish that you could join us.
Cecil Rafferty

Enclosed please find an invitation to the Midsummer party at Oakley Park.

I *know* the route. I know it in my sleep. Still, I fold open the map one more time, staring at the names of villages and rivers in very small letters. Instead of tomorrow's route, my eyes turn to the south-west, find the Channel coast, then Dorset. My finger traces the route from Dorset to London; from Dorset to White Waltham.

Lately I have been thinking of Timothy Squire. *He'll come back the same old boy who left. The Royal Engineers can't change a boy that stubborn.*

Sliding open the small drawer at the bedside table, I reach for the letter inside. The party invitation from Cecil Rafferty. He must have sent one of these to every girl on the base. '*It is my deepest wish that you could join us...*'

I snatch my hand away as the bedroom door creaks open. Joy is holding two cups. With a sigh, she sits on the bed, pushes a tea towards me. I nudge the drawer closed with my elbow.

'Thanks,' I say, taking a sip; I won't be able to sleep tonight anyway. My throat fills with a horrible burn. 'Oh, God, what's wrong with it?'

'Rum.'

'Rum?'

'Had to make it drinkable somehow, didn't I?' She smiles. 'Go on, Coop. You need something to calm you down.'

I brave another sip. *Coop?* That's the first time anyone's called me that since my games teacher in second form. *I like it.* Maybe the rum will help me sleep – if it doesn't keep me up all night being sick.

Americans have a bad reputation, mainly for doing whatever they please and looking down on everyone. But in their minds they've come to help us, so why wouldn't they expect to be treated as saviours? Most people are simply too knackered to bother, but others get pretty wound up about it.

I used to think of Joy as someone almost impossible – a black American female pilot – but she is even more impossible than all that. She is just a regular girl, relaxed and carefree. *And my only real friend.*

'I'm not like you, Joy,' I say. 'I'm... scared something might go wrong up there.'

Twice in a row I've made a heavy landing. *Heavy, but in one piece*, I remind myself.

'Flying is scary, Coop, no two ways about it. But it's also the future, and women can have a part in it, same as men. Black or white, old or young. And this is your deciding moment. So drink your rum.'

10

Saturday, 1 May 1943

It is a hot day, so I am in my summer flying uniform –
white shirt, dark tie, sleeves rolled over elbows, the
reassuring weight of the shoulder straps, brown suede
leather flying boots, leather gloves with white silk liners –
as I take my final walk around the plane.

My eyes latch on to a figure in the distance by the
hangar. Who is that?

Since that day my father appeared at Traitors' Gate,
I have seen him everywhere – down corridors, atop the
battlements. Even now, in the middle of the countryside,
surrounded by RAF pilots and security, I still see *someone*,
in the corner of the hangar, hiding, waiting…

I blink my eyes and he is gone. *It is only Westin, on
his way off to lunch perhaps*. Father is not here. Under
threat from Oakes and Timothy Squire he has returned to
Germany, never to set foot on British shores again.

It would have been better if he really had drowned.

The thought thuds in my mind like a weight. I take a long

breath and circle the plane a final time. Commander Gower appears not to have noticed my very painstaking inspection. She sits, composed, in the front cockpit seat. I step up on to the wing, hoist myself into the rear seat. I watch as she plugs in her speaking tube. But no sound comes.

I wave to the flight engineer to spin the propeller. Westin could have at least stayed to see our plane off. He must think himself too distinguished to waste his time on Moths.

The engine throbs to life. A glance at the map spread across my knees, steady my breath. I have the route memorized – the sequence of roads, the church, the railway, the low hills, the edge of the forest. Looking now will only confuse me. I fold it away and clear my thoughts of strange men watching me from the shadows.

The Moth ahead takes off. Turning into the wind, I follow, opening the throttle and easing forward the stick to lift the tail: 40 mph. My fingers gripping through the gloves, I pull back on the stick: 50 mph.

It rained overnight, and we splash across the runway until we are climbing, up to 1,800 feet, levelling off just before the bank of low clouds. I'd like to climb higher, but given all that Gower has warned us of clouds, I move into a low cruising position.

Straight away I see the steeple. *One of the pinpoints.*

No. That is a different steeple – they all look the same. One country church is the same as any other. Is that Shottesbrooke? Is it possible that I am *already* off course?

Looks it, by seven miles south at least. First turning point is coming up and I am off track. Glancing down at

the map, I confirm my position. Checking the map constantly means looking away from where I'm flying.

The plane flies itself, Cooper.

Unless I mess it up, and we stall or spin. I adjust my
course, make for the first turning point: the railway. Now
the landmarks come up as and when they should. The
road; the wood, glinting green in a flash of sun; the long
hedge. In my head I tick them off on the map. I see other
things, too, not on the map – bright spots of colour are
clothes in the garden, hanging on the line to dry. Gower is
silent in front. Like a great old stone in the cockpit.

I look down at my watch – at Timothy Squire's watch.
Twenty minutes and I am exactly where I should be. Just
as I relax and take pleasure in the smoke climbing from
chimneys below, a stern voice crackles through the head-
phones.

'What is the name of that village?'

She is testing me – my navigation skills. *What is the
name of that village? Woolworth?* Instantly I can't see.
The world is gone. *Thank God.*

'Sorry, Commander,' I yell into the mouthpiece.
'Clouds have rolled in.' *What is the name of that village?
Wheatworth?*

Gower says nothing. *Will she take over the controls?
I will fail the moment she does.* The scud becomes a sudden,
instant thick wall of cloud. Greyness presses down and I
feel the seriousness of it. I make a shallow turn, peering
to the left, to the right. Nothing. A fogbank, unforecast.
Thanks, Malcolm.

For a moment I can only see directly beneath me, then that too is swallowed up. The map is now useless. How can I pick my way along roads and rail tracks if I can see nothing? A wall of cloud and rain and I don't know what to do. Does the whiter cloud beneath mean land is close? If only I could recognize something from the map.

This is madness. Up and down are meaningless, there is nothing but white. If only I could use the instruments. *Why isn't she taking the controls?*

I stand the Moth on its wingtip, peer into the smallest gap of cloud. Something – there – that could be the rail tracks. If it is, four and a half minutes on a course of 240 degrees should put me down over base. I right the aircraft, adjust the course, and start counting down.

Silence from in front of me. For a moment I had forgotten all about her. *She has to be well impressed.* Time to climb to lose some speed. I open the throttle.

Nothing happens. I try again – nothing. It is closed.

'I'm afraid you've had an engine failure,' comes the voice. 'You will have to make a forced landing.'

Oh, come on.

Gower has cut the throttle on me. She wants to see how I react to an emergency. *And if I mess up?* Will she just sit up there, holding the throttle closed? At 6,000 feet, I put the plane into a shallow dive. At 1,000, we are still in cloud, so I settle into a glide and turn my nose towards the runway. We break out of the thin clouds at 100 mph and 800 feet, into a curtain of rain.

Keep your nose up.

My final turn is into the wind, wheels down for extra drag, and I enter the circuit at 60 mph, the exact speed recommended in the Notes. The ship rolls to a stop.

I start to climb out but stop, balancing on the wing, grey light falling through the break in the clouds. Gower is calling to me, congratulating me, but I don't turn around. I keep standing, on the wing, staring up at the white clouds.

'Sorry, Commander Gower. Ran into that cloud just over Datchworth.'

There is a smile in her eyes. *She knows I've only just remembered the name.*

'Here,' says Gower. 'Your passport to the skies.'

I take the Flight Authorization Card, slipping it into my pocket, trying to control my giant grin. 'Class I' ferrying, of light, single-engined aircraft.

'Any operative tries to tell you a thing or two,' Gower says sternly, 'show him that. And take this to the store before you leave.'

Nothing in her voice betrays the excitement of the moment. But I know what the note is. I march to the store. The worry that has gnawed at my stomach for weeks – for months – is gone.

'This,' I slide the paper across to the staring woman, 'is for my wings.'

Monday, 21 June 1943

I drop the half-burned cigarette, stomp it out. Some day I will enjoy the taste, maybe, but not now. Straightening my uniform, I wonder how bloody Lightwood does it. By the afternoon his uniform is still perfect and untouched – like he only just buttoned it a moment before. Face like a horse, but a horse in a perfect trim jacket. I adjust my shirt again, muttering a curse: 7:30 a.m. parade, and the company second-in-command is about to inspect the lines.

'Well, second time's a charm.' Lightwood is smiling.

Yes, we both passed the training, received our uniforms, earned our titles. Real sappers, pinch me if it isn't true. But there's no time to celebrate. We're being trained for a bigger task. Once again I am sharing a barracks with Lightwood, just off the cookhouse at the far end of the camp. He doesn't get any *less* annoying. And our day's ration is still pitiful.

I straighten up as Captain Pascoe, the second-in-command with his combed-back hair, marches up the path from his fancy hut. Well, a sight more fancy than our huts at any rate.

Anna is furious with me. She reckons I've got fond of Flo.

Have you? comes a quiet voice from somewhere. I don't have time to think about girls, not here in Dorset surrounded by bloody eager soldiers. Two months in this windy valley under fat grey skies.

This is my last chance. I can't ever go back to Quarter and the docks. What would Anna think?

It's an important job, so they've taken all the sappers

– boys under-age, raw recruits – to see how many will be ready for action. How long will it be? Another two months? Six months? How long can we wait?

I risk a last glance at the thin smoke drifting from the cookhouse before snapping to attention and bringing up my palm in salute.

'All right, lads,' booms Captain Pascoe. 'Let's hope none of you are afraid of heights.'

Wednesday, 23 *June* 1943

'Local skies look good.'

That was the last thing Malcolm said before Joy and I entered the hangar. In his voice was some hesitation, an unsaid warning.

We are leaving local skies.

We will be fine, Malcolm, thank you very much. I survived your 'perfect conditions' for my flight test, I can handle this. Joy has the map; she will help with the navigation. We may not be like Cecil and his dashing bomber crew, but I am the captain of this ship and I trust my co-pilot.

Another measly lunch at the Mess hall. But that's not the only cause for the hollow feeling in my stomach. It's almost 1 p.m. White Waltham to Preswick: 400 miles, one of the longest flights we do. In the west of Scotland the sun doesn't set until 10 p.m., and we may need that extra light.

Westin is here, for some reason deigning to help the take-off of a lowly Moth. Of course, with him watching, my take-off is not great. The ship staggers into the air, unwilling – Gower will have some words for me when she hears about it – but I am up in the sky now. *Flying by myself.* Let Westin snigger.

Some light clouds, but not worth manoeuvring around. I steer directly into the cloud bank. For a moment, there is nothing but white. I am still holding my breath as we burst through the other side, our green plane flashing in the sun. I give out a great whoop, the smile wide on my face.

'Feeling pretty good back there, Coop?'

We follow a rail line, then the bright reflection of a river, all the while I inhale the familiar smells of the cockpit: wood and petrol, the leather of the helmet, the scouring freshness of the sky. I pull back on the stick, warm from the sun.

A black speck on the horizon grows, becomes familiar. A returning Moth. She passes us and tips her wings – a hello – and as I tip mine back, I am laughing. I feel like the RAF fighters, flying out to repel the German bombers.

We fly over the chequered green fields, follow the London to Edinburgh train line. Sheep and cattle graze below. After a time, the landscape starts to look different, a thick haze over the Midlands; then the Trent River below, a thin cut of blue. The air gets colder as we move north. I can see cars, too, curving along roads.

I think of Flo's dad, how he drove past me on my bike. What is she doing now? Probably stuck in some clammy classroom, studying Latin or trigonometry. I open the throttle, shooting through the broken clouds at fantastic speed, veering west. The first two hours pass swiftly.

We are approaching the north, where people came to be safe from the Blitz. Kate was sent here; even Timothy Squire, who spent weeks in some village near Manchester before he sneaked back to London. *Where is he sneaking off to now?*

Petrol gauge is soon low, and we land at Ternhill, where we refuel. We take off again and follow the railway line past Oxenholme, the mountains of the Lake District on our left, the Yorkshire Dales on our right. A Moth has only two hours in the tank, so we are forced to stop in Carlisle to change over fuel tanks before setting off once again.

Perhaps Joy is right; there *is* something to flying. More than just doing 'my bit' – some escaping from the world, narrowing life to the one moment. To this. Chasing the sun across the sky. It is also the future.

The hollow feeling in my stomach has not gone away long enough for me to be hungry. But if it does, I am prepared. Wrapped in newspaper in my kit are a sandwich and a flask of tea, as well as a slab of chocolate and boiled sweets.

There it is, just like it says on the map: Hadrian's Wall. We are passing into Scotland. Uncle told me all about this ancient wall, once the limit of the Roman Empire. The wall itself looks more like a farm wall, extending east to west. Did that really keep the Scots out of England?

This *is* a different country; I can see that already as we cross the Solway Firth, up the Nith valley and the hard

Ayrshire hills rising into regal mountains, rolling off into the north. Below, the landscape looks prehistoric. I'm sure that's heather down there; heather and thistles. England has nothing like this.

We are alone, silent, motionless, hovering above the earth. The grey sky robs you of height, of distance. This is freedom. Suddenly I remember Mabel, how I brought her back only to watch her fly away again. I can see them, right now, the two mated birds, Mabel and Grip, vanishing into the sky above London.

Things soon become rather drab, and definitely freezing. The temperature says minus 12.

With a great bark, the engine coughs and spits.

There is something wrong. The exact sensation as when Gower cut the throttle. What is going on? The cold?

We are losing height. *What the hell is going on?* Why doesn't Joy take control?

With a bang the throttle kicks in, and we jump up wildly, hurtling through the sky. I right us, test the throttle. *All seems fine again.* My whole body is tensed like a coil.

Seeing the coast and the bright water below, I don't need to confirm with the map. Turnberry lighthouse. We turn, descending towards the aerodrome. The runway is lit. We have managed to beat the sunset, but the light is failing. Small glowing lights show the landing path.

The wind offers some trouble, but I descend as fast as the cross-winds will let me – correct the drift – and at the last moment the wind dies away.

With a sudden jolt of speed, we land.

Two female engineers rush out to lift me from the open cockpit. I am almost frozen, my fingers struggling to undo the straps. The same is happening to Joy in front.

'Tiger Moths,' says one of the voices. 'You'll be all right in a second, my loves.'

We are helped to a large, shabby bus, where a heater is on. Shivering, laughing, in the dirty seats, Joy and I rub our arms. I wish I'd brought another jumper in my kit.

'What happened back there?' Joy asks.

'Nothing,' I say, without a thought. 'Just got a bit mixed up.'

She laughs, pats me on the shoulder. 'Knew you had it. See, you've got a knack for it, Coop.'

Why did I lie to Joy? *Because I don't want to believe in her bloody conspiracy.* It's enough having the Germans coming here to try and kill us without our own men doing it, too.

The engine was likely frozen. I practically was. *Besides, here I am, safe and sound and on the ground.* I will mention it in the snag report, used to make note of any faults incurred during delivery, but that's it.

My face aches, a dull, satisfied ache, red from the wind and firmed from sun. After twenty cold minutes, someone comes with soup and tea. She also hands me tickets for the train. Of course it was clear enough on the chit. *Delivery only.* Nothing here to collect.

'It's the sleeper. You'll be at St Pancras by breakfast.' She smiles again, taking away the soup bowl. 'In time to do it all again.'

The next week will be filled with flights, but none will be as far or as cold as Prestwick. With no berths in the sleeper carriage, we have to lie on our parachutes in the frozen corridor. Even Joy stopped laughing after an hour.

'You have a sweetheart out there?'

'What?' I say, shifting uncomfortably.

She looks at me from across the train floor. 'Anyone you write to? I always see you writing stuff down.'

'Not really. I just like to write, that's all.'

I am silent. Timothy Squire and Flo. *Timothy*, racing around in the mud and dirt, stealing food like a bloody street urchin. *What would Flo think of that?* I can see him now, cursing and smoking with his buddies down at the docks. *Mr Swift would be* thrilled *to meet him.* Is he even going off for training this time? Or is it just another lie?

Laughing with Joy earlier reminds me of laughing with Flo, that time on Speech Day – I worried I was going to choke, I couldn't stop. Flo was laughing too, tears streaming down her face. And now she is off laughing with Timothy Squire.

She was always so competitive. Getting mad at me when I couldn't figure out games she wanted to play – mad because she wouldn't have the chance to beat me. If I didn't know the rules, if I wasn't properly trying, then it didn't count. For some reason I also remember Flo complaining about how that annoying boy Dudley fell madly in love with her – how he was always trying to kiss her. 'I swear, Anna, all he wants to do is kiss me.'

Joy doesn't say anything else, but an image hangs in my thoughts: Timothy Squire at the dinner table with Flo's family.

'What about you, Joy? Someone back home, in New York?'

She shakes her head. 'Nah. Not any more. It's a long way.'

I see, just as she turns, the glimmer of tears in her eyes.

'What about that pilot at the Lansdowne?'

Joy laughs, and I look down not to notice her wiping her eyes. Again we fall silent, the heavy clattering of the tracks the only sound. *It is clear that, if something is upsetting her, she doesn't want to talk about it. Even Americans don't want to talk about* everything.

The train stops at Darlington. I remember all these towns, I realize, from memorizing the cross-country routes. And I know just where we are. How close we are.

I have a sudden thought, a mad thought. *A mad, mad thought.*

Joy may be on leave now, but I'm not. Still, I could be home by 10 a.m. for first chits. *It's possible, risky – mad – but it's possible. It's midsummer and we are practically in his neighbourhood. How could we not?*

'Get up. Get ready.'

Joy blinks in confusion, but moves to stand. 'Ready for what?'

My smile feels more like a frown. I am standing. *This is madness.* 'We're getting off at the next stop.'

Joy leans towards me as the train begins to slow. 'Are you sure?' she asks for the hundredth time.

'I'm sure.'

'As long as you're not doing this for me. I'm happy to travel alone, been doing it my whole life. Do you even have a leave coming up?'

'I am not doing it *for* you, Joy. I am doing it *with* you. You are a visitor to this country after all, and it is only right for me to show you around.'

She gives me her annoying, knowing smile. I glance towards the door, the trees blurring past. Warm air streams through the open window.

'I've never seen the Tower of London, either,' she says.

'Plenty of time to see that,' I answer quickly. 'And that's *home* for me, Joy. I think I need a holiday. A real one. And you should see a proper English midsummer.'

'So this has nothing to do with the party at the handsome pilot's estate?'

She is grinning now, but I am not. The trees have slowed,

become real. The train is pulling in to the station. *And we are getting off.*

Cecil is kind, and good and noble. He says ridiculous things like 'Good show' and 'quite right', and he does think rather a lot of himself. *But he doesn't lie to me.* And he'd never give Flo a second look.

Maybe some of the others will be in uniform. Is it that sort of party? *What am I doing?*

I don't even have the invitation with me. It is in the drawer next to my bed in Mrs Wells's house. *Proof I did not plan for this to happen.*

The train lurches, then settles in the station. Swiftly, without time for another thought, I lean out of the window, reach outside, and pull the handle. The door swings open and I step on to the platform. Joy steps down beside me, her eyes wide in disbelief.

'Don't go getting yourself in any trouble.'

Too late now. I try to give her my best smile. 'Sometimes, Joy, you gotta live like your hair's on fire.'

Music and laughter fill the night air, and tiny lights bloom in the trees. It's all a bit of a dream. I simply asked the taxi driver to take us to Oakley Manor – 'you mean Oakley Park?' – and we were met at the door and guided down to the celebrations.

I feel none of my earlier exhaustion. The glittering trees,

the cool wind and warm flames, the comforting smell of burning wood. *Just wood. I'd forgotten how good fire can smell.* A stand of tall green trees – poplars? – and bushes and benches down the rolling valley to the pond. Nothing looks as though it could be any other way.

A perfect country garden, even grander in its way than Hyde Park. The ravens would love it here. Instead of the narrow stone passages, the stumpy plane trees, the single patch of green grass – Yeoman Brodie still insisting it is not to be walked over! – and the high walls, they could preen and cache in this paradise.

Joy is standing under the branches, happily chatting with a grinning officer. *She seems to have come around.* And we fit in perfectly in our uniforms. Though I can't say I *feel* like I belong. I half turn towards Cecil, who is standing at my side. He is even taller than I remember.

'Is this your home? We are so sorry, by the way, for just showing up like this – I mean, *I* am sorry, the whole thing was my idea…'

Cecil smiles. He has been smiling ever since we appeared – unannounced – in his back garden. 'I am so glad you were able to come, Anna. This is the family home, yes. I grew up here, and come back as often as I can. Under no circumstances would Mother and Father allow me to miss a midsummer.'

'Oh, are they here now? Your parents?'

'Sadly, they had to retire early. They are up at the house, though it wouldn't be entirely out of character for Father to wander back down for a goodnight tipple. I shall introduce you.'

272

'Oh, thank you.' I offer a big smile of my own. 'I just can't believe you live here. I mean… it is incredible.'

'You approve?'

A man in a white uniform brings over a tray of wine glasses. I accept one with a smile. 'I could get used to this.'

It's the wrong thing to say and I know it instantly. His face grows serious, strange. *What do I say now?* I take a long drink of the wine but all sensible thoughts seem to have abandoned me.

'Westin!' I call out. I've never been more glad to see the dour man, who comes reluctantly closer. 'How are you? Westin got us off the ground today, as usual. Did you take the train up, Westin?'

He does not look at me. 'I did.'

'Feels a bit boring after aeroplanes, doesn't it? Do you ever want to fly yourself, Westin?'

'I'm an engineer, not a pilot.'

'I'm sorry – I didn't mean any offence—'

'None taken,' Cecil interrupts. 'Westin's happy on the ground, aren't you, West? And we're all happy to have him there. He's one of the best engineers Britain's got.'

This could hardly go any worse. *At least Isabella Pomeroy isn't here.* But I do see, smoking a cigarette over by the poplars, a very familiar figure. Nell. *Of course.* Wearing the sleek blue dress again. *Does she have no other dresses?* I will simply ignore her.

After another awkward moment of silence, Westin makes an excuse, wanders off towards the pond.

'I don't think he likes me much.'

Cecil laughs. 'Oh, that's just West. Sour as a lemon, but a heart of gold.'

'He never shows it to the female pilots.'

'He never shows it to *any* pilots, Anna. I suspect he took his failure at flight school somewhat harder than most.'

I should have guessed. How would I feel if I was kicked out, and everyone around got to fly planes? It's almost enough to make me feel sorry for him.

Cecil takes a drink, moves a little closer to the fire. His sleeves are rolled up; I notice his strong, bare arms. I remember his hands, steady, sure – not the fumbling hands of Timothy Squire. I try to stare, like him, into the flames.

'"Setting the watch", it's called,' he says. 'Fire to keep away evil spirits. Not sure it will work with the Germans. Getting more fires over *there* would be more effective.'

He laughs, a low chuckle. I stiffen at the words, but say nothing. Not here, not now. *Flo and her wild rumours of firestorms.*

'I apologize,' he says. 'I am being unforgiveably dull. I am very glad you were able to join us.'

'You really wanted me to come?'

'Truly.' He does that thing where he holds my gaze for a little too long. My stomach does a somersault. 'You more than anyone else, Anna Cooper.'

The white uniformed man appears, taking my empty glass and replacing it with a full one. I do not take a sip.

'Have you had a chance to talk to Joy?' I manage to ask.

'Not yet. She appears preoccupied at the moment.'

Joy's conversation with the other pilot has become more

intimate. I stare for a moment in awe at her confidence. *How does she do it?* She didn't even want to come.

'She is a great pilot,' I say, stupidly.

'So are you, Anna, I am certain of it. I knew you had a head for it all along.'

I pause, my mind still buzzing. 'What do you mean… "all along"?'

He smiles, turning a little red. 'Well, I gave Gower some advance warning of you.'

'"Advance warning"?'

'Anna. They don't let just anyone into the ATA, you know.'

Gower's words come back to me. *You come highly recommended.* Not by Queen Bee; of course not.

'So I put in a good word for you,' he says with that smile. 'I had to, after I'd got you in such hot water with that flight. Commander Gower is a considerable person in the ATA.'

I nod, confused.

'It's a good fit for you,' he says. 'Anna, are you OK? Let me get you a jumper.'

I am staring. Cecil put in a word for me? He's the only reason I'm here. Because he felt guilty, because he thought he'd got me thrown out? No, like he said, I *am* a good pilot. And I have to take every chance I can get. But he's looking at me again.

'Some of our pilots crashed,' I blurt out. I am too embarrassed to control my thoughts. *What am I doing here?*

'There is no more dangerous position in this war.'

275

'For technical reasons, I mean. Strange errors, which aren't the fault of the pilots or the engineers.'

He looks at me for a long moment. 'You mean sabotage. German spies in your midst. It's possible,' he adds after a moment. 'Christ, anything's possible from these villains. But don't fear, Anna. Just keep your eyes open and tell your Commanding Officer if there's anything strange at work.'

'Joy said… she said it might be sabotage from within. Is that possible? From the RAF, she said. Because they resent women flying planes.'

I say the last words in a great rush. It is too late now, I've said them. But Cecil's reaction is not at all what I ever imagined. Laughter at the whole notion of it, I half expected – outrage, I was nearly sure of. But not this.

He is smiling. A tiny, I've-got-a-secret smile.

'Well?' I say when he doesn't answer. When he does nothing but stand there with his little smile. 'Is it possible?'

'Anna. The RAF is not the demon you girls have dreamed it. Far from it.'

There is something in his tone I do not like. 'So it doesn't bother you that we do the same job as you?'

'Your job is quite different from mine, Anna.'

'But we are pilots, too – more than capable of flying the same planes as the RAF, should anyone ever allow such a thing.'

'I am proud of you, Anna. Of all of you.'

'What about when the war is over? And RAF pilots won't have jobs to come home to because female pilots have taken their jobs.'

276

'Let's just win the war first,' he says, giving me his best smile. 'And we'll worry about all the rest when Hitler is finally good and dead.'

I know that he wants to make peace – his best smile, his friendly tone – he even reached out for my arm, and the thrill of his touch was very real. I remember dancing at the Lansdowne, the feel of his body against me.

'Anna, the RAF is fighting the same war as the ATA. For King and country.'

'No.' I shake my head. 'It is not the same. We are not fighting for the good old days, Cecil. We're fighting for our future.'

The wind sweeps higher, blowing west. It seems like neither of us will ever speak again. The bonfire crackles, shooting up sparks into the darkness.

I wander off towards the pond, grateful for the cover of night. Joy is too engrossed for me to lure her away, but the moment she looks towards me, I am taking her and we are getting out of here. *What a disaster*. I basically had an argument with Cecil about the RAF – thanks to Joy's mad suspicions.

'I would never have thought it of you. Little Anna Cooper.'

I nearly curse out loud. I have forgotten all about Nell. There was no glow of a cigarette to tip me off.

'Thought what of me, Nell?'

'Come here to claim your prize, did you? Guess it's true that Cecil is looking for someone… more polished.'

I shake my head, try to meet her eyes. 'He's not my prize, Nell.'

She lights a cigarette now, taking no care to blow the smoke away from me. 'You came to see me then, is that it? Oh no, the last thing you would have expected was to see me here.'

'Nell—'

'Bit much, I know. An East End girl at a fancy midsummer party. You were never one of us, Anna Cooper. Just some posh girl taking cover in the Tower, waiting for her chance to head back west. Me being here must be too much for you. I've overstepped, I wager.'

I suddenly feel horrible for mocking how she reuses her dresses. *Oh, what would Mum say to that?*

'Nell, you belong here more than I do.'

A long haul, and the cigarette glows red and angry. 'Then what are you doing here?'

'I don't know.'

A rustle in the grass announces an approaching figure. *Oh, please don't be Cecil.* I feel the pressure of a hand on my arm.

'You ladies having a nice evening?'

At the sound of Joy's voice I exhale loudly.

'What do you want, Yank?'

Joy does not blink, but meets Nell's gaze for a long moment before turning to me. 'Come on, Coop. This party is getting awfully dull, even by British standards. Let's go home.'

Thursday, 24 *June* 1943

A smoky white morning greets us. Lightwood and I are now officially part of Major Roland's D Company of the 2nd Battalion. We are the only two sappers, and most of the lads are from Oxfordshire and Buckinghamshire Light Infantry. Good enough lads. Lightwood and I have been trained to stop everything, demolition charges, plastic explosives, and all types of fuses. Our final test was to save an unsuspecting cement bridge from its personal Armageddon. Now we'll only need to do it again in German territory.

But first we need to be ready.

We ignore the wooden gliders parked in the grass. Major Roland has not made us go near the plywood contraptions yet, for which I am thankful. Almost thankful. Instead, we run. We run and run, for ever, across country.

'The peak of our fitness,' is the major's goal, and soon I begin eyeing the plywood gliders wistfully. *At least I could be sitting down as we crash into a mountainside.*

'If you're not fast enough, if you're not fit enough,' he yells, 'you will not be part of the invasion drop!'

For some reason this makes us all pick up the pace. We also practise running in a crouch, an awkward and painful thing.

'Never run standing up,' he calls at us, easily keeping pace with his troops, despite his grey hair. 'Spread out, find trees, find cover, but keep moving. Get to the target.'

Rifle training takes the place of one-on-one combat, for reasons clearly stated.

'Never let them get that close,' Major Roland says. 'If you can see them, shoot them. If you see a puff of smoke, shoot at it. If you're worrying about where to kick some bastard, you're already dead.'

We learn many vital things. Brown blood means you're bleeding to death. Never use the middle of a road, always keep to the sides. And that all of this running makes you properly ravenous. *I'm just as hungry after I stand up from eating in the Mess as I was before I sat down.* Soldiers' hours make dockers' hours seem lazy.

Most of all, our orders are drilled into our heads: get to the target. No stopping. No fighting. No helping. Get to the target.

We all know what the target is. And we all know how we'll be getting there.

Sunday, 27 June 1943

I was worried about the idea of taking a ship over – cramped up, tossed on the sea – but *this*. I'd never even thought about this. Lightwood is properly alarmed, and I'm certain I've done him no favours by bringing him away from the docks.

'These things will burst apart if they hit the ground at any speed,' he says. 'They're basically matchsticks. That's if we make it across the Channel. The Germans have control of Jersey and Guernsey – the islands will open fire on us if we're spotted.'

Defusing ticking bombs is fine; it's the means of getting to the bombs where things get a bit sticky. A plywood box with an 88-foot wingspan being towed through the night sky by a Halifax bomber. Major calls the gliders Horsas, but the men have taken to calling them Hearses.

We all know how it's meant to go. Tow lines will be cast off at 5,000 feet, where the glider pilots take over, steering the box and the twenty-eight lads inside into the rushing wind towards the drop site. The pressure on the ears is so painful, we're told to 'hold your noses and blow as hard as you can'. We're not told that most gliders break apart during landing.

Either way, every trip in a glider is a one-way trip.

Hitler will be expecting an invasion at Pas de Calais, the shortest distance across the Channel – a bare 25 miles from Dover. Naturally, then, given Major Roland's love of suffering, we shall be arriving at Normandy, the *longest* possible distance at close to 100 miles.

Assuming we don't crash-land, there is no shortage of possible disasters. Maps have been handed out, in case we're 'dropped on the wrong side of the river'. We also spend an afternoon learning 'duck calls', should we lose our maps and ourselves.

I will not be killed quacking in some French marsh.

Other happy news: the river may be in flood, turning the whole region into marshland, with water waist-deep or higher. The danger of drowning is 'high'. Then, if we're lucky enough to land in the proper place, we face barbed wire, minefields, and machine-gun positions. I've never killed anyone – I've never seen a person die! I struggle to push the black thoughts away – it's like I can feel the oily feathers, crowding out all other thoughts. *Get out!*

I stare ahead at the glider, knowing soon it will be us inside, wishing I could pull my shirt from my skin, or adjust my uniform to catch cool air. *There is no cool air here. Only sun and running and bloody murderous gliders.*

And once we secure the bloody bridge, all we have to do is 'hold until relieved'.

'You ever worry, Squire?' Lightwood looks up at me, eyes serious. 'About not making it.'

I give a start at the echo of my own thoughts. 'What? Come off it, Lightwood. We've got plenty to do before dinner.'

'It's just... I can see it. All these bodies, thousands and thousands of them, floating in the water. We'll never make it on the beaches. Rommel will stop us.'

Jesus. 'Lightwood, get a grip. We're not landing on the beach – we'll be in some bloody apple orchard next to a village filled with beautiful French girls who love a liberator. We'll be heroes, and we don't have to do sod all except *not* blow up a bridge. Forget Rommel, the Germans have been standing guard there for four years now – they'll likely be asleep when we land. Piece of cake. Yeah?'

If only I believed a word of it. Lightwood doesn't believe it either. He knows the orders as well as I do.

You've got five minutes, lads. Any longer, and Rommel himself will be down on you.

11

The day is hot at first light. And I am ready. After a few weeks of drop-offs, taking ships to Hatfield and Hamble, from Radcliffe to Cosford, with one-night stays in hotels and hardly enough sleep, I am looking forward to the warmth of Mrs Wells's house. I am not meant for the nomad life.

But I am eager to embark on this next delivery. *Priority.* A short flight, but an important one. This plane is going where it's needed most. To Biggin Hill, the heart of Fighter Command. Timothy Squire's voice comes back to me. *The only way it could work is if we throw everything at them – every plane, every tank, every soldier.*

I will see this one safely there. *I am ready.*

What I am not ready for is Cecil Rafferty standing in front of the hangar in his uniform.

'Anna. I am sorry to simply show up here. I hope you're not at all embarrassed. I only wanted to apologize, for our little disagreement at the party. It was utterly my fault, and I'm sorry for it. Anna?'

I am shocked into silence. It took Timothy Squire six months to apologize. *And Cecil didn't really need to apologize at all.*

'I wanted to come here – to the base – to speak with you. I fear I've made a frightful mess of everything.'

Not the best timing. I am loaded down; bag with goggles, helmet, maps; logbook and Blue Bible under my arm; parachute slung over my shoulder.

'I've thought about what you said.'

I look up at him, the image of an RAF pilot. 'What did I say...?'

'Pilots don't live long. So I've decided to take matters into my own hands.' He scans the runway, his eyes resting on nothing for long. 'I am on my way to a new assignment – naturally I can't say much about it, but I will be helping end the war as swiftly as possible.'

Boys and their secrets. I shake my head. 'Are you here to pick up a Lancaster? I haven't seen one in our hangar.'

'I'm not here for a Lancaster.'

'A Halifax? Because—'

'No,' he says, with a flash of irritation.

'Then why?'

'As you said before...' He smiles, clearly forcing himself back on track. 'Pilots don't live long. And even this new mission is risky – as a matter of fact, it is a great deal *more* risky, for me at any rate...' He digs around in his pocket, muttering as he does. 'It's the only way I can imagine leaving again. Knowing that I had something – the best thing – to come back to.'

What is he going on about? I can see my aircraft waiting by the hangar behind him. A Tempest, of course, and one of the new models. The Mark IV? I've never even seen one up close. The contour is unusual, I can tell that even from here. The cockpit is bulbous. Why is it so bulbous? Perhaps it is because they've replaced the heavier Sabre engine.

'What I am trying to say...' Cecil carefully extracts something from his coat. A little box. And then, in a swift motion that paralyses me, he has one knee on the runway. All thoughts of the bulbous fighter vanish.

'I don't want one of your rings, Cecil.'

'This isn't just one of my rings. This is the only ring that matters.'

His eyes are looking into mine, and he is holding open the box. The ring inside could be made of anything, I don't even see it. I only see his brown eyes, nervous, excited, locked on my own.

'Anna Cooper. Will you marry me?'

What do I do? Cecil lets me talk, he doesn't carry on and on about bombs and rats and rubbish. He even listens to me, though I never seem to know quite what to say. I mean, what can you say to Cecil Rafferty? He's been to Eton, he's in Bomber Command, he spends evenings at clubs with Nell and Isabella Pomeroy. He put in a good word for me with Gower, even though I never asked him to. *He doesn't* lie *to me.*

He gives rings to everyone. Not wedding rings. He's on his knees on the runway. Someone will see. *Oh, God, what do I do?*

He doesn't love me. He doesn't know a thing about me. We've barely even spoken to each other.

War makes strangers wed.

Nothing in my life seemed as hard as looking away from his eyes.

'Cecil, I can't.'

'What do you mean?'

'You're a pilot, Cecil. I can't – I can't lose anyone, not now. Not after my father, my mum, my uncle – I can't. I'm sorry.'

I apologize again to him in my mind – and add an apology to Portia and Rogan, and the life they could have had at Oakley Park. *Oh, how Flo would have squirmed! I could have invited Mr and Mrs Swift to dinner and sent* them *home with leftovers.*

Cecil stands, as stiff as a stork. A quick glance over my shoulder proves no one is watching. The box snaps shut over the ring. 'Who is he?'

'What?'

'What's his name?'

I blink to see Cecil tilting his head alarmingly towards me. Maybe Bella was right, and he has grown used to all the girls jumping for him.

'There is no one. I am too young, and the war is on…'

'But there is someone.' It is not a question. The only sound is the roar of a distant take-off. I swallow hard. *Well, I'm not about to become a liar myself.*

'A pilot in Bomber Command? Fighter Command?'

'No,' I say. 'He's training to be a sapper. He lived at the Tower with me – he helped me look after the ravens.'

'Ravens?'

'Yes. That was my – our – job. But he's just a… boy.'

Cecil nods without expression. He is angry, but more shocked I think. Shocked and trying to be graceful. *Even now, he is so handsome. Especially now.* He is used to getting everything he wants. That is not his fault. For one bizarre moment my mind swings to Flo.

'So that's it then?' he says, his voice rough.

For a brief instant he looks like a scared boy, no older or wiser than Timothy Squire. I move towards him, drawn by his pained look, but he takes a careful step back, slipping the box into his pocket.

'I'm sorry,' I say softly, softly.

'Good morning, Miss Cooper.'

I hand my chit to Westin behind the desk. He takes it, squints, accepts it. My mind is a tangle of confusion. *What just happened? I'm sorry, Cecil.* Westin reaches down, pulls out a lump of papers.

'What's all this?'

'This certificate of safety is to be signed by an engineer – I'll do that. These petrol vouchers you must sign – yes, here and here. This is a form 700 – you do know what that is, don't you? Good, that's a daily inspection sheet. Use it carefully. I'll be out to help your take-off.'

He keeps the certificate of safety. The second form is to be signed at the destination as proof of receipt. *I can't believe Cecil asked me to marry him!* No, I must focus. The third sheet is the snag report. Fingers crossed there will be nothing to report. I take the bundle, add it to my logbooks, and march off in search of my aircraft. The parachute is *so* heavy that I begin to worry I may not make it to the plane without falling over.

There it is, gleaming in the sun – my Tempest Mk IV. No weapons, of course, due to the ban on women flying military aircraft. Without weapons equipped, though, this is just like any other plane for delivery.

Any other plane with a Rolls-Royce Griffon 61 piston engine.

Standing a few feet from the Tempest, I adjust the straps of my chute, listening to the deep engine rumble. Westin does a slow circle of the craft, inspecting. The rigger, as always, has a hand on the wingtip. In the cockpit, the fitter does his final engine tests, climbs free of the plane without a word, stands ready.

'All set, Cooper,' says Westin. Finally, a smile. Maybe my first fighter makes me a real pilot in his eyes. *Even if the flight will be over in a few exhilarating moments.*

I nod, and make my way to the plane. To my plane. Climbing up the walkway to the wing, I step into the cockpit, pull the door shut. I can't hold back a smile as the aircraft trembles with life. A quick check of my own things – Blue Bible, maps, door shut, helmet on, parachute hooked up – and a glance around the cockpit. Oil pressure – check; fuel pressure – fine; radiator temperatures – good.

Nothing has been tampered with. Of course not.

I wave to Westin and the fitter to take away the chocks. *I hope I have not just made a great mistake. What will I tell Flo?* A man proposed to me today. Cecil Bleeding Rafferty! I think of the deliberately vile Isabella Pomeroy and a smile comes to my lips. But I can't imagine ever telling Nell about this.

Brakes off – the hiss of air somehow louder than the throbbing engine – and ease open the throttle. We are moving, all of us, the rigger and the fitter holding a wingtip each, Westin marching alongside. All eyes on me.

I wave them clear, and they let go of the wings, fall back. Alone, I taxi ahead. My last sight is of Westin, giving a salute. With the green light, I open up the throttle. Here we go. Keep it straight as I surge down the runway.

Accelerating, gaining, a slight bump, another, more throttle, and the nose pointing up. I lift into the air like a banner caught in the wind. I reach for the safety catch, and before we've climbed 500 feet I raise the undercarriage. *Getting the wheels up*, Joy calls it. A little early, but no matter, the ground shrinks as we begin a climbing turn to starboard.

Of course Malcolm predicted perfect flying conditions

all along the short route – when I challenged him on his previous mistakes, he blamed the restless English weather. So far, only low racing scud, and in no time I am above it, my shadow racing across the white clouds below. Above the clouds there is only the blue of the sky. I feel warm, free. I am flying.

Life after the war. I think about it, often, but it never takes any solid shape. Timothy Squire is there, though. *Isn't he?* Could it be Cecil? Oakley Park? *You will have to land any second now. Then you will have to go back, deal with Cecil, deal with it all. But not yet.*

The pure joy of an empty mind. It is hard to believe that I once found it oppressive, the huge, depthless blue. Now it is the perfect escape. But I am not alone up here, and as I prepare for my descent, I am aware of the increased traffic, all heading south, all heading towards the heart of Fighter Command.

There it is, on the high plateau. *Biggin Hill.*

My hands are shaking as I turn to land. *Relax, you've done this plenty of times.* Land this plane and put it to bed, Joy would say. Two miles before the end of the runway, I push the lever forward to lower the undercarriage.

The lever does not budge.

I push again, as hard as I can, but I can't move it an inch. The thought enters my mind with the slowness of a nightmare. Without the landing wheels, I cannot land the plane.

The lever is jammed. I strike it with all my force, cursing. I smash the lever, bruising my palm, skinning my thumb, again and again, as waves of panic break over me.

The nightmare is real.

Nothing happens.

Congestion on the runway is mad, with fighters landing and taking off every few moments. With a whispered curse, I am forced to flyover.

How did this happen? I think of Joy, and her mad insistence that the RAF is trying to sabotage the female pilots. Or is it my fault? I spent all my time on Trainers, without landing gear to worry over. This is a sophisticated plane and I was only half present.

No, I tell myself firmly, I know how to fly this plane.

Then just what the hell is going on?

If only I could use the radio, I could explain to the control tower; they must be mighty concerned watching this display from below. Or at least ask for help. I was not focused – my mind is a mess! – and now look what's happened.

I am panicking. *Think*. What do I do? Fly until I am low enough in petrol that my chances of crash-landing will be slim? What else *can* I do, try to turn back, circle White Waltham? Why? What can they do? Fly out and save me?

I swoop again, not coming in to land. I am stuck, trapped inside this tiny cockpit; I can't move; there is no air. My thoughts race to the parachute.

Prising off my helmet, I take a deep gulp of air. Sweat

plasters my hair across my forehead. I remember my time in the hangar with Westin. A Tempest has a landing speed of no more than 100 mph. My thoughts turn again to the parachute.

Never bail over a built-up area.

The area below could not be more built up, with hundreds of aircraft and countless pilots and crew. Far, far too dangerous to bail out. My eyes blink furiously, my ears ring like struck bells. A bolt of fear shoots through me, over and over. I must focus. I must land this plane.

Congestion is still heavy, more and more fighters landing – but I see an opening, if I speed towards it now. I have to take it. I press on the throttle, roar into the space between approaching aircraft. I am in the landing queue now, and I begin my descent.

The landing gear has to open. It *has* to. A new plane appears instantly behind me, approaching the landing strip.

Every word of the Notes is clear in my mind. I speak them – yell them – as I drop towards the runway.

'Emergency. Select DOWN. Press both emergency pedals forward firmly. If unsuccessful, yaw aircraft violently at 130–250 mph. Wheels will extend automatically. Why don't you bloody *extend*?'

I am yawing the bloody aircraft, my feet stomping the rudder – right, left, right, left – the Tempest's nose swerving back and forth. My stomach heaves but I don't care. Again I yaw the plane, thrashing madly as I plunge through the sky.

Yaw does nothing. I am too far into my descent to pull

up now. I must land. I do it again, the nose turning sharply. A hissing sound; the landing gear, my engine, I don't know.

'Come on!'

Nothing.

Taking a long breath I pause with my feet over the rudder, and step smoothly down, left foot, then right, left, right, left—

A jarring rasp of metal. I feel it, tearing out the belly of the plane.

We have wheels. The increased drag catches me off guard, and the nose dips. A touch of throttle and trim, and I swiftly pull the flap level – full flaps down.

Lots of traffic now, planes everywhere, but the landing gear is sorted. I manoeuvre through the barrage balloon corridor, a little careless, like a bullet dropping to earth, but the flaps work like a charm.

We sink to the tarmac.

A crash wagon is waiting. They will have seen the chaos of my approach. My first thought is that I have let Gower down; that I have proved the RAF and the experts right. No; this was *not* my fault. Casting the second form aside, I tear off the snag sheet and hand it to the flight engineer as I exit the cockpit.

'Undercarriage needs to be looked at,' I say.

He recoils at the harshness in my voice. 'What?'

'I'm the pilot and I say the undercarriage is faulty. Do not let another pilot near this plane until it is fixed.'

He nods, dazed, as I go back to the cockpit, grab the chit and the forms. A man in a car collects me, takes me to a hut where I sign the form 700 – 'flight distance 37 miles' – and search for some tea. *Hopefully with rum.* My hair is slick with sweat.

The Mess hall is a ten-minute walk from the hut. The whole time questions rush into my mind, but I have no answer. Almost the entire length of the aerodrome, the field is more mud than grass. Pilots and ground crew swarm everywhere. But everyone is silent, focused. No one looks anywhere but straight ahead. My own footsteps thud loudly in the space between fitters warming up engines and distant hammering. What will I tell Gower?

A NAAFI van drives past, and I instantly think of Mrs Barrett and her canteen. *No one was trying to kill me there.*

A Spitfire is taxiing. I watch as it turns into the wind, and races down the runway. I will wait in the Mess for my new ship – a Barracuda – to be fuelled up and readied. Every safety measure on this plane will be thoroughly checked.

I will make it back to White Waltham and find out just what the hell is going on.

I take off without incident, the Barracuda a little heavy but clearly in working shape. My pulse still races.

The glint of metal in the distance. My first thought is lightning and for a moment my mind fills in the rumble of thunder. But no, it is not the weather. Again the glint, brighter, and I see that it is a plane approaching, coming fast.

Not to worry, it's not close enough for me to adjust my flight path. An RAF pilot, or another ATA pilot, maybe, delivering to Biggin Hill.

Arrow-straight, too fast to make out, blazing silver under the sudden sun. My stomach throbs heavily. It rushes on, coming closer, finally seeming to slow, so at 500 feet I get my first clear view. As the plane runs along the cloud bank, I cry out, my heart clutching in my chest.

The yellow nose. The sign on the plane – the black cross on the fuselage. And on the tail, the twisted black symbol of the swastika. A Nazi fighter. A Messerschmitt.

He sees me.

Thoughts abandon me. There is nowhere to go; he has the high ground, and I could never pull up into the clouds. I'd be lost and as good as dead up there. More planes are likely behind him – huge bombers, being escorted.

I have no guns, no radio. No chance. *Once they have sight, they'll never lose it.*

But the German pulls up, rushes past in an angry boom of wind. The moment stretches out, on and on, as the roaring engine dies away into the distance.

Nothing else comes.

What was a Messerschmitt 109 doing here? The last plane in an escort, returning home now that he's low on fuel? Or has there been an air raid – London, maybe White

Waltham? *Why didn't he fire?* I definitely didn't lose him; I didn't even try to move. I froze, and I am lucky to be alive – he ducked me.

Why didn't he fire?

He saw an RAF plane and, low on fuel, decided not to risk it. He hoped I didn't see him. But why am I certain there was something else, something *more*?

I go in to land, suddenly aware that if there *has* been an air raid, the gunners will be mighty touchy. How can I tell them? If they'd only let us use the radio... no, no use in that. What can I do? An old instruction surfaces in my mind. Joy or Gower, I don't know, but it seems sensible. *Lower your wheels nice and early so the anti-aircraft guns know not to fire on you.*

Please, God, let the undercarriage work. It does, my wheels are down. I come in, land safely, and, once I've rolled to a stop, breathe again.

Clearly, there has been no air raid here. A scout, perhaps. I will warn Gower, but first things first.

Westin is hunkered over the engine of a Hurricane. 'You killed Diana Gaines.'

He doesn't even look up. 'Killed what?'

'Diana Gaines. The pilot. Her engine failed.'

Now he glances up, casual as you like. 'Fighters are difficult.'

I speak through my teeth. 'And the undercarriage in my Tempest was locked.'

He smiles, a slow, cruel smile. He holds it a long moment before going back to his engine. 'It's a prototype. And you have to go easy on the big engines—'

'Why? Because you failed to become a pilot? Because you failed and a bunch of women succeeded? Is that it?'

It was him all along, watching me, waiting for his chance. I *was* being watched by this petty, vindictive villain.

'Don't flatter yourself. You're not a real pilot, Miss Cooper – none of you are. The second the war is over this little programme will be the first thing to go, mark my words. No one will remember it but as an embarrassment.'

A heart of gold, Cecil said.

'Go to hell, you traitor.'

If I tell Gower about Westin, she'll be less likely to believe me about the 109. That is far more important. Westin won't budge – he'll sit there, calling my bluff, until I can find a policeman to have him arrested. Gower can't help with Westin. But only she can help stop the 109s.

'A Messerschmitt. He was spying, Commander. I am sure of it.'

She won't believe it. But she does seem, immediately, to believe it.

'He fired on you?'

'No. I think maybe he was too low on fuel to go chasing after a Barracuda. He was in a real hurry.'

She is looking at me. 'Where did you see him?'

'West. Headed home. I doubt they know about us here, Commander. But I have a feeling he found… something.'

She pauses, clearly thinking. *Thinking about what? That I am mad? That she should revoke my wings?*

She nods. 'OK, thank you, Cooper.'

'Also… Commander. My Tempest was damaged. Faulty landing gear.'

Gower stares at me, not at all pleased.

'You are certain?'

'Emergency measures barely worked – the yaw did nothing, the wheels wouldn't extend. It was deliberate. And I'm certain I know who did this. Cam Westin, the engineer, he sabotaged my plane.'

She is silent, her face creased with worry.

'I know it, Commander Gower. You have to believe me.'

Gower sighs. 'I thought maybe… during one of your practice flights… I thought the engine sounded a little off. I took the controls and landed it. Mechanic ended up scrapping that engine. Couldn't tell how it'd got so clogged up. I never thought – Westin wasn't even working that day—'

'He never was, when you were around. I may have told him about today, may have bragged about how I was going solo. I promise you that I am telling the truth about him.'

She sighs. Then raises her voice. 'Robertson,' she calls. 'Come in here.'

A stern woman with a gun at her belt enters. 'Yes, Commander?'

'Find Cam Westin and bring him to my office.'

No one is in the hangar. Only a Moth, its hood open, abandoned mid-service. Despite my fear I almost laugh. *Did he run? From me?* Muffled footsteps behind me, and I whirl around to see Malcolm, looking pale and confused.

'Where is Westin?' Robertson demands. 'The engineer.'

'Gone.'

'Gone where?' I ask.

Malcolm seems to turn even paler. 'No clue. But he took all his stuff with him.'

'What?' I say. Robertson hurries, her boots echoing in the silence.

An anger scaling towards rage courses through me. *He's run away.* But another feeling overwhelms it all, a heavy sense of disappointment. *It really was him.* He was the one watching me, planning his attempt; I knew I wasn't mad.

He had signed the safety certificate himself. It would have looked like it was all my fault. Just a dumb girl pretending to be a pilot.

Christ, why?

Malcolm stands before me, peering at me with wide eyes. 'Anna? Are you OK? What happened?'

A tiredness beyond sleep, beyond tears and anger, over-whelms me. 'He's a traitor. He sabotaged my plane.'

'Westin?' Malcolm gazes into the distance, his eyes burning. 'Anna, I will find him. I promise you. If it takes me ten years, I will find him and have him arrested. I promise.'

As Joy talks and talks over dinner, Mrs Wells nodding along, I tell them I am knackered. But I do not go to sleep. I slip out into the back garden as night thickens. I can't tell Joy about Westin – she'd think her RAF conspiracy has been proven true. Westin is only one man, and a uniquely horrible one. This is his doing, not the RAF's.

In all the madness I have forgotten about Cecil. About his proposal.

Could I change my mind, once the war is over? *Like he'd ever take me, now.*

My head has never hurt *this* much. On the cold grass I sit, folding and unfolding my hands. My head is going to explode – not even the darkness seems to help. Shoving aside the pain, I stare up at the night sky.

The Great Bear stares back down.

V

THE SHADOW OF

HER WINGS

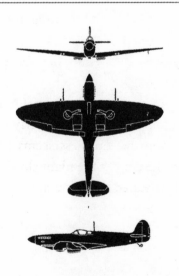

"SPITFIRE"

'They are supposed to be coming. Why don't they come?'

Joseph Goebbels, Nazi propaganda minister

12

Sunday, 1 August 1943

'We have an emergency. Thanks to some reconnaissance from one of our own pilots' – Gower tilts her head at me – 'we have some forewarning. Not a lot, but it might be enough.'

Silence in the crew room. It is first thing in the morning. Gower marched in before Minx and Bella played the first hand of bridge. Cards and money lie forgotten on the table.

'The Germans have found our Spitfires. Their scouting planes have located the Vickers factory at Castle Bromwich. We've had radio confirmation. The RAF is doing all they can, but can't get enough pilots there in time.

'Hundreds of brand-new planes lined up like ducks on the grass, with only a few balloons guarding them. We need to get there before the Luftwaffe and get those planes out of there. We need everyone on this.

'Ansons are being fuelled now. Take a load of pilots, and get moving.'

The Germans have found the Spitfire factory. This is serious enough that they have even dropped the ban on women flying military aircraft.

I *know* how serious this is. Timothy Squire has been going on about it for months. The invasion. *The only way it could ever work is if we throw everything at them – every plane, every tank, every soldier. And then we're going to need some proper bloody luck.*

If only I could have fired on him, then I could have stopped all this. No, the Nazis would have sent out dozens – hundreds – of reconnaissance planes. All I would have done is got myself shot down.

The pilots file to the door, leaving only me behind.

'Commander,' I call as Gower turns to follow the others out. My voice sounds high and loud in the suddenly empty room.

'Cooper?' she says, her impatience clear.

'I should go too, Commander. We need every pilot out there.'

'No chance, Cooper. The pilots are coming back in Spits.'

'So will I.'

'You've only two months' flying under your belt. The others are all supremely capable pilots.'

'I can do it. Castle Bromwich is only a hundred miles away.' I am shocked to hear my voice come out almost normal.

'You've got a Class I card. And after that business with the landing gear… I appreciate your help in alerting us to this, Cooper. We'll take it from here.'

And that's when Joy appears in the doorway. 'She can do it, Commander.'

Gower sighs, gestures her inside. For a long moment she just stares at the two of us.

'Sending a pilot with such minimal training could be the death blow to the ATA. You run the risk of ruining it for everyone. Should a male pilot damage an aircraft, it would of course be a black mark. But if one of us were to damage a Spitfire, if a woman were to damage one, even with a locked undercarriage, well…'

'The Air Ministry keeps a very close eye on the pilots' logbooks. If there is a *scratch* on that aeroplane, and Sir Francis sees that a pilot without her requisite five hundred plus hours of flying… Can you fly this aircraft, Anna Cooper?'

Joy steps forward. 'She can, I—'

'I am asking Aircraftwoman Cooper. If she can't speak for herself, I'm certainly not going to let her near a Spitfire.'

I fold my hands behind my back to keep them from shaking. 'Yes, Commander Gower. I can fly the Spitfire.'

'Manoeuvre through a corridor of barrage balloons?'

'I will follow Joy. Use her slipstream.'

Commander Gower is looking at me, a cat watching a robin. 'And if she crashes, can you fly on and bring the Spit back here? It is vital that we recover each and every plane.'

I swallow, nodding. 'I will fly on, Commander. I will bring the Spit back. You have my word.'

Gower takes a long breath. '"Women are not built to fly fighter aircraft," the officials say. "Their minds are not conditioned for it." The first time we had a pilot burst a tyre – after a *year* of clean flying – they grounded all flights. Held an inquest. Men from the RAF came down, conducted a full review of airwomen: leg strength, powers of concentration, reaction times.'

Gower looks back at us, her eyes bright with anger.

'On you go. Fast now. Cooper, never let that tail end out of your sight. And those bloody Spits better get here *shining* new.'

'But… we can't,' I say, casting my eyes to make out the distant church spire. Nothing can be seen. *It is an utter washout.*

Minx shakes her head. 'A hole will open up. Let's go.'

I squint ahead. *Can we really get through?* We march in our groups of five, Minx taxiing me, Joy, Canada, and Bella. We sit as the engine warms up, quiet. Unconsciously, my hand goes to the Flight Authorization Card in my top pocket. I can do this. I can fly a Spitfire.

Minx begins our taxi to the east end of the runway. The sky is dark. All at once, there is a burst of colour in the sky. A red flare soaring above the control tower.

We all watch it, motionless, as it hovers over us.

Green: *proceed*. Red: *unsafe*.

It is advice only, the ATA covering themselves. We have no choice. The flare is red but we are flying. No sound

306

comes from the pilots beside me. Just as we lurch into the clouds another flare blossoms in the sky behind us, glowing red and angry.

Sunday, 1 August 1943

I have mastered all kinds of fuses and bombs over these past gruelling months. I am a real sapper. And I could run right to London and back without breaking a sweat. Not even Quarter could doubt I'm a proper soldier now. It's what's next that frightens me.

We are being introduced to Mr RAF pilot. I stand upright, my eyes on Major Roland as he says some introductory words.

'Don't worry, he'll put you in the right spot. One of the RAF's finest pilots, the captain here has flown the route multiple times in preparation. Once the bomber lets go of the tow line, the glider pilots will take over. They know the exact orchard, and they will get you there.'

I've never been to France. I've never been outside England. They're just going to drop us in some field – some orchard – with a wrench and a map? I can't worry too much. The Ox and Bucks lads are considered some of the best soldiers in the British army. I've seen them with my own eyes heaving themselves across barbed wire so the troops behind them had stepping stones over the barricades.

That's if we land without busting into a million pieces.

Then Mr RAF pilot will fly back and collect some more poor sods to drop off in our place. Major sees that my mind is drifting, and fixes me with his dark eyes.

'Do you want to be part of this invasion drop, Squire!'

'No, sir.'

A moment of skidding silence. 'What's that, Squire?'

I cough, trying to find my voice. 'I'm a builder, sir – by training. And those Hearses are made of plywood, sir.'

Major Roland does the most extraordinary thing possible – he laughs. 'Well, hell. That they are. But they'll take you there in one piece – if you're in one piece when you take off. Can you keep it together, Squire? A whole country is counting on you.'

'Yes, sir.'

'Good. Well, say hello to your new pilot.'

Mr RAF goes down the line, swiftly saluting and shaking hands. When he gets to me, he smiles his best public school smile.

'Fair point, sapper. Those boxes wouldn't stand a fall. Don't worry, I'll have you safely across the Channel, and the glider pilots will see you to the landing point. You lads just take it from there.'

Not such a bad bloke this toff. Looks like a hero straight out of a comic book, too. *Dashing*, Anna would say, if she wasn't too busy laughing at his slicked-back hair. Just another of the Brylcreem Boys, but hopefully he's got enough sense to do his job properly. *If he's such a great pilot, let's get him in the glider.*

'Timothy Squire,' I say, extending my hand.

He only hesitates a moment before taking it. The war is destroying the officer class, Lightwood told me. No more barriers. *Pay us what you pay these pilots and maybe I'll have the cash to waste on wads of Brylcreem.*

His grip is strong. 'Captain Cecil Rafferty.'

Our test flight begins as Rafferty and his bomber tow us into the sky. The lads sit facing each other across the narrow fuselage, holding helmets in their hands. The reason is clear enough once I spot the green tinge to some faces. I breathe in, slow. *Rafferty knows his business; and the glider has two pilots. No need to fear.*

But I'd rather be anywhere else. Send me back to Disley, where nothing has happened in a hundred years. Two days will seem like a week. I remember when Dad took me to see the pub, and then we spent an afternoon staring at the golf course. The family who took us in – the Gibsons – couldn't believe we'd had enough of walking the course after only ten days.

I will miss you both, Mum and Dad. I will come home.

With a great stagger we are pulled upwards into the clouds. My stomach goes west.

There is no way I am going to be sick into my helmet. Desperate to look away from all the green faces surrounding me, I glance at the porthole. Empty blue sky streams past. The major's words echo in my head.

'Once released from the towing aircraft, you are committed to making a landing. Go-arounds and second attempts are quite impossible. The glider is completely powerless.'

The glider pilots cut us loose from the bomber. We are plunging, helpless, and I grip the seat with all my strength as we drop from the sky. As we come to land – to crash? – I vomit noisily on the floor. *Steady on, Squire.*

'Sapper,' a voice calls after we have landed intact and made our way back to the parade ground. I hear the bombers touching down across the yard. 'Never do that. You make the floor slippery; you could cost a man his life.'

I nod, swallowing hard and forcing my eyes open.

'You OK, Sapper?' Rafferty asks, hurrying over. His face is distinctly un-green.

'Fine, yeah, Captain.'

'Good man.' He clasps my shoulder, walks away. *Decent bloke, him.* A real-life Rockfist Rogan, a strapping young RAF pilot. *Glad he's on our side.*

We are loading up the glider again. *I can do this.* My stomach is empty, my nerves under control. Captain Rafferty stands out front, the men in their kit queuing to get in.

His eyes slide over the troops, find mine.

'Where are you from, Sapper?'

'East,' I say. Like he needs me to tell him. Truth is, he doesn't seem to be listening at all.

'You've seen the worst of the bombing, I'll wager. Hitler took it to the east.'

'He did, sir.'

'Women, children. Civilians dead.' I nod, but he's just gazing around. 'You seem a reasonable chap.'

A reasonable chap? 'Thank you, Captain.'

'You know a bit about bombs. Firestorms.'

Firestorms again. Why is that all everyone wants to talk about? I should introduce Captain Toff to Anna, they could talk about firestorms until they both fall asleep. The thought immediately curdles. *There is no way I'd introduce this guy to Anna.* Not that she'd ever go for a stiff like this bloke. She doesn't care about good breeding and pots of money.

'Sapper here knows all about the Blitz,' pipes up one of the Ox and Bucks lads. 'Grew up in the Tower of London.'

Captain's head turns slowly to face me, the clouds gone from his eyes.

'The Tower of London?'

'Squire looked after the ravens. Bit of a bird tamer, aren't you, Squire?'

Now how did that daft nickname follow me here? Lightwood, you blighter. Not sure if Captain Rafferty's heard it before, but he's staring at me like I've got horns.

'Timothy Squire from the Tower of London? Looks after the ravens?'

Before I can answer Rafferty lets out a terrible growl and lurches at me. I hold out my arms to block him but the impact throws me down. Pain floods up my neck. I rise but the weight of the giant posh bastard tumbles me back to the tarmac. *The bleeding captain is attacking me.*

It occurs to me in that flash of pain that I thought of Rafferty as a real-life Rockfist Rogan. *Rockfist was a champion boxer.*

Suddenly the weight is lifted, and I roll away, finding my feet. The muttered curses tell me it's over. One of the Ox and Bucks lads is leading Rafferty away.

My bloody pilot, trying to kill me before we even get over there. And here I thought my luck was back. Lightwood is here, and it looks like he's earned himself a crack in the nose for trying to gentle this raving toff. *Christ, maybe he* is *a champion boxer. Well, Lightwood deserves that, for spreading that daft nickname around the base.*

'Bang on time, mate,' I say.

He pulls back bloody fingers, and I wince as he wipes them on his pristine uniform. 'What's that all about then?'

'How should I know? But I owe you, Lightwood. Again.'

'We might not have a chance for a third. Bloody captain trying to kill you.'

In truth, he seems more annoyed than hurt. I clutch his shoulder, give him a grin that only slightly hurts my neck. 'Next round's on me, Lightwood.'

13

Pilots, both RAF and ATA, scurry to the Spits on the grass. There must be fifty planes still here, or more. No chits, no ground crew, no control tower. Scrambling from our Anson, we abandon it next to the empty hut. Even on the ground the winds buffet us mercilessly.

The Spits aren't like the one I saw at the base, not quite. Khaki on the top, blue on the underside; and fully equipped with weapons. *Ready for the invasion. And we'll need every one to even have a chance.* 'Take one and follow me,' Minx calls, taking her own advice. The winds whip away her next words. 'Keep the formation.'

Standing before the plane, I slide back my coat sleeve. The light catches the large silver watch on my wrist before vanishing under my sleeve. I climb surefooted on to the wing, squeeze into the cockpit. It is small, barely wider than my shoulders. My hands are rigid on the stick. I start the engine and power roars through me. *No time for check-ups here.*

Swallowing deeply, I grab the oxygen mask and loop

313

it on as fast as I can, turning on the valve and setting the height. But I can't move swifter than the thought: *it feels just like a gas mask.*

Mum.

I can't think of her, not here. I *must* focus.

Spitfire after Spitfire rolls forward and takes off. I watch Minx and Bella go, and then Joy signals to me; I pull up behind her, the Spit surprisingly nose-heavy and sluggish. My growing fear is difficult to hide even at this distance.

My helmet feels too tight, the goggles seem to narrow my vision. My suit, too, pinches at my throat. The thick rubber mask makes it hard to breathe. *It's an oxygen mask. Once we get above 10,000 feet, it will* help *me breathe.*

Canada appears in the mirror behind me. We are the last to go.

Joy doesn't waste a moment, her wheels spinning and bumping along the runway. I urge myself on with a smile.

'Right. I can do this.'

Joy takes off and I open the throttle and follow her into the clouds.

The Spitfire's awkwardness on the ground vanishes in flight. The sky is its element. With the stick much higher up, I simply twist my wrist to turn. The smooth acceleration, the pinpoint turns, the speed. The balance is perfect. The Spit practically *sings*.

But strong cross-winds gust from the right. I open up the starboard throttle, straightening the plane, then close it. The winds are strong – 60 mph at least – sending even a Spit bucking like we're on the sea. I flip the oxygen on.

In a hurry the sky has grown deeply unfriendly. Great climbing towers of black ahead soon reach out, grab at us, but Joy edges away and I shadow her. Joy at least knows how to use the instruments; she knows where we are. I can see no one else, but can sense them around me. Astonishing to think that such huge aircraft can all be invisible in the same patch of sky. All I can hear is the sound of the wind and my own muffled breathing. Then an echo of something inside the dark clouds.

The air in the cockpit has turned frozen, my fingers and hands shaking. *It is not the cold.* I am terrified. Something is out there.

Directly in front of me wings suddenly harden from the clouds. I scream through my oxygen mask, swerving the plane wildly.

It is nothing. Only a flicker. Clouds do mad things. *I am too suspicious.* But I do have a strange feeling, a feeling there is something *above* me, almost possible to glimpse through the grey. My hands are shaking madly, and sweat-soaked hair clings to my forehead.

I must keep my head. Opening the throttle, I catch up to the plane in front, which in the half-light I can see is Joy. I can see, too, Canada behind me. We are going to make it.

A heavy sound as a great weight tears through the clouds. Fast and slow all at once, the yellow nose of a fighter materializes, flashing golden. A great golden hawk, with the taste for blood.

Without thinking I heave to the left. I could have slammed right into Canada, but the moment I swerved, I saw it. An angry, bright light.

Machine-gun fire.

Unbelieving, I pull up, crashing through the last bank of cloud. I'm out. And there they are. A squad of 109s – at least a dozen Nazi fighters, clearly leading the bombers to Castle Bromwich. The world slips away.

They have found the Spitfires after all.

We can't get away fast enough. All over the sky the 109s hurl themselves at us, locking on to our positions. Around me white light flickers, angry, insistent.

Once they have sight, they'll never lose it.

Panting, I fumble with the throttle, force the plane to move. *Move.* One is on me. He is too fast. He's got me. He's on my tail and I can't shake him. My hands are rigid on the stick. I am too slow, too slow.

Pray to whoever you pray to.

Any prayer is shattered in a blast of machine-gun fire from the tailing Messerschmitt. He misses, but he is gaining. I'm doomed.

Joy, ahead, swings back, and is lost in the clouds. I try to follow her, but the 109 has latched on to me, moving impossibly fast now, gaining, gaining. I watch him veer as I do, cutting a steep arc that mirrors my own, always drawing closer. An arrow, aimed at me, that cannot miss. Finally, he seems to slow, which means he has caught me; from this distance his machine guns will easily find their target.

I stare ahead, past the horizon, my final thoughts on Maida Vale and home. I remember being with Mum in the old sitting room, opposite the fireplace.

The air raid siren wails. Practised, precise, Mum draws the front drapes while I slam the shutters and bolt the front door. Mum hurries to fill the sink with water.

Wordlessly, we rush up the stairs, and drag her mattress back down. The distant sound of bombs grows as we position the mattress in the centre of the room.

'Is it close?' I ask. 'I don't want to go outside – the Anderson shelter is so cold and there's no loo.'

'We'll get all the blankets if we have to go out. Here.' She hands me ear plugs. 'Cotton wool is more comfortable.'

'They are coming, aren't they? The Germans.'

'Don't let your imagination get away from you, dear.'

'I'm not brave like you.'

Mum reaches out, fixes my hair with an easy gesture. 'No one is brave, Anna, not truly. We only do what we have to do. It's all we can do.'

From nowhere Joy reappears behind the 109s. Is she hoping to scare him off? *Joy, get out of there – are you mad?* Another one will be hunting her.

An explosion of fire. I scream again, wordlessly, pointlessly. *Joy!*

But it is the 109 on my tail that is plummeting to the earth.

She *shot* him down! Joy shot down a Messerschmitt. I am cheering, tears running down my face in shock, in relief, my hands shaking on the stick. Then I see it. She is off, but instantly another 109 is on her tail. She rolls, tightly, a true air circus pilot, but he is glued to her tail.

Up in the distance, she fights to break free, ducking, dodging, until clouds erupt from her wing.

He got her. This time it is Joy.

She is reeling out. Joy is on fire; she is going down. Again I am screaming, screaming for help, but no voice responds. There is no one listening. There is no one. The 109 circles back into the clouds. Joy's Spit drops, the black smoke mixing with the grey cloud. She vanishes into the storm below.

Joy.

She is gone. I speed over, engine at full blast. *Live*, my mind shouts the word. *Live*. Did she get her chute up? I pull the nose up into a slow arc. My lips are cracked behind the mask, my tongue dry – my whole body burns with fear and anger. I have to go back, turn around.

Back into the storm? Madness. The 109s will hunt me down in seconds.

Canada shoots past and I know that I should, too. I should follow her, get back to base, report the crash so Gower can send someone.

I can't turn back.

Joy came back to save me. I can't abandon her. Canada

is long gone ahead of me. I should follow. I should open the throttle, get away from the storm before it traps me again. The 109s are in there.

Opening the throttle, I fly on. What if Joy is hurt? What if she is dead? This is not the time for frantic thoughts. I can't go back. And I promised Gower – I swore to do my duty. *Bring back the Spit.* I said that I would, that I was ready for this.

For a moment my mind whirls. Can I radio Nell at the WAAF? She's a controller; she can tell me where the air-craft is. I stare at the controls in front of me, certain there's a radio in here somewhere. Only I don't have the first idea how to use it.

What can I do?

No one is brave, Anna, not truly. We only do what we have to do.

I'm going back for Joy.

Break port, that's what it's called. I pull the aircraft into a tight turn on the port side and the world disappears. Through the windscreen there is only grey. Even as I drop, the blanket of cloud thickens, turns black. My blood is racing from the quick turn, the steep fall. I can't breathe. *The oxygen.* The mask has pulled away from my face. I struggle, tighten the mask, swiftly adjust the goggles.

Bloody hell.

What was my compass reading before the blackout? I can't remember. I have been in the clouds too long. Don't look outside. Look down, look at the instruments. It's only me and the control panel. *Stop looking outside.*

That's where the 109s are.

It doesn't matter; if they're still prowling around, I'm as good as toast. Nothing I can do about them now. But I can figure out the control panel. The instrument gauges and levels stare back at me. *Oh, Joy, why didn't I listen to you?* The plane is just above the horizon bar. I know what this means. I need to turn: 180-degree turn, straighten out, and land. I've done it a dozen times.

Never blind.

I tighten the harness, close the throttle. Too late. I am heading in way too fast to land. Whatever is behind these clouds, I will never be able to dodge in time.

It is too tight, too close, I can see nothing. And the bloody weapons – I will be blown sky high. There is only one choice. Gower prepared me for this; she forced it on me once before.

But that was a test. She was holding the throttle closed. If I got it wrong, I failed. If I get it wrong now…

Without another thought, I cut the engine. Silence as the blades click and freeze, and I am floating, sinking, into the mist. The altitude says it is diving. Too far to land safely. I drop the wheels, feel the extra drag. *Keep your nose up.*

A flash of green. Just a flash, that is all, and I yank the stick. I am turning, gliding away, from a certain death on a hillside. The hill appeared like a fist from the clouds. I am barely free.

But I saw it, in that brief second – a white parachute.

My wheels crunch on the earth. I have landed without flaps – heavy, far too heavy. I squeeze the brake on second touchdown, but hold the brakes an instant too long, and the undercarriage shatters. The aircraft tips over. I feel the wingtip dig, and then hear it snap.

My head bashes the control panel. Without time to turn, my mask takes the impact. And even without the gush of blood, I know the dull crack is my teeth. My head spins and spins, and I feel the warm salty taste of blood, the deep thudding pain in my jaw. I rip off the broken mask, pull off my helmet.

Joy.

My arms work, and my hands, and I switch off the ignition, release the buckle and shoulder the cockpit open. I can't see her.

But I can see something else, all around me. My Spit is on fire.

My mind has gone empty. Nothing but fire behind me, and Joy somewhere ahead. My feet run, stumbling on the rocky, uneven ground, the shock to the lungs of the cold, wet air; my eyes blink, blink, but Joy is not there. I am trying to run but my leg has been hurt in the landing. I hobble, unable to bend my right knee, drawing breath in sharp, painful gasps. My legs push me forward, feet hot, face cold, my chest aching, I blink and blink.

Joy.

It is her.

Having willed Joy to appear, my mind suddenly screams for the opposite. 'Joy! Run!'

The words are muffled through broken teeth. In my mind, I hear Westin, calmly walking me through some mechanics.

From room temperature to 3,000 degrees Celsius in under ten seconds.

I try to gather speed, to round my knee, forcing myself to move. I run, a strange clumsy motion, throwing my leg forward, willing my body to follow. Joy is there, just beyond, the white chute spilling behind her, staring at me with huge wide eyes.

You have four seconds to get out...

I am flying through the air, pushed by the explosion behind me. The world becomes searing white light.

Friday, 6 August 1943

A view of the steep blue sky from the window; stone walls, storing in the cold; a comfortable bed, with crisp white sheets; the air heavy with the smell of iodine. Every morning I wake up in this room, I think it must be a dream, a twisted memory. *Almost two years ago, I lay in this same bed.* But it is not a dream. I am in the hospital room, one I recognize all too well.

That time, Uncle came in to tell me it had been Oakes who had dragged me from the fire. *And even after that I thought he was a spy.* That time, I saved Malcolm's life.

This time, I didn't save anyone. All I did was destroy a Spitfire and help light a beacon for the ATA to come and collect us. All I did was lose a warplane we needed for the invasion. I groan, trying to rise.

'I always worried...' says a voice, slow and soft. Timothy Squire is perched on the stone window ledge, wearing his sapper's uniform. He is smoking a cigarette, careful to blow the smoke away from me. 'I always worried that my luck had run out. That I'd spent my ration of it. But you – you have more luck than anyone, Magpie.'

I smile, my lips still split and sore. But I am glad my face is no longer bruised and swollen. It has been a long five days. As I come up to a seated position, my lower back shoots with pain. This time, I hold back the groan.

'I'm glad you're home safe, too, Timothy Squire.' I reach a hand to my mouth, gently prodding the strange new teeth. Those three hours at the dentist were nearly as bad as the six Joy and I waited to be picked up. Nearly.

'Back to your old self now, though. Teeth and all.'

He is laughing and so am I. *Last time, I lost all my hair. He didn't see me then.*

'Will your friend be all right?' he asks.

'Joy was hurt badly when she landed with her chute. Her back... she'll be in the hospital for a while. Much longer than I will.'

'You'll be fine in no time, Magpie.'

'How are the ravens?'

'Yugo is fully grown,' he says. 'So we've taken the nest down. He's going to be a fighter. Can't seem to get Oliver on to any other words. Tried a few things that might bother Stackhouse, but they haven't caught on. Yet.'

He has changed, become harder – a real soldier. But not everything has changed. His grin still has more fox than wolf in it.

'I'm glad you're here, Timothy Squire.'

'I've been here as much as I could.'

I remember, through the haze, him coming and going, making a great fuss over me. Even now, he looks at me with open kindness. *He would make a great nurse, if he weren't so obsessed with blowing things up.* And we need people willing to blow things up; we must fight in order to win the war.

I try to think, questions tumbling over each other in my head. I don't even want to ask but I hear myself saying the words. 'Did Flo come to see me?'

'Everyone came to see you, Anna.' He is missing his grin. The silence is heavy after the laughter. Suddenly he looks slightly ridiculous perched in the window, a cigarette burning in his hand.

'Yes,' I say, my voice high. 'But what I asked was, did Flo come? Did you talk to her?'

'She was here, yeah. She was really worried about you.'

'Are you in love with her?'

He slides free of the window, his face slack, pale. 'In love with… her?'

Intently, he crushes out the cigarette in the ashtray, then looks down at his feet. Anywhere but at me. 'I met a friend of yours over at the base in Dorset. Captain Cecil Rafferty. You know him?'

My mind goes blank with shock.

'He's a pilot.' I watch him, horrified by what he might say next. *Cecil is in Dorset, too? What is going on?*

'Didn't seem too keen to meet me, I have to say. Next time I see the toff, he's likely to go for my throat. Not that I'm afraid of a blighter like him.'

'Timothy Squire—'

'Anna, I don't care if you love him. It doesn't change anything.'

I can't seem to find my breath. 'What do you mean?'

'You must've taken a right hit to the head,' he mutters. Then he sticks out his chest and raises his head to meet my eyes. 'Anna, I'm in love with you, OK? And Flo can't change that, and neither can Cecil Sodding Rafferty.'

14

Friday, 1 October 1943

'It makes no sense,' I say.

We are walking, one step at a time, across Tower Green.

'What doesn't?' Timothy Squire asks, carefully avoiding my eyes. He has taken my arm to help me walk, and I can feel his nervousness. These past two months he has come and gone, but he is always so nervous.

'Love. I thought maybe I couldn't... love... someone who could go off and get killed. But you're the most reckless person I've ever met, Timothy Squire.'

His eyes swim up to mine, and the tension in him vanishes. His eyes are sky-blue, without a cloud. 'I'm coming back, Anna. To see you. I promise.'

I shake my head. He didn't give me the details, but he told me enough – the invasion is starting, and he's going with it. 'No. You can't promise that. Just promise that you won't do anything too reckless. And here, take this.'

I unfasten the watch, now a little dented, and hold it towards him.

'Please. It kept me safe. You need it now. And promise me to be careful.'

He takes the watch, gently, and slips it on to his wrist. Then he kisses me, once, and once again. 'I promise.'

The loud croak of a raven. *Of course.*

As I look up, my face hot, I see a figure by the roost. Not Oakes.

'Is that…?'

Together, grinning like fools, Timothy Squire and I walk over to the roost. Yeoman Stackhouse raises a hand in greeting; his other hand holds the tin bucket. All around him the ravens flap and play.

'Pretty smart, these birds,' he says, positively beaming. 'I'm sure you've heard, Oliver's picked up a new word. Oliver, can you say your new word for the young lad and lass here? Go on, have a crack at it.'

Oliver speaks and Stackhouse's grin threatens to split his face. 'Hear that? That's my name. Lad's taken a shine to me, seems like.'

He is far too proud and happy for me to laugh, but it takes all of my will. It wasn't *quite* his name, and I'm more than certain that Timothy Squire has been the one doing the training.

'Sickhouse!' calls Oliver and again Stackhouse beams.

'Good lad, Oliver. Now it's time for bed, mate. On you go.'

I raise my eyebrows at Timothy Squire, who winks back at me. Seems like he's a good teacher.

It would be a hard heart that isn't won over by these amazing birds, and I smile to watch Stackhouse gather them all for bed.

'See, Magpie? It's all in good hands. Before you know it, I'll be back again. And if you've still got those future plans for us, I'd be well up for hearing them.'

It is so strange. Just two months ago I was hunched among rocks with Joy, surrounded by our burning planes. Now I am home again, walking across Tower Green, watching the ravens play. The last letter I received from Joy said she was at the Royal Canadian Hospital at Taplow, being treated for a broken back. She cannot walk for at least another month, and the doctor won't say when she can fly again. But she will. *Of course she will.*

And what will Gower have to say? What will she say to me, after I promised to return with the Spit, even if Joy was in trouble? I will find out soon enough.

Timothy Squire has returned to his unit. At least we have both said the words – *I love you* – and now, I expect, he'll find the time to write some letters. I will miss him. Most of the time we simply walked to the roost, looping around the Green, extending the journey, our own private ritual. 'Let's take the old way,' one of us would say. Now I spend my time doing the same walk, remembering our goodbye, and occasionally waving at the smiling figure of Yeoman Stackhouse.

It does not take long to stroll around the Green, which is scarcely bigger than Flo's garden, so I cross it again and again. But even Yeoman Brodie, who rails about how the grass shouldn't be 'trod upon', turns a blind eye to my habit. I am in no mood for the stone corridors and twisting passages of the Inner Ward. Here at least there is air, a great open space of wind and emptiness.

I am still weak, my back sore, my legs threatening to buckle. My jaw feels… different since the crash. And the weather has cooled; I should have worn a jumper. But I will enjoy my time here, my time at home because, soon, I must return to my duties.

I realize, staring up at the grey sky above, that I never flew over the city, over the Tower. Once I feared to, with all the congestion and balloons everywhere, but now I wish I had; I wish I'd been able to see it from up there.

As usual, it is cold, the Tower sunk in mist, the air filled with directionless croaking. *Home.* It's been three long days of rain. Patches of the Green shift to mud; water rattles the gutters and cascades down the drains cut into the cobblestones. The ravens, indifferent, perch and cache, hiding food for later, hiding trinkets from one another. The rain pours down, swelling the Thames, washing the Tower clean.

Taking a quick break, I lean against the back wall of Bloody Tower. I cast a glance over at Traitors' Gate, now filled with the tide water. The portcullis gleams. *There is no one there. Father has not returned.*

No one can sneak in, and no one can sneak out. *You did,*

comes an inner voice, but I ignore it, turning back to the Green and the calling ravens.

The new chick, Yugo, has definitely bonded with Timothy Squire, putting up a right fuss when anyone else tries to get him back in his cage. By the speed of his growth, I would guess Yugo is still getting more than his share of meals, too. He *is* fully grown. He has that look, that he *knows* you; he gets that from his mother.

The other ravens hop along, beaks hanging open despite the cool day. Oliver, preening and dancing, his croak occasionally taking on the sound *Anna* or *Sickhouse*; Stan, biting at anything and everything; Portia, dignified and silent; Cronk, living up to his name. Rogan is calmly settled on the rail, his dominance not in question. Lyra and Corax are both wise to the snack they know I'm carrying; Corax marching around my feet, Lyra being patient and wanting me to know it. *I see you, Lyra.*

The ravens and I have established our routine, which Stackhouse largely stays out of. After dusk feeding, a large bowl of water is brought for the birds to bathe in (though Stan inevitably tips it over – not an accident, I am certain), and I usually make two or three water trips before all seven are bathed. Then they preen and dry their feathers on various perches, before agreeing to retire for the night. I am certain that spending time with the ravens improves my health more than any of the doctor's orders.

Yeoman Oakes comes to visit me just as I sit down on my bench. He smells only of coffee today.

'We have to stick together, remember?' He smiles. 'No more dogfights for you, Anna Cooper.'

'It was hardly a dogfight, Mr Oakes.' I still can't bring myself to call him Gregory, no matter what he says.

He has helped me to recover, too, yesterday taking me to see Hew Draper's carving in Salt Tower. I recalled, as we crossed the battlements to the old tower, my first time going there – how terrified I was of Oakes, of this place and its strange carvings in walls and whispers of sorcerers and ghosts. Yesterday, I only smiled. Especially to see Oakes, excitedly telling me all about the history of Hew Draper's imprisonment, and how he's going to include it all in his book.

It is the furthest I have seen him venture from the Bloody Tower since Uncle died.

'As I'm feeling better, Yeoman Oakes, perhaps tomorrow we could go and visit St Paul's? I haven't been there since you took Timothy Squire and me during the Blitz.'

He smiles a slow smile. 'Yes, that would be nice. I'm overdue to see some of the volunteers down there. Thank you, Anna. Yes, I'd very much like to go.'

The barracks clock rings and I leave Oakes thinking about our outing, keeping as quick a pace as I can towards the north-east of the Tower.

Oakes is not my only visitor today, and I am running late.

'You found it.'

Flo is looking around, eyes wide. 'What is this place?'

'The raven graveyard. No one else knows about it.'

I come and sit beside her on the stone ledge. We are quiet, staring at the two lines of wooden crosses planted in the row of dirt.

'Are they actually...?'

I shake my head. 'Uncle just wanted to mark them. To remember.'

'And no one else comes here?'

'Only me.'

Flo breaks into a grin. 'It's like the old tool shed.'

I laugh, loudly, at the thought of us sneaking into Mrs Morgan's tool shed and trying to imagine what the old junk in there could possibly be. 'If Mrs Morgan had ever caught us in there, we'd still be running.'

Flo laughs, too.

Memories of home flood my thoughts. Home in Warwick Avenue. Me, waiting, impatient, in the sitting room. The dark night at the window.

I stare at the door, the brown wooden door closed tight; from inside comes the jarring stop and go of someone practising the violin. I finally go to the door, knock gently. The music stops.

'Yes, dear?' Mum's voice is tired.

I push the door open and step into the study with its pens and pencils, make-up cases, and yellow wrappers from those hard candies. The violin is back in its case.

'What is it, Anna?'

'*You forgot to say goodnight.*'

Flo shifts at my side, bringing me back into the present.

'When will the Tower open to the public again?'

'Not until the war is over.'

Oakes said there would be tourists queuing in the streets then, in their hundreds, all waiting to pour down the lanes and battlements and squawk in front of the roost. What will these visitors make of the ravens? *Likely they'll be terrified.* I was, when I first came here.

'I'm sorry, Anna,' Flo says. 'Not about what I think, what I believe – but I shouldn't have lost my temper. We both just want the war to end, and for everyone to come back home again.'

I can't believe the war will ever end.

It all rests on the invasion. And it'll take Timothy Squire's own luck.

Do you truly want the war to end? says a voice in my head. *What will you do then?* I chase away the thought.

'And I'm sorry about everything I said, too. About Canada. I should really like to go some day, and try chewing gum and watch ice hockey.'

'I thought you'd come to Montreal,' she says as her laugher dies away. Her voice is soft, distant. 'I would wait on the steps, not even looking up at the giant clock. It was cold, it was always cold, but I didn't mind. I knew you were coming. Seems mad now, to think it. But then I just knew, knew you'd find the Notre-Dame Basilica, and meet me on the steps – just like you said.'

I pause, unsure how to answer.

'I wanted to, Flo. More than anything. I tried,' I say, remembering my doomed attempts to find a boat willing to take a terrified twelve-year-old off to Canada. 'When the war's over, we'll go together. I promise. We'll drink soda until we're too sick to move off those stairs. We'll sleep there, on the stone steps, until the snow covers us up and the world forgets about us.'

With a smile she says, 'You are mad, Anna Cooper.'

Maybe she's right. But as we sit in that stone graveyard, with faraway smiles, I know we are both picturing it.

My last visitor today is the most surprising of all: Nell, wearing trousers and smoking a cigarette, her dark hair shorter now, though still longer than mine.

'Fag?' She offers a pack but I shake my head.

Together we pace the battlements, venturing into the Inner Ward, crossing on to the high battlements. Nell doesn't like the ravens – she thinks them ridiculous and loud. *All of us take some getting used to.* She is mostly quiet, walking and smoking, and I stay quiet, too.

'Sorry about midsummer, Cooper. One too many of those fancy cocktails.'

She even has the grace to sound embarrassed.

I try to smile. 'I'm sorry about Cecil Rafferty. Have you heard anything…?'

A curt shake of her head. 'Figured you two would be a hot item now.'

'No.' I look up and see the clouds have paled, thinned. It will be a glorious sunset. 'I think he's looking for someone a little more... polished.'

She laughs, a rich smoky laugh. *I'm certain I've never heard Nell laugh before.*

'A girl's got to wonder whether men are worth all the fuss?'

I am hugging her, aware as always of how beautiful she is – far more beautiful than the violet-eyed Isabel Pomeroy. *Cecil will be lucky to have her.*

'Great lippy,' she says as she pulls away. 'Looking snappy, Cooper. Come and see me at the WAAF sometime. You know the way.'

When she says she'd better be getting back, she pats me on the shoulder, gives a brilliant smile, and strides off towards the West Gate in a puff of smoke. I watch until she is long gone. *Nell Singer.*

Time to feed the ravens.

'I'll be back. It's almost bedtime, so no wandering off.' The ravens give a series of croaks and honks in response. I hoist the empty bucket, letting them know dinner is over.

I cross the Parade Ground, looking up at the White Tower, the stone glowing orange in the sunset. I walk on, to rid myself of thoughts of the war, how it has changed us all: Oakes, Timothy Squire, Flo, Nell. Me.

New clouds hang in the sky, white and clean. Soon I will fly again; soon I will have to face Gower. Soon. Turning to the left after Bloody Tower, I follow the stone walls down to the flashing of the river. The empty bucket swings with my steps.

VI

ACROSS THE SEA

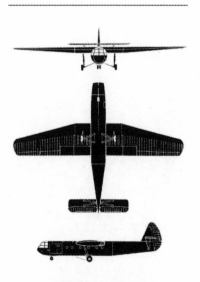

"HORSA GLIDER"

'So far the Commanders who are engaged report that everything is proceeding according to plan. And what a plan! This vast operation is undoubtedly the most complicated and difficult that has ever occurred.'

Churchill, address to the House of Commons, 6 June 1944

15

Sunday, 9 April 1944

After an amazing descent over Stonehenge, and neighbouring the bustling port of Southampton, there is Hamble, the only all-women's ferry pool. Everyone on site is a woman – the drivers, the office staff, the weather forecasters, the operation officers – more than sixty of us, all together, including Commander Gower herself, taking a short leave from White Waltham.

No need to worry about trusting the flight engineers here.

Joy is still on medical leave. When I visited her she was well on her way back to us. She's due to arrive before the end of summer.

I know something of long recoveries. Eight months ago now. It feels like years. The past few months have left me thinned, drained – but eager. I have also been made a second officer, a promotion that I never thought I'd receive. *Especially as I destroyed a Spitfire in the process.* Turns out Pauline Gower *can* change her mind. A narrow stripe is now sewed on next to the broad one. She did not go as far as to honour my 'sacrifice', but she did say she was proud of me. And I could tell that she meant it.

Wearing my uniform is almost beginning to feel... normal. The chase through the sky, the dogfight some-where over the Midlands, already feels like a half dream.

Hamble is small, a single-storey brick building, where cold draughts drift through the tall windows. We have a Mess, a fair-sized lounge (much less glamorous than White Waltham), and a locker room. It is small, clean, and quiet. I've not had a headache since I've been posted here. And Timothy Squire has written me four letters already, the last of which was a full neatly written page. All of them ended with, *Take care, Magpie. I love you. Timothy Squire.*

I also received a letter from Malcolm, who assures me that he will track down Westin and see that the foul man rots in gaol. I wish him the best of luck, even if I doubt the outcome.

Again there are no barracks, so I am staying with a quiet family twenty minutes off base. They have a well-fed dog and let me ride their son's spare bike to the airfield. Mrs Young is a fine cook, and she smiles and calls me 'a real hero' when I leave in the mornings. The house is like a sweet cottage, with coloured shutters and wistaria trained up the stonework. I store my things – including Timothy Squire's letters – in a drawer next to the small bed. From the square window I can watch the River Hamble as it flows south. Broader than the Thames that runs in front of the Tower, the water is smooth – though Mrs Young says the tide current is strong.

Not everything is peaceful, especially not today. Rumours swirl about a Second Front about to open up, maybe this very night. Visiting the coast has been banned – no day trips to East Anglia or holidays in Cornwall. Armoured tanks now crunch through the cobbled streets of quiet villages, and motorcycles roar down country lanes. Can I believe the rumours?

Only certain flight routes are allowed; much of the sky falls under a new 'restricted area'. The girls say it can only mean one thing. I nod in agreement, my mind fumbling back to the words of Timothy Squire, and Cecil Rafferty. It was only matter of time.

Our invasion is starting.

Thursday, 1 June 1944

Thirty-seven training flights in that bleeding glider – and only twice did I lose my stomach. Now, not one of us so much as frowns as the pressure from the steep dive bores into our ears; simply hold your nose, and blow as hard as you can.

Back at base, the men are well chuffed, relaxed, even happy. And why not? Cinema shows, increased beer rations, dance music playing from the loudspeakers.

The men are blind. We have been confined to the base, and all the music and beer in England can't change what that means.

'Things are looking up, eh, Squire?'

You're the worst of them, Lightwood. You're blind as a worm.

I knew to be on my guard when Major passed me in the Mess this morning. 'Fine day, Squire.'

I almost stumbled. 'Yes, sir. It is, sir.'

'Keep up the good work, Squire.'

Something is desperately wrong, even if Lightwood thinks we're having the time of our lives. He's still smiling up at me.

'They're offering leave passes, Squire.'

I keep the frown out of my voice. 'Leave passes?'

'Yep. Twenty-four hours.'

Lightwood, the idiot, never stops grinning. We have been distracted, deceived, fattened up for the slaughter. Now we are getting our twenty-four-hour leave.

It is time.

'Here!'

A pint is thrust towards me. I reach out, the slosh running down my arm.

The soldier clinks the glass hard, threatening to spill it again, then immediately empties his pint into his mouth. Head tilted back, eyes closed – I can see his throat, swallowing, swallowing.

He bangs the empty mug on the table and stares at me with red unseeing eyes. I worry he expects me to do the same, but he only laughs – a deep, hearty, terrifying sound – and turns back to the crowded bar.

If only Lightwood were here, instead of dashing off to visit his brother. I seem to have been stationed with the only fool mad enough not to know what's going on. These lads here know right well what's what. The pub heaves with soldiers, wild and roaring, taking their last chance to get drunk.

No, not their last chance. Not my last chance. I fight it, but the black feeling doesn't go away.

Friday, 2 June 1944

Three nights we've been trapped in here.

Lightwood was as shocked as a fish plucked out of the Thames. Not that the invasion has come, but that he'd missed his own big send-off. 'We'll just have to have another,' I told him. He was still smiling – but that was two days ago.

Seventy-two hours penned up in this hangar. Nothing to do but stare at one another, and try to avoid watching the Americans, oiling their guns over and over. The Red Cross girls are a fair enough distraction, serving doughnuts and flashing the odd smile, but after another day in this hot, stale air, even they lose interest for us. Some of the lads are gambling on cards, and records blast out music, but nothing makes the air less close and heavy.

Outside the sun is high, and hot enough to roast a chicken. I chase away the thought of real food. *Doughnuts and weak tea.*

Cecil Bleeding Rafferty is in the starboard corner, looking for the all the world like he's waiting for his subjects to kneel to him. I spotted him earlier in the day – just when I figured it couldn't get any more grim – and my eyes keep being drawn back to the lordly fool and his shiny little head. Shiny, even across a crowded room, hazy with the drifting sunlight. He's noticed me as well, staring back with a blank look. Rafferty obviously loves Anna. Did she fall for his pilot's wings? How could she?

Thoughts of Flo make me feel guilty. Not that I ever *really* thought about Flo like that, only... she is pretty, and she says the most shocking things. She makes me feel clever, too; not like Anna, who's always correcting me. But I don't even know Flo, and I've loved Anna for years. And now I've finally told her.

And now I'm going off with the invasion.

Still, though. Cecil Rafferty? What a tit. Imagine Anna falling for a tit like that. I can feel my lip curling as I look at him.

That's done it. Here he comes.

There's nowhere to go, the hangar is too crowded. I bang into a card table to get clear of him. He's a fast bastard, and has my arm before I can get free. I try to kick him, but he pulls me towards him. One of the Red Cross girls cries out. Where the hell is Major?

I take a solid punch to the ribs before Rafferty is pushed off and all I see is the beautiful face of Arthur Lightwood. He could be straight out of a poem from school.

I try not to stare around in panic as he helps yank me

to my feet. My ribs scream in pain. *Where is Rafferty?* Officers have gathered around, including Major. Feeling as if my ribs are broken, I struggle to stand upright. There's Rafferty, safely behind a few of his toff pals. I look back, salute Major, who looks a quite violent shade of red.

'Right, whatever in the name of Christ is going on here, can you two put it aside for the sake of smashing Hitler?'

'Yes, sir.'

'Yes, sir.'

Rafferty has a bright swelling on his cheek. *Attaboy, Lightwood.*

'Let us see. If either of you comes within ten feet of the other before you're on that bloody glider, you are both dismissed with disgrace from His Majesty's armed forces. I mean it, Rafferty, I don't care who your father is, I'll find another pilot in a heartbeat. Another pilot who is not a complete insubordinate fool. And you, Sapper, you can crawl back under whatever rock you came from and take your little enforcer with you. Do you both understand me?'

'Yes, sir.'

'Yes, sir.'

Sunday, 4 June 1944

My pockets and pouches bulge with chocolate bars, grenades, spare socks and underwear, and a French phrase book. I also carry a shoulder bag with six Mills 36 grenades, four 77 phosphorous smoke grenades, and fuel for the small Tommy cooker, along with a lighter and cigarettes, sheets of toilet paper, and a water-purifier kit.

Tea bags are stuffed inside both trouser legs. *Ruined, if Lord Rafferty ditches us in marshland.* The weight of it all is enormous. I take a step, almost fall, find my balance. I will not be moving quickly with this on my back. *And with this bruise on my ribs.*

A slightly smaller bag is slung around the neck – escape kit: map printed on silk, compass, knife, and money. And, of course, my first-aid box: bandages, and two needles of morphine.

One for pain, two for eternity.

Base is like a kicked anthill, but Major calls us to order. The gliders are ready for loading. We are set to leave in the hours before dawn. But Major has his customary few words – in fact, he says very little, instead reading us a message from General Eisenhower, the Supreme Commander, every word of which sends shivers running up and down my back.

'Soldiers, sailors, and airmen of the Allied Expeditionary Force! You are about to embark upon the Great Crusade, towards which we have striven these many months. The eyes of the world are upon you. The hopes and prayers of liberty-loving people everywhere march with you. In company with our brave allies and brothers in arms on the other fronts, you will bring about the destruction of the German war machine, the elimination of Nazi tyranny over the oppressed peoples of Europe, and security for ourselves in a free world.'

So this is finally it; we are going over. *Time to go and meet Rommel.* Time to board a bleeding glider that's supposed to carry us to the Desert Fox and his waiting armies. Hold until relieved. *Hold until relieved.*

Of course I am afraid – terrified – but I am also committed. I truly *am* ready, or as ready as I can ever be. All I need is to think of the panic, the fear inside Bethnal Green Station. If I let myself, I can still *feel* the bodies.

We can't go on living like this. We have to go over there and smash these bastards. The eyes of the world are on us.

I glance down at my watch. My grampa's watch. It kept him safe; it kept Anna safe. Maybe it'll give me the luck I need. It is time to go. But no one is cracking on yet. I watch, through the small window, the half-moon rise and rise.

A grey snarl of clouds surrounds us, filling the sky. Great climbing towers of cloud from the west and gales from the north – the massive downpour and high winds have sent the seas berserk. My prayers did not work.

Or maybe they did.

Midnight has dawned with a storm. We are going over, but not in the blasting rain. Not today. The lads sense it. I haven't the heart to look at them, now that they're all blacked-up and properly terrifying. Of course we've done the same – my face is smeared in soot – but to see them all, the whole group of Ox and Bucks lads, looking like ghosts… I turn back to the clouds.

'Looks like we're staying put,' says Lightwood, the relief in his voice too clear.

'Maybe,' I say.

'Right, lads,' calls Major's voice, cracking like a whip. 'Back inside.'

My whole body melts with relief, and a smile shoots on to my face before I can force it down. Even the pack suddenly feels light.

Some kind of second chance. *For what?*

Monday, 5 June 1944

'Better here than out there,' Lightwood says. The sounds of rain lash the hangar.

I nod. I know what he means. It's difficult to imagine the thousands – the *tens of thousands* – of men in boats anchored to the coast thrown around and blasted by waves. Just the thought of it makes my stomach lurch.

The bleeding Phoenix, finally being put to use. I hope to God that the harbours – or whatever they are – won't sink on account of some dodgy rebar. *I tied the steel bars as well as I could.* And it's far too late to worry now.

But there is little else to do as the slow hours pass. A soldier, looking dead asleep, half-opens his eyes to peek before dropping them shut again. I would wager most of the men with their eyes closed are faking it. No one could sleep, not knowing what's to come. *And knowing what has to come, sooner or later.*

The air sneaking through the window is warm. Summer has chased away the spring chill. A long spring – a good spring. But I am not thinking about the spring. I am thinking, of all things, of a game of Monopoly Anna and I played in her hospital room. Anna rolling her dice and laughing. During the Blitz, we used to spend hours in the study before it burned down, playing games and sharing a Thermos of tea. I can still hear her cackling away at some great move, some lucky roll. *Steady on, Squire.*

I light a cigarette. 'Lightwood?'

He declines and after another puff, I crush mine out, too.

A heavy force hits my back and I leap away, certain Rafferty has resumed his attack. But the eyes that meet mine flash with humour. 'You Limeys need to relax,' a tall American says. He must be on stilts, looming over me like some great cocky tree. 'We'll take care of you out there.'

He slaps me on the back again and walks away. Lightwood watches him go, likely grateful not to have been manhandled in passing. I am more than thrilled for the paratroopers' help – they are big, strong, and clearly know what they're doing with their weapons.

But I know the truth.

We're going first. D Company is the first group to take off, ahead of the pathfinders, the paratroopers, the most battle-hardened American Airborne Division. *Hold until relieved.* Our mad Captain Rafferty will see ours are the first feet on the ground. *And then he'll fly off to safety.*

I decide to try again with another cigarette. This time Lightwood accepts, too. American soldiers file past the window, faces blackened, helmets pulled low. I watch their faces, marvelling at how calm they are. My own reflection mirrors back at me, like a terrified boy playing dress-up. Still, I stare through the window, ignoring my own face in the glass, focusing on those men on the other side, strong, confident. None of them look over; they simply march past, vanishing from sight.

All at once it hits me, like another sucker punch in the ribs, and the cigarette slips, burning, from my fingers. *The man in the window. Across the street from 78 Catesby Street.*

He's been there the whole time, watching to see who comes.

Anna's father.

Of course he didn't give me his real address. He's been hiding across the street, watching. Watching and laughing at me and Lightwood.

What if he comes after Anna? No one knows he's there. If Rafferty's landing kills me… I have to tell her the truth.

I turn from the window, wishing the last thing I saw wasn't my own terrified expression. 'I have to leave.'

Lightwood looks at me calmly. 'No one can leave.'

'It's important. It's about… Anna.'

'She knows you love her, mate.'

I blink in shock, but don't have time to try and under-stand Lightwood. *How does he know?*

'Listen to me. This is important. There is someone I have to see – something I have to do – in order to keep her safe.'

'Now?'

'There is no later, Lightwood. Not for me.'

Lightwood squints his eyes at me. 'You mean to try getting out of here?'

I let the immense weight of the pack slide to the ground, start unloading my pockets and pouches. A sapper's got to use his head.

'You just watch my kit – please, mate. I'll scrub my face off, dash off, be back before nightfall.'

'You're going to dash off? Squire, the second this rain stops, we're leaving.'

'The rain won't stop – I have time. I'll be in Southampton in less than an hour. Just – please, mate. Watch my kit, and cover if anyone asks for me. Yeah?'

'Southampton—?'

I am already walking away. My excuse, I can only hope as I wash my face clean in the sink, is mad enough to work. *This is well beyond mad, even for me.*

'Where are you off to, Sapper?'

'Chemist,' I say, meeting the guard's eyes. My heart is beating so loud I'm certain he can hear it, too. 'Major's orders, on account of all the rain: two hundred French letters for keeping the rifles dry. He says if we can't keep the barrels dry, there's no sense carrying the bloody things around. Didn't want me going with the face paint, though – keeping everything secret and all. Do you think I can borrow that motorcycle? Yeah, I figure no one will be using it for a while. Thanks, mate. Back in two ticks.'

I stand in front of the abandoned house. Of course the bloody rain has dried up but I can't think about that. It took me nearly three hours to get here; the motorcycle ride to Southampton took close to an hour. I barely even got to enjoy it. The train journey to London took an hour and a half and I didn't enjoy that at all.

The moment I told Anna the truth, she was off like a shot to see him. I could do nothing but follow along. At least she promised to stay out of sight until I've confirmed the German has no weapons. *Will she let me arrest him?*

I have to confront the bastard. He lied to Anna, he's likely helping organize an attack on Britain. Now, with all the training, the hundreds of miles, the combat drills, *I am ready.*

The abandoned house stares back at me.

They will leave without you. Lightwood can't disarm the bridge himself – not in the five minutes he's got; I'll go to gaol for this. The lads are leaving *now.*

Not yet.

Let him see me. As soon as he does, he will come. Now that I am alone, not a threat. Just a boy walking into a trap.

The air is heavy, damp – I could squeeze water from it with my fists. *Where is he?* My heart is thumping like I'm about to leap out of a glider without a bloody pack. I almost wish I was. *If I'm wrong about this...*

'Ah, the young friend.'

I turn slowly to watch him advance. No hat this time. Blood pounds in my ears. The German approaches from across the street, where he's been hiding. Where he's been the whole time. The truth of it burns like bleeding hell.

Likely he's getting ready to gloat about it now, that quiet small smile on his face. 'You've come alone this time.'

'No, he hasn't,' comes a voice.

From behind the wall steps Anna.

He is looking at me. Father.

His hair, pale as moonlight, is cut short. He does not seem so thin, so wild, this time. He looks almost like the man from the photograph. *He is the man from the photograph. Isn't he?*

I couldn't believe it, when Timothy Squire arrived at Hamble on a motorcycle. I'd written the number for Hamble in a letter; he could have rung, even if the R/T operator thought it was a sweetheart calling. But he said it was urgent, that we had to get to Southampton Station *this moment*, and so we came together. He explained what he could on the shuddering train to Waterloo.

I am grateful to be in my uniform. Somehow I feel braver. Though not as brave as Timothy Squire, who is tall and strong in his green sapper's uniform. He looks proud, dark from the sun. Older. *He stole a motorcycle; he risked his job – his freedom – to bring me here. To finally tell me the truth*.

He made me promise to wait, to make sure the German didn't have a weapon, before I showed myself. *But I've waited long enough*.

The German looks shocked and immediately nervous. Are there others, he must be thinking – Yeoman Oakes, the police?

'You came.'

I shiver, but do not look away. 'You stayed.'

'Anna. Anna, I am sorry about your mother.'

'Are you?' I manage to ask, tearing my eyes away from his face. Timothy Squire stands just a few feet to the side. Respectful, but wary.

'I knew she was... distressed. I should have done more.'

'Then why did you leave? Why then, and not now?'

His face tightens, the high cheekbones drawn in. *Like mine*. His ears, though, are nothing like mine, sticking out at the top. 'I had to come back for you, no matter what the danger. I tried, but I couldn't come sooner. But when I heard about your mother... If Gregory Oakes hadn't lied to me, I would have found you earlier—'

'What was the song?'

We stare at each other in the stunned silence that

354

follows. I know nothing about this man. All I remember is some music from behind the study door.

'What was the song?' I ask again, this time breaking through. 'The song you played in your study. I remember it, your violin.'

'There were many.' His voice is raw. *With what – Sadness? Grief? Anger?* 'I believe the one you mean is called, "The Lark Ascending".'

'Mum tried to play it. I would hear her, behind the closed door, trying to play it. You left your violin behind.'

Oh, Mum. You just made up his memory, created him from nothing. A violinist who drowned when I was too young to memorize anything about him. Only an old photograph and some song about a lark.

'I had to leave, Anna. I had an... opportunity. I had to return to Germany.'

I am surprised how steady my voice is. 'You are a scientist?'

'An engineer.'

Timothy Squire's head swivels at this, but I don't have time to worry about him. This strange man – this engineer – is looking at me with pleading eyes.

'There is something coming, and you cannot be here when it does. You must believe me. I... worked there. For a time. It is why I left England, though I did not know...' He trails off, but finds his thoughts once more. 'The Nazis have new weapons. They will be ready now, I am sure of it.'

Worked there? Oakes's words come back to me: *He left*

355

to take some scientific post. Why will no one tell me the truth? *We all have secrets. We all try to do what is best.*

Timothy Squire interrupts. 'I wouldn't worry about *you* – you Nazis – attacking.'

The German shakes his head dismissively. 'Hitler knew Churchill would try to invade. He has the weapons ready. The FZG-76 – two tons, twenty-five feet long, a wingspan of sixteen feet. A warhead with two thousand pounds of explosives. *Vergeltungswaffen*, they are called. Vengeance Weapons.'

Timothy Squire moves between us, facing the German. 'I don't care what he calls them,' Timothy Squire says. 'A self-propelled missile is *impossible*.'

'They are rockets. With a range of two hundred and fifty miles, they can be launched from Holland. If the technology has been perfected... there is nothing you can do.'

'Bollocks. They could never be accurately targeted—'

'Of course not. That is precisely their use.'

'It's time for Hitler to experience *our* blitzkrieg!' Timothy Squire's voice is hot with anger.

'They must test them,' I say, my mind snatching at any chance. 'Where?'

The man turns to me. 'Poland.'

'You know where the building site is? We must alert Bomber Command.'

'They've already been. The research site was destroyed last year. They have moved into the mountains now. Maybe even inside the mountains. We can't get at them now.'

'"*We*"?' comes Timothy Squire's outraged voice.

I feel confused, dizzy, and worry for a moment that I might sick up. The new weapon, targeting us even as we target them. The V1s.

And Mum's words, from so long ago. *Wars are always lost.*

'You must go,' I say, and both sets of eyes sweep back to me. The German's eyes are blue, and filled with concern. That always-serious face – never the hint of a smile. I push the image of the photograph from my mind. He is useful; he can help us, somehow. *He said 'we'.* 'You must trust me.'

'I do,' he says, simply.

Timothy Squire says nothing. I will explain to him later.

'Go to Ireland.' My throat constricts but again I say the words. 'I will write to you there.'

I can feel Timothy Squire lurch. His voice comes as though from a great distance. 'Anna, no—'

'I will wait for you, Anna,' the man, Will Esser, says. Hope washes the anger from his voice.

I can't let Timothy Squire have him arrested. I think of Oakes's story, of the sad man playing the violin in his cell the night before his execution. I can hear the music, that song I heard on the radio back in the crew room – 'The Lark Ascending' – and I know it is the same music I heard from Father's study. The only thing I remembered about him.

I hear it now, and I see him – his blue eyes, his heavily lined face, his hair, pale as moonlight – playing the violin in his gaol cell.

I look at Timothy Squire, his face fixed in horror, clearly sorry to have brought me here, to have ever told me the truth, and then my gaze turns to the German. His hopeful blue eyes, the hint of a smile. Will Esser.

My father.

Monday, 5 June 1943

Helmets are netted and painted in green and brown camouflage. Boots are tight as possible, straps even tighter. Faces are smeared in coal. Lightwood pulls out two fags, lights them both, hands me mine.

'Luckiest prick in Britain. Glad you'll be with us.'

I nod in thanks, my heart still throbbing in my chest. It took even longer to get back, nearly four hours – I almost ran out of petrol on the forest road – and I've missed the entire day. A different guard, thank the Lord, was at the gate, and after I told him the chemist story he was smirking as he let me past.

No one is smirking now. We're so heavy in armour and gear, like those bleeding knights from the Tower display trying to mount horses. *The Line of Kings*. There are no kings here, no great leader at the head of the charge. Just some good lads and that bollocks Rafferty.

And the Yanks. Instead of the stove soot we have used, the Americans have added some kind of polish – their faces have streaks of white, strange, fearful patterns. All of them have shaved their heads bald. The Yanks who have even more gear than us – guns strapped across chests in what looked like instrument cases, machine guns, bazookas, great commando knives and revolvers, patches of eagles and American flags on their shoulders. *And parachutes.* Shouldn't we all have parachutes? *The glider has a parachute, I remind myself.*

Three gliders are headed to the Caen Canal; three to the Orne River. Luckily, both missions have a glider full of Yanks alongside the two British ones. Some of the lads grumble that we've already had too much of a war, and the Yanks haven't had a bit of one. For myself, I'm more than grateful to have them take care of the Germans guarding the bridges. All I have to worry about is defusing the bombs. *Which I can do in my sleep.*

The days of rain have left the runway skimmed with puddles. I waddle ahead, the end of a shrinking queue. Nine more lads and I'm on board. We've got forty minutes to load the gliders – take-off time is 22:56 – and we're set to use every second. We are glider number three, right in the middle of the pack – now crammed tight with a Jeep and two anti-tank guns.

I mucked everything up bringing Anna along with me. She can't hate the man; he's her father. *What will she do now?* I have to warn someone. Not the police, they'll have him arrested on the spot, and Anna will go off on me. Should I post a letter to Oakes? No, he'd rally the Warders and the Scots Guard and God knows who else. What am I meant to do?

Now that he's seen her, he'll do anything to be with her.

I can't leave Anna at the mercy of a madman, even if he is her father.

I have to tell someone, and fast.

Six more lads and I'm on. Stuffed in the plywood box with vehicles and massive guns, men on both sides of me, men across from me, all as calm as they can trick themselves to be. All certain that this might well be the end. *One hour in the air, then we're across.* I've done this thirty-seven times.

Then we land.

We've all seen the aerial photos, to get the lay of the countryside. We've also seen the great forests of anti-glider stakes – 'Rommel's asparagus', the lads call them – waiting for our arrival. We are part of the airborne landing; the seaborne landing won't be far behind. The largest force ever put to sea – a new, bigger Armada. *The Great Crusade.* And the Germans don't know it's coming.

At least we pray they don't.

The invasion will work. It never has before, but it will now. *It has to.*

I've got my own trick, of course. The black wings are still in my mind, but they are not death, not any more. They are Yugo's wings, the fighter. He will fight, he will survive this war – the rations, the bombings, and whatever Hitler can throw at us – and so will I.

I'll see you again, mate. Until then keep an eye out for Stackhouse and his measly portions. Mum and Dad, I'll be back – no horrid letter from the Minister of War for you, Mum. *I promise.*

And I did what I could for Anna. *What else could I do?*

She'll be fine, too. Somehow. *I love you, Anna Cooper. I will come home. I have my own plans for us.* Looks like I've missed my chance to warn someone about her father. I can only pray she'll keep away from him.

The lads inch towards our glider. One more, an almost portly fellow called Morton, who'll drive the Jeep once we land, and then it'll be me climbing in the glider. I swallow, hard. The Germans don't know we're coming. *Unless it's a trap.*

I glance for the first time at the great bomber that will tow us across the Channel. I reckon Rafferty is still relaxing in the hangar with his bloody feet up. *Better than having to look at him out here.*

A Yank paratrooper has broken away from his queue to approach ours.

'All right, you limeys. Don't you dare take any prisoners.' The Yank doesn't raise his voice, and his words are all the more chilling for it. 'Those Nazis have a plan for any paratrooper they find – your privates cut off and stuffed in your mouth. Your body is used for bayonet practice. You want that? You see a Nazi, you shoot a Nazi. No prisoners.'

There is little enough to say to that. The Yank walks away, his boots scraping the tarmac.

'All right, lads!' The major's voice roars into the silence. 'You've all had excellent training, and your orders are clear. Do not be daunted should chaos greet you on the other side. It undoubtedly will. Remember your training, remember your orders, and you will see this mission complete.'

A smattering of cheers and one aborted *hip-hip-hurrah.*

'Sir,' comes Lightwood's voice just behind me. 'I reckon I'd better go now instead of later.'

'What's that, Sapper?'

'The toilet, sir. I have to go and spend a penny, sir.'

Before the major can reply, three other voices have piped up, including the almost portly lad. Major's face swings to me.

'What about you, Squire? You need to go back and have a wee?'

My mind says *no*, but I don't bring the word to my lips. *One last bit of luck*. 'Yes, sir. I do, sir.'

'Christ's sake,' he grumbles. 'Everyone who needs to go shake hands with the vicar, you have five minutes. And it takes fifteen to get out of that suit. So I'd hurry.'

I am already pushing away, scanning the troops, knowing he's in here somewhere, knowing I will find him. *One last bit of luck*. Men stream past, Lightwood calls my name, but I don't listen. *There*. I see him. Rafferty, thank Christ, is standing alone, staring at the window like the bugger that he is. *Near enough to having his feet up*. I am on him in an instant.

'Lord Toff, me and you need to have a quick chat.'

'Why are you telling me this?' asks Rafferty, his eyes wide. 'You've been to see her, is that it – I'm supposed to be envious. Of you?'

He leans close to my face. Too close. *All right, mate*. 'Because you're coming back, you tosspot. I'll be over there swimming in whatever marsh you drop us in. You get to come back here.'

Lightwood, smelling trouble, has raced over but I hold out a hand, keeping him back. Rafferty is staring at me like I'm some bug on his boot heel. My voice drops almost to a whisper. 'And she might need you. She won't admit it, of course. I reckon she's confused – he's her father and all, but the man's a bleeding Nazi.'

I don't tell him that the man is likely some mad Nazi scientist, that he should be arrested and questioned and executed. *I only care about Anna being safe.* And I'm a bigger fool than a room full of Arthur Lightwoods.

Rafferty stares at me for far too long. 'Why?' he finally says.

'Just don't tell her I told you. Deal?'

He pulls his head back, still looking hard at my face. 'You're a crap hero, Squire.'

'You're a crap human, Rafferty.'

He holds out a lordly hand and, God forgive me, I shake it.

Monday, 5 June 1943

The night is slow in coming, and double summertime gives us the light to sit by the river. We are told that despite the sudden nice weather, no one will be flying tomorrow. This only adds to the strange feeling I've had all day. None of our current aircraft are fighters – not a single Hurricane,

Tempest, or Spit in the hangar. In fact, we only have wooden Trainers and taxis. Whenever deliveries resume, I do not look forward to inching across the sky in a Moth. *But it will be many years, if ever, before I've earned the right to complain to Gower.*

Down by the river we drink coffee and the other pilots laugh, enjoying the unexpected free evening. The days of rain release the smells of the countryside, the flowers, grass, trees. I am sitting still, watching the sky and the windblown clouds, wondering what is going to happen, as the last light goes from the sky.

My conversation with Will Esser chases through my mind. He is not an evil man, at any rate. I will not betray his secret, should he choose to stay, but I will not help him. He is still the enemy, no matter his promise that he means no harm to England, or any Englishman.

The sky is low tonight, Polaris almost touching the crown of the oak tree on the opposite bank. Canada jerks to her feet, knocking her teacup, spilling tea on to her trousers.

'Canada—'

But she doesn't even flinch. She is standing, staring.

Out of the shadows comes the prow of a boat. And another. And another.

And another.

It is a dream, a vision – like nothing I have ever seen. It seems never to end. Barges, fishing vessels, ferries, with camouflage webbing, guns bolted on, canons mounted. A massive, river-filling armada of boats, burdened with thousands upon thousands of soldiers, packed in like lambs. The moon glints off uniforms and helmets, the faces lean, painted dark, stern.

A noise shatters the silence. The loud, proud squeal of the bagpipes. I can see the man, in the prow of the boat, in battledress with a kilt, the bagpipes in his hands. I know the tune, too, somehow, from some faraway memory. *Road to the Isles.*

Our great hope, our dreaded fear, has come. The tune dies away as the lead boat vanishes downriver. *The invasion is starting.*

All night we sit by the water, stunned, as the endless boats pour ahead. The navy, army, Scots Guard, Free French, Canadians, Americans, Australians, New Zealanders. Some men sing Cockney songs, high and loud; other boats blast music from their loudspeakers as they pass. *The Marseillaise. A-Hunting We Will Go.* Timothy Squire's face I do not see. *He is there, among them. He is going. The docks, the preparation, the great secret.*

This is why he was so urgent to meet, to finally tell me the truth.

Above, the sky suddenly throbs with engines. Nothing, not even the dark days of the Blitz, were like this. I squint into the night, Canada and the other pilots around me, all of us staring up, seeing the black shapes above, feeling a huge terrifying thrill. *This is not possible.* Spits, Hurricanes, but mainly bombers, heavy four-engine beasts crawling across the sky. Aircraft stretch for miles, disappearing out of sight. It must be everything we have that can fly.

It must be everything that we have. The sky, the river, the whole world seems fanning out, pouring south in endless numbers.

The only way it could ever work is if we throw everything at them – every plane, every tank, every soldier. And then we're going to need some proper bloody luck.

Our invasion is beginning.

And we are being left behind.

Tuesday, 6 June 1944

The sun has just risen, but we are ready. We must join the invasion force. The word is six thousand boats, twelve thousand aircraft, fifty thousand vehicles, all making their way across the Channel. Every aircraft is needed, and every pilot here wants to help. But Gower's frowning face tells us all what is to come.

Bella has her chin held high. 'Don't we need to be briefed and inoculated?'

'No female pilots are allowed to cross the Channel.'

No one bothers to ask why. Bella drops her helmet on the ground and walks out. 'I quit.'

In the silent wake of Bella's departure no one breathes. We all stare at the abandoned helmet lying on its side.

'I don't want to be left behind,' I say, stepping forward. My words seem to snap Gower back to life.

'Left behind? What do you imagine we've been doing this past year? Ferrying Spitfires here, taking bombers there. You're done your part, Cooper. You just didn't know it at the time.'

That should be enough, I know. I see Canada bowing her head, and Minx turns to stare after Bella's exit. It should be enough. *But it isn't.*

Cecil must be up in the sky, heading over there. Cecil in the air, Timothy Squire across the water. I can't think straight, mad thoughts rising up.

Amy Johnson and the officer. Did she somehow survive – is it even possible? No, she died, helpless with cold, dragged to the river's depths along with the poor officer.

Timothy Squire doesn't understand. He thought I would arrest Will Esser, or send him away – and make everything right. They are all trying to protect me. Cecil, Malcolm, Oakes, Joy – and Timothy Squire, who never could stop lying, even now. Father has been here all along, and he knew. *Oh, Timothy Squire.*

Maybe this is the end. Maybe the invasion will stop the war. And then what? Will they shut down the ATA? Will women still be able to fly?

What will I do?

These rockets – the V1s – are coming, the moment Hitler senses our troops have landed. *Oh yes, he will have his vengeance weapons ready.*

I look at the old wooden Moth. My battle is not out

there. That much I have been told. We are not allowed to fight for the kingdom. But we can defend it; we *must* defend it.

For a moment I hear the legend again. *If the ravens leave the Tower, the kingdom will fall.* Well, the legend didn't account for flying rockets. Britain needs all the guardians it can get.

Will Esser. *Father.* He helped develop the rockets. If I can get him to safety, I can find out all about these weapons, and I can find out how to stop them.

As I stare at the aircraft, I don't think of any of them – guardians, protectors, friends – even Timothy Squire. I turn back to the base, the grey sunrise, the empty tarmac. No pilot, no aircraft approaches.

'I am sorry,' I say in a whisper.

Drawing a breath, I take swift steps towards the hangar and the waiting Moth.

THE END

Acknowledgements

This book is dedicated to the memory of my grandparents, Jean McIntyre, who worked in the RCAF at a Commonwealth Air Training base in New Brunswick, Canada during World War Two, and John McIntyre, from Alloa, who worked for forty years at the Saint John shipyard.

Special thanks to the Arts Council England for their generous support for these novels and for funding the series of learning and literacy events, *Beyond the Book: These Dark Wings at the Tower of London*.

I am exceedingly grateful for the partnership of Megan Gooch and Ceri Fox at Historic Royal Palaces, who combine their expertise and determination with enthusiasm and good humour. Bridget Clifford at the Royal Armouries Museum has, as always, been so generous with her time and knowledge. My thanks also to Chris Skaife, the real Ravenmaster at the Tower of London, for sharing his knowledge of and passion for the ravens.

Thanks to the team at Head of Zeus, particularly to my publisher Nicholas Cheetham, for his feedback, insight, and patience, and to my editors Helen Gray and Madeleine O'Shea for their insight and efficiency.

To Bill and Jill, for their continued support and grace. To my parents, Greg and Bronwyn, for their endless encouragement and love.

I am indebted to the kids of the Shiranamikai karate club for inspiring the names (and some of the personalities) for the ravens.

A special thanks to my brothers, who've encouraged me since we were boys. To Andrew, who drew detailed maps in the front of my stories and helped to legitimize the whole enterprise; and to Simon, for being both my favourite character to portray and my most generous reader. I'd never have had the guts to do something like this if it hadn't been for you two.

And to Jackie, my co-pilot, for everything.